THE
HEARTS

A family of substance

DONNA CALDWELL

A Family of Substance © 2024 Donna Caldwell
www.DonnaCaldwellAuthor.com

ISBN 978-1-915962-43-0
Published by Compass-Publishing UK 2024

Designed by The Book Refinery Ltd
www.thebookrefinery.com

The right of Donna Caldwell to be identified as the author of this work
has been asserted in accordance with the Copyright,
Designs and Patents Act, 1988.

All rights reserved. No part of this publication may be reproduced or
transmitted in any form or by any means, electronically or mechanically,
including photocopying, recording, or any information storage or
retrieval system, without either prior permission in writing from the
author or a licence permitting restricted copying.

This is a work of fiction. Names, characters, places, and incidents either
are the product of the author's imagination or are used fictitiously. Any
resemblance to actual persons, living or dead, events, or locales is
entirely coincidental.

All rights reserved. No parts of this manuscript may be reproduced or
used in any manner without the permission of the copyright owner.

A CIP catalogue record for this book is available from the
British Library.

Disclaimer:
This book is suitable for readers 18+ and deals with adult themes,
please consult my website for further information,
www.donnacaldwellauthor.com/trigger-warnings.

Stephen

Enjoy the but
Seems... your Melanie
to may give you
some Ideas. :)

*Dedicated to my best friend and husband Neil.
Couldn't have done it without you*

Dee Caldwell
x

Darcey:

After an urgent and rather intriguing phone call from the very efficient Doris at Office Angels job agency this morning, I found myself sitting in the opulent reception area of Heart Industries within the hour, as instructed. I nestled my handbag into my lap like a protective shield to smother the growls from my stomach as it protested at my lack of food.

The moment I'd stepped through the gargantuan glass doors, I'd felt dishevelled and out of place. I was a mess. I was, however, grateful to finally be out of the harsh and punishing rain. In my best charity-shop bargain dress, my long hair hastily tied in the nape of my neck with a black satin ribbon, I was thoroughly drenched. I was also altogether too warm from my mad dash to get here.

Consciously drawing in a deep breath to help calm my racing heart, I raised my eyes from the spectacular, tiled floor in front of me to take in the grandeur of the mammoth glass and steel foyer. I knew my face would be a divine shade of red, and smiled inwardly as I remembered that, when I was a child, my proper, well-put-together mother would say, "Ladies do not sweat. We glow." Well, I was now glowing like last year's Christmas lights, and the rivulets of sweat and rainwater competed with each other as they ran down the valley between my ample breasts, soaking me to the core.

From the moment I'd opened my eyes that morning, the gods had conspired to make my day a total misery. I'd woken to find Fred – my pet goldfish, the keeper of my deepest, darkest secrets – floating belly-up in his bowl. He'd been such a fabulous listener. On many an evening, I'd poured my heart out to him, with details of my incredibly boring dating life (or lack thereof). Fred was the only pet I could afford and had ever owned. Without allowing myself time to shed a tear, I'd flushed him unceremoniously down the toilet, giving him a small salute as I finished brushing my teeth.

My mood had darkened further as I realised I'd run out of coffee. Not that it mattered because I noticed I had no milk either. In addition, I hadn't had enough change to use the tumble dryer at the launderette the previous evening. Unaware I'd be needing the dress I'd just washed so soon, I'd hung my little black number, reserved for interviews and funerals, from the shower curtain rail in my bathroom, and it was still damp. Unfortunately, I'd had to make do as I had no choice. I needed this job and had to create a good first impression.

Stepping into the slightly moist, cold fabric, a shiver ran up my spine. As soon as the damp material grazed my butt and slid up around my breasts, it felt as though I'd slipped into a wrung-out swimsuit. My nipples beaded to hard peaks in protest; so much so, that I could have put someone's eyes out with them.

I'd set foot outside my sad little bedsit, or "the shoebox" as I lovingly referred to it, and the heavens had opened. On the bright side, such a torrential downpour on my dash to the train station meant I needn't have stressed about wearing a damp dress. If I'd put my clothes on wet straight from the washer the resulting look would have been the same.

To say cash was tight would be an understatement. When I opened my purse, the metaphorical moths flew out. If I'd been given more notice regarding this job interview, I would have done my usual trick and called into one of the very kind, thoughtful department stores en route. It would be rude not to take full advantage of their hospitality and free samples of foundation, lipstick and the latest designer perfume. I never felt guilty about doing this; after all, as soon as I won the lottery, I might actually be able to afford to buy some of them.

My stomach had begun to churn and grumble, partly with nerves but mainly because I'd had the unenviable choice of either buying a bagel and coffee for breakfast or having enough money to make the entire journey here on the train. After I'd bought my ticket, I'd had the grand total of one pound twenty-five pence left in my purse, and a huge blister on my foot the size of a ten-pence piece that throbbed to the rhythm of my pulse. However, I'd quickly been distracted by having to jostle for a place on the crowded train, or tin can as I referred to it; which was quite apt as I was forced to travel like a sardine, packed with other sardines.

I'd found my head positioned next to a filthy, overall-wearing man's armpit. The man clearly had an aversion to soap. I was soon counting the stops until I could depart the train. I'd begun to feel lightheaded as I'd been holding my breath for so long when, to my horror, the guy started to smile at me, showing bright yellow, plaque-covered teeth. He then tried to strike up a conversation. I'd never thought of myself as a snob until this point. But now I knew I was. Even though they were making me feel physically sick, I couldn't take my eyes off those foul teeth. Nor could I decide which was more offensive – his breath or his armpit.

Inwardly, I'd felt devastated. If this was the kind of guy I attracted, I was doomed to be single forever. I may as well give up now and buy a cat or three; I was obviously destined to become an eccentric, single cat-lady.

Thankfully, the sound of the train doors opening saved me from having to respond to his obvious interest. I was swept up the platform with the throng of bodies moving like lemmings towards the escalators. Then, when I'd finally got out of the train station, I'd been met with an onslaught of rain even heavier than before. It appeared to be hitting the pavement so hard that it bounced back and soaked me all over again. All I could do was send up a silent prayer in the desperate hope that I would somehow secure this position, even though by now I no doubt resembled a bedraggled, rumpled dog.

Having finally arrived at this pillar of industry, I'd walked over to the reception desk with an air of confidence I didn't feel, and announced myself. I may have looked like a hot mess but there was no need to act like it. Fake it till you make it, right? I'd been ushered to some seating on the right-hand side of the reception area and advised someone would be along shortly.

Desperately needing to just sit down and rest my poor, blistered foot, I'd discreetly toed off my shoe. I usually loved to people-watch; my seat gave me the perfect viewing platform but, as I'd taken in my surroundings, I'd groaned silently as I noted that the women striding in and out were immaculately turned out, like little Stepford wives. They marched confidently through the foyer in their designer power suits and skyscraper designer heels, with matching accessories. The men were no different with their modern, slim-fit suits, slick haircuts and manicured fingernails. They all looked like generic, highly groomed, metrosexual GQ models. I grabbed my handbag even tighter, beginning to feel rather self-conscious in my now wrinkled dress and too-tight shoes, wondering why the hell Doris had sent me here ...

I was pulled from my internal ramblings by a beautiful, mature-looking woman with kind eyes and a ready smile.

"Hi there, you must be Darcey? I'm Gloria – Mr Heart's personal assistant."

Before I knew it, Gloria was shaking my hand, chattering away as though we were old friends and indicating to me what looked like a private elevator. I attempted to rise from the soft plush seating as gracefully as I could, considering my foot felt like it was on fire and I was sure the blister had just burst inside my shoe ... nice. Really nice ... What next? As I smoothed out my soggy dress, I glanced down and you guessed it. There, on the beautiful seating, I had managed to leave a perfect silhouette of my wet butt.

"Darcey? Is everything all right, my dear?" Gloria's voice pulled me back to the conversation as we reached the elevator doors. "You seem to be limping. What have you done to your foot?"

Whether due to nerves, embarrassment or sheer desperation, I found myself blurting out much of my uncensored inner turmoil to this kind-faced, motherly-looking lady. At this point, I imagined I'd blown the interview by my appearance alone, so what the heck? After all, I may as well get everything off my chest. It might just make me feel better – a trouble shared is a trouble halved and all that. Poor Gloria was bombarded with a blast of my unfiltered thoughts. It was as if my filter had taken a sabbatical, leaving me to ramble on like a complete loon: the reality that I didn't have enough money in my purse to cover my bus fare home and figured I'd have to walk through central London barefoot with a burst blister the size of a ten-pence piece; the fact that I never normally wore heeled shoes; the misery of being soaked through to my underwear but all the while trying to make a good impression as I desperately needed this job.

Gloria looked at my pathetic, rain-drenched face – and burst out laughing. Not exactly the reaction I expected, but I couldn't help myself and joined in too. Her laughter was infectious and if I hadn't giggled along, I think I might have cried.

Linking her arm through mine, Gloria patted my hand in a reassuring gesture, and the pair of us rode the elevator like two long-lost friends. She even let me into the secret that she only wore her dress shoes on the journey to and from work and, occasionally, if she was called into a meeting with Mr Heart.

Leaning in conspiratorially, she revealed, "I'm a secret slipper aficionado."

I smiled, and the churning in my stomach abated slightly as we made our way to the top floor. I knew I liked Gloria already.

Gloria:

I knew I'd made the right choice. I had always been a shrewd woman with the ability to sniff out a gold digger or fraudster at fifty paces. My talents in that department had served me and Heart Industries well over the years.

I'd been looking for the right replacement for my position for months now, and took an instant liking to Darcey. There was a refreshing honesty and innocence about her. The girl was also able to find humour in dire circumstances. And I was in no doubt that Darcey's circumstances were dire. There had been many other candidates with excellent qualifications, who would have sold their own grandmother for this opportunity. But, after seeing the photograph and reading the resumé and personal note attached to Darcey's file by Doris from the agency, I knew I was on to a winner. The knowledge that Darcey had walked out of a position at Abington's was the icing on the cake.

Yes, without a shadow of a doubt, Darcey Robson was the woman I'd been searching for. I made a mental note to send a thank-you bouquet to Doris, as she had far exceeded my expectations this time. Darcey was highly qualified, well read and naturally sexy, with a charmingly unpretentious air about her. I had the feeling she wasn't even aware of her natural beauty and raw sex appeal. With her large, almond-shaped eyes and thick, curving lashes, Darcey was both striking and intelligent, with a rare wit.

However, the poor dear did look as though she'd never had any female guidance. She somehow resembled a sack tied in the middle, but a stunning sack all the same: slim, tall and elegant, with curves in all the right places, which even made the hideous, shapeless dress she was wearing look passable. I'd have to fight the urge to take her under my wing. She just seemed so vulnerable. But, having read the personal note from Doris, I knew Darcey had integrity, wisdom beyond her years and a rod of steel for a spine. All this young woman needed was a break – and a little spit and polish before being introduced to Mr Heart.

Darcey:

When the elevator doors opened, I stood in awe. Mr Heart's reception area was magnificent; like a bright white, modern, spacious living room out of a glossy magazine. My whole bedsit could fit into this room ten times over. As I took in my surroundings, Gloria slipped off her shoes, headed for her desk and grabbed her slippers, iPad, and a few other things she had got ready.

We made our way over to the stylish, white, L-shaped leather sofa. Gloria put what she was carrying down on a glass and chrome coffee table, slid her feet into her slippers and casually walked across to what can only be described as an executive kitchen area. There was an impressive coffee machine, a mini bar, a chilled wine rack, an assortment of snacks and a stunning fruit display on the granite-topped workbench. I tried not to salivate and wondered if I could pack a doggy bag before leaving. Then the aroma of fresh-ground coffee hit my caffeine-starved senses and they began to do a happy dance.

It was the moment Gloria handed me my coffee that my stomach chose to growl like a starved bear. Turning beetroot red, I apologised profusely. Once again, Gloria simply laughed and added a plate of delicious-looking bagels, croissants and pastries to the table, encouraging me to eat. As we settled on the butter-soft leather sofa, I could feel myself begin to relax.

When Gloria spoke of Mr Heart, I could see the love and respect shining in her eyes. I presumed she must have worked for him for a long time. At first, I thought perhaps she had some sort of crush on her elusive boss, but I ruled that out almost instantly. Gloria had been nothing but professional and efficient. I'd heard of Heart Industries but hadn't had the time to Google and research the man himself. Normally, I liked to be prepared well in advance of any interview and do my due diligence. But this meeting had been set up at very short notice and my home laptop had died months ago. I found myself picturing a commanding, handsome, silver fox of a man.

I began to wonder how long Gloria had worked for Mr Heart. I listened intently as she filled me in on what the personal assistant job entailed. I would have the use of a company car should I need to run errands, a clothing allowance, medical insurance, dental care; the list went on. I couldn't help wondering what the catch was. The salary was double what everyone else was paying and, my money situation being as it was – i.e. I had no money – I would have been willing to clean the bathrooms if Gloria had asked me to.

After an hour of going through company policy, procedures and training, Gloria informed me the job was mine if I wanted it and I could start immediately. I couldn't believe such a prestigious position was being handed to me on a plate, especially as I was expecting at least two or three further interview stages. I sat poised, waiting for the "BUT" to come ... and it didn't. I could feel myself exhale at her words. The remaining stress I held in my shoulders seemed to melt away completely.

I also began to tear up. Oh, my god – what was that about? I was going to make a complete idiot of myself twice in one day. I just couldn't stop the onslaught of tears that rolled down my cheeks. Then, obviously, my nose began to run for good measure, and I kept thanking Gloria over and over, explaining repeatedly that this was the first break I'd been given in a long time.

Since walking out of Abington's almost six months ago, I'd had a feeling that Rodger Abington, the creepy, pompous arse, had been responsible for my lack of employment. As soon as prospective employers discovered where I'd worked previously, I never got invited back for a second interview, or my references weren't followed up. It got to a point where I asked Doris to mention my former boss as soon as my details were put forward to potential employers. Saved me from wasting bus fares travelling around the city.

But I couldn't have stayed there. It wasn't dictation that Mr Abington had wanted me to take down.

Not only that, he frequently had shady-looking visitors in his office. They made me feel uncomfortable, always watching me and staring. I'd recognised two of his guests once. They had recently been featured on the local news channel TVW during a report on the court proceedings of a local, corrupt land developer. It turned out they had also been embroiled in the cash-for-land scandal and had been questioned by police. I couldn't understand why Mr Abington would want to be seen doing business with people like that.

The man had an unpredictable temper on him too. One of my duties was to handle his personal files once he'd put a new business proposal together. But when I took a dock development proposal he'd been working on off his desk one day, he totally flew off the handle.

"Don't meddle in things that are none of your fucking business!" he'd yelled, red-faced, spittle flying out of his mouth.

And I had no idea why. It was my job to deal with these files. Whatever was it about, this particular one, that made him behave like that? I spotted a few strange shipping reports but he ripped the paperwork out of my hands before I had the chance to get a proper look.

The man was odious. Now, months later, every time I thought of the sleaze bag, a cold shiver ran down my spine.

As I sat today in this immaculate space, I felt I could finally see the light at the end of a very long tunnel. Gloria grabbed my hand and a box of tissues and, with a knowing smile, told me I would be perfect for the job. Bizarrely, she then tucked a wayward lock of my unruly hair behind my ear and wrapped me in a warm, genuine, motherly embrace.

We chatted a little more until I'd gotten a grip on myself. Gloria then suggested I should have a look around and familiarise myself with where everything was, explaining that Mr Heart was not expected back till late this week or possibly next week. I gathered that I would liaise with him remotely the majority of the time and attend a few functions occasionally when he was in town, but I wouldn't have much interaction with him in person, which was fine by me as he was predominantly working away.

Gloria left me alone temporarily, saying she would be back shortly as she had contracts and a non-disclosure document for me to sign – a requirement for all new employees. She used a different elevator to the one we'd arrived in. I hadn't even noticed it as it was more or less concealed behind a stunning potted palm and planted container.

I felt like Alice falling down the rabbit hole after such a curious turn of events. Gloria had told me to acquaint myself with my new surroundings and I was keen to find out more about the mysterious Mr Heart. So obviously I went snooping. I wandered around, looking in the various rooms and cupboards, and peered into the office of the man himself. Although hoping to gain some insight into my new employer, whom I imagined as a powerful, commanding CEO – an alfa male in his sixties – I was sadly disappointed. The office was huge and devoid of anything personal; almost clinical in appearance. There were no pictures of family, no mementoes, just a scrupulously tidy desk. Mr Heart was away on business most of the time, Gloria had said, and I would have the whole top floor to myself. I could use the gym up here whilst he was out of the office if I wished to.

The bathroom, I discovered, was much like his office – immaculately clean, with steel-grey slate tiles, white sinks and a huge mirror. There was a pile of fluffy white towels on a chrome shelf. I was compelled to run my hand over them because they looked so thick and soft, they seemed like fluffy clouds. The bathroom was actually a wet room and was truly exquisite.

There were numerous beautiful, smoked-glass, coloured bottles in a recess built into the wall next to the shower.

Wow – this man took his hygiene seriously (unlike the man from the train this morning). The glass bottles called to me and I lifted one to my nose and took a long, deep sniff. It smelled masculine, expensive; clean and fresh with a hint of sandalwood and something spicy.

Replacing the bottle, next I peeked into the gym and was equally impressed with all the modern equipment. I also lit up when I spied the punch bag in the corner, suspended on huge, galvanised chains. Sadly, my mixed martial arts classes had been the first thing to go when I'd lost my job. I used to love taking all my frustrations out on that bag. My only hope now was that my new boss wouldn't be as much of an arse as Mr Abington Senior. Or Mr Abington Junior for that matter.

My curiosity satisfied for now, I figured I'd better take a seat behind my new desk out front. I sent a silent prayer of thanks skywards. Hopefully, I'd be able to make the rent this month without killing myself doing three different jobs. Maybe I'd also get to eat more than just supermarket-branded instant noodles for the foreseeable future.

The elevator sounded and I looked up expecting to see Gloria. Instead, I saw a mature gentleman, in a mail room uniform and with a dazzling smile, pushing a trolley.

"Hey, you must be Darcey."

I smiled back. The man's name badge read, "Mike Huggins".

"Gloria said she was taking someone on to cover while she was in hospital for her surgery. It's nice to meet you."

At that moment, the elevator sounded again and Gloria returned. "Hi, Mike. How's the grandkids? Mike, here, is the eyes and ears of Heart Industries, Darcey. Anything you need to know, just ask Mike. He's also a terrible old flirt and a gossip."

"Oh, I wouldn't say that, Gloria," Mike replied. "You know there's only you in my life."

I thought I caught a twinkle in Gloria's eye as she continued to chat with the smooth-talking Mr Huggins. I found myself liking him instantly.

Gloria handed me a sticking plaster for my blister, then asked me to read through my work contract and sign all relevant paperwork for security passes etc. This struck me as a little odd. Gloria hadn't been gone very long, yet here she was with my contract and other documents ready for me to complete and sign. It was as if it was a given that I'd been going to get the job all along. She also asked me to get acquainted with Mr Heart's current projects and his diary, informing me that she had been to see Human Resources about initiating my benefits package with immediate effect and that someone would be up to see me soon.

I sat behind my immense new desk in my space-age, leather office chair, still trying to absorb the whirlwind of events that had been my morning thus far. Even my discomfort at having damp breasts, soggy underwear and a huge blister couldn't spoil my freshly lifted mood.

Opening the drawers, I was delighted to find everything I could possibly need. I am meticulous when it comes to my work and I love stationery. I know it's sad, but I just adore the smell of a newly opened memo pad or post-it note block and a brand-new marker pen. It's the little things in life that make me happy. Honestly, I still get a frisson of excitement at a large contract, and I've always found spreadsheets and figures satisfying and somewhat sexy.

I caressed the stationery fondly. Feeling a renewed sense of pride and self-worth, I dived into my tasks with anticipation because I knew I was good at what I did. I would prove to Gloria that she had made the right choice in hiring me. A cheesy grin spread across my face as I discreetly slipped out of my evil, ill-fitting shoe and wiggled my poor toes. Fixing the plaster in place on my sore foot, I felt human again.

As I began to lose myself in costings, reports and findings, Mike said, "If you get five minutes free, you should pop down to the post room and I'll introduce you to the team. And if you ever get sick of drinking that posh coffee and fancy slumming it with some instant, there'll always be a cup with your name on it."

I had every intention of taking Mike up on his offer and stopping by. I always made a point of getting to know the people I worked with, regardless of their position within a firm. I just loved to be around others. It made me feel less lonely.

The rest of the morning flew by. I didn't look up once from my desk until Gloria asked me to join her for lunch. I was starving but had to tell her I was fine and just needed to work through. I didn't have any lunch with me and the reality was I couldn't afford to eat out. In fact, I couldn't afford to eat period; I'd lived on a meagre diet of fresh air, dust and smart-price instant noodles for the last six months.

"Nonsense," Gloria said. "I've put out a little sandwich for you."

I walked over to the white leather sofa and looked at the impressive array of well-presented food and deli sandwiches on the glass coffee table. The varied assortment of goodies was far from a "little sandwich". I had to try not to salivate on the beautiful white cushions. Gloria told me lunch was always catered for, as she never left the office in case Mr Heart needed her.

We chatted about work and her upcoming operation. She informed me the position was for six months while she had the surgery on her knee and then recuperated. I promised her I would try to look after Mr Heart as well as she did and thanked her yet again for the opportunity.

The sound of the elevator doors interrupted us and a rather handsome, if somewhat austere-looking, man came striding over with purpose, dragging a small metal wheelie trolley with a load of boxes piled up on it. Gloria stood and introduced me to Michael from I.T. He quietly and efficiently set up my brand-new Mac desktop computer as well as a laptop, iPad and iPhone.

There was only one thing more satisfying to me than spreadsheets and new stationery, and that was new tech. It felt like Christmas; especially as Heart Industries even provided quiet eye candy. I might not have had time (or the money) for a personal life, but I could appreciate a nice firm butt as much as the next person. My day was getting better and better.

I had used Apple computers before whilst temping and at university, so I was familiar with the programs. And as nice as Michael and his butt were to look at, I just wanted him gone so I could play with my new toys. In no time, I'd set up a diary for Mr Heart, cross-referencing all his appointments, meetings and functions; doing what I did best.

After filling in all the necessary paperwork for the Human Resources department and appearing to sign my life away, I agreed to a full medical and background check. Gloria told me it was standard procedure. She said I would also need to purchase suitable work attire and keep a small overnight bag in the office with a couple of changes of clothes, some toiletries, personal items etc, in case I needed to accompany Mr Heart out of the city at short notice and stay overnight during negotiations or business dealings.

Rather nonchalantly, Gloria added that an appointment had been made for me at Balbier's to pick out some clothes. I almost choked on my coffee and instantly broke out into a hot sweat. One blouse from Balbier's would cost more than a month's wages. I was still having palpitations when Gloria mentioned I would need a cocktail dress and an elegant evening gown too.

"Don't worry, dear," she said, a playful smile on her lips. "With your figure, Susan will have a field day and likely blow the budget. An appointment has also been made for you at Franco's, so you'll have access to an open account. You'll need to have your hair styled, get waxed, plucked and buffed within an inch of your life for the events you'll be expected to attend."

I stared. "What ...?"

I always kept my lady garden neat and trimmed don't you know, and the thought of having my pubic hair ripped from my body made my eyes water. I couldn't begin to fathom what pain the styling, plucking and buffing would entail and

I found myself clenching. Franco's was where all the celebs went for their fancy hairdos and treatments, not the Darceys of this world. I thought I was being extravagant by shaving my legs and underarms, which otherwise, in their hairy state, were another way of keeping warm in the winter. What must I look like to Gloria if she thought I needed so much help?

She must have read my thoughts and she chuckled. "It's just a perk of the job and I'm sure you'll love it. You'll be expected to work long, unsociable hours at times. I'm sure Doris mentioned this to you."

Since I didn't have any social life, dependants or money, the hours made no difference. I would have to give up two out of my current three jobs, but I could still work for Mr Rumis. He really did need me and I owed him a debt.

Even so, I couldn't help wondering – what was I letting myself in for and, more to the point, could I do this?

As the surprising but exhausting day came to an end, the thought of having to put my shoe back on my poor, blistered foot and make my way home made me wince. I grabbed my handbag, computer case and other gadgetry, and made to head out. But Gloria, bless her heart, had instructed the company town car to pick me up outside. She hugged me; said I'd done really well today and deserved a little break in life. And I knew I liked this woman.

She told me to take the elevator we'd come up in that morning, as it was private and would take me down to Mr Heart's garage. Paul, the driver, would be waiting there to whisk me home in the company car. She said this arrangement was just until my own car was issued. Somehow, I seemed to have landed the best job I could ever have imagined. And I hadn't even had to jump through any hoops to get it. That made me nervous. Was it all too good to be true? I was waiting for the other shoe to drop. I couldn't help thinking Gloria would soon realise she'd made a mistake.

I walked through the door of my lonely bedsit, kicked off my torturous shoes on autopilot and headed for my bedroom. There, I deposited all my new tech and my handbag onto the bed, stripped off and dived into my pathetic excuse for a shower. The warm water washed over my body while I tried to process the day. As a shiver of excitement ran up my spine, I was overcome with the need to do a happy shower dance.

Putting on my comfy sweats, I headed to Mr and Mrs Shoemocker's on the first floor of my building. They were a lovely old couple, who had no children, so I'd kind of become their surrogate daughter. I would run errands for them, do their grocery shopping and cook them a hearty meal twice a week. They didn't have much but they did have each other. I would sit and listen to Mrs Shoemocker tell me stories of their youth and how her husband was the true love of her life. She would squeeze his hand and look at him with complete adoration.

When they were younger, they had loved to dance. So now, quite often, I would sing for them. They would roll up the rug and take hold of each other in a loving embrace. Mr Shoemocker sadly had dementia, which was quite advanced, but the love they still shared was palpable. When I sang, it was as if it helped to reconnect them, and he would come back to her. To truly find the love of your life – that one person with whom your world begins and ends – is rare, but I knew it was possible. The Shoemockers had restored my faith in the power of love.

Mrs Shoemocker's hands were riddled with arthritis so the pair of us fell into an easy routine. I would cook while she imparted family recipes to me that produced the most wonderful aromas, and the food I was able to create tasted simply out of this world. No money would ever change hands in payment for my time, but I would sit and share a hot, hearty meal with them. There were times when that was the only solid, warm food I'd had in several days and, for that, I would be eternally grateful – as would my grumbling stomach. Money had been tight for months, with trying to make the rent and pay off the ever-growing pile of bills. When I'd walked out of Abington's it was the right thing to do, but having a strong moral compass didn't put food in my belly. And I soon learned I wasn't entitled to any state help because I'd left of my own free will.

As I sat with the Shoemockers that evening, memories of my Andy played in my mind like an old movie. He'd been my rock; my first love. But tragically, he was killed whilst on a tour of duty in Afghanistan. We'd been due to get engaged and married but I'd wanted to get my Business and Marketing degree first.

With a heavy heart and tired feet, I finally let myself back into my bedsit and succumbed to a night of deep sleep.

The next morning, as my alarm sounded, I woke wondering if the previous day had just been an amazingly vivid dream. But I took one look at my old, shabby dressing table and there, neatly piled up, was all the new tech I'd brought home the evening before. As if I needed further proof that any of yesterday's events had happened, when I walked into my small kitchen, there on the bench was Fred's empty bowl.

I brushed my teeth and showered quickly, with a sense of excitement I had never experienced before. I was actually looking forward to going to work. I donned yet another of my charity shop bargains, this time a blouse and skirt combo. I brushed and braided my waist-length hair and laced up my comfy, old, battered black Converses. I'd had them since my student days but, hey, there were a good few miles left in them yet. With my torturous shoes in my bag to change into once I'd made it to the office, I headed out of my building in record time. My laptop was strapped across my body and I was ready to walk the whole way to the business district. But, as I stepped out onto the street, I was met by Paul, smiling at me from the pavement, with the company car door open wide.

"Goodness, I could kiss you!" I called.

Laughing, Paul closed the door behind me and I set off to my new job, in the lap of luxury.

We chatted the whole way to work. With my laptop slung untidily across me, I must have looked like some sort of rumpled hobo. Not only that, but my security pass didn't work when I tried to access the private elevator, so Paul had to let me in with his. However, his card would only allow me as far as the first floor, so I had to go to the main security desk at reception to report the issue with my card. This obviously involved me crossing the beautiful foyer, past the perfectly made-up Stepford wives and the Ken dolls in their immaculately pressed and tailored power suits, before I even got to the security desk. Just to add to my humiliation, I was halfway across the foyer when I realised I was still wearing my old, tatty, battered Converses.

When I finally made it to the office, I set the coffee machine going and took in the delivery of fresh fruit and muffins. I'd arrived in good time, so was even able to pop into the mail room to collect our post and see Mike and his colleagues for ten minutes.

Once back at my desk, I rifled through my bag and slipped into the evil professional shoes. Then I powered up my laptop and iPad, and a calendar of events popped up to remind me that I had an appointment at Franco's at 11:00 a.m. To say I was filled with dread was an understatement. The words "hot wax" were enough to instil the fear of God into me. It was the thought of ripping unwanted hair out by the roots; it sounded barbaric.

Just as I was about to veer off into my mental ramblings again, Gloria walked through the door.

"Morning, dear. Are you ready for your day of pampering?"

My concerns must have been written all over my face, as Gloria advised me she would accompany me to Franco's. I felt I was being ungrateful but I couldn't understand what the shape of my bikini line or the colour of my hair had to do with Heart Industries.

Once again, Gloria seemed to read my mind. She explained that I would be representing Heart Industries at numerous events, on the arm of Mr Heart no less, quite often acting as his plus one.

My heart plummeted. Now I knew what the downside of this job was; and I began to feel a little nauseous. But I was in no financial position to walk away this time, moral compass or not. I would have to manage, I thought, as long as that's ALL I was required to do and he kept his hands to himself. Vivid memories of Mr Rodger Abington the Third came to mind: his constant inappropriate sexual innuendos, his cold, clammy hands, his putrid breath against my neck. I swallowed the bile and instinctively drew my arms across my chest. The man made my flesh crawl.

Chapter Two

Darcey:

We pulled up outside Franco's and Gloria exited the car as gracefully as a ballerina. Me, not so much. My heel caught on the hem of my over-long skirt as I tried to get out and I fell in a heap on the pavement, scraping the skin off one elbow and knee and putting a huge hole in my tights at the same time. Holy mother of fudge – that hurt! I swear it could only happen to me. This, of course, was directly in front of the glass-fronted shop doorway, just for that extra level of embarrassment and humiliation, because why not announce yourself so dramatically to the whole salon?

Paul was there in a flash but I could see he was trying to suppress a chuckle. He pulled out a wet wipe and proceeded to wipe my hands and clean my boo-boos up as though I were a five-year-old. Not quite the air of sophistication I'd wanted to portray on my first visit to this exclusive salon.

Gloria was laughing so hard, there were tears in her eyes. "Come on, darling, let's get you pampered – I think you need it," and she ushered me through the glass doors furnished with handsome, scrolled-metalwork handles.

All my senses were awakened as we entered the salon. The aroma was magnificent: a pure essential oil blend that smelled warm, relaxing, inviting – and screamed money. There was an elegant front desk adorned with a whimsical, stylish flower display. I was dying to reach out and touch it as I wasn't sure if the flowers were real or not.

Gloria introduced me to Franco himself and his stunning-looking team. Wow. He was absolutely beautiful. His face looked as though it had been carved. He was an Adonis of a man with a lean and fit-looking physique. He was also fabulously camp and I loved him instantly.

Gloria then proceeded to tell the team I needed "the works", and I saw her wink at one of the ladies. I was offered a glass of champagne with a raspberry in it – and I felt so out of place. Especially when I looked down and saw that my heel had torn a hole in the hem of my skirt. Also, I had bobby pins in the damn thing. The waist had been too big on me and I couldn't sew, so I'd folded it over and secured it with half a dozen clips.

I was led through an exquisite seating area, where there was a huge glass water jug with a tap and cute little glasses on a stunning but simple side table. The water had lemons, limes, ice and pretty flowers floating in it. There appeared to be crystals at the bottom too. I didn't know if they were for enhancing the water in some way or for decoration. From there, I was escorted into a warm, fabulous-smelling treatment room decorated in gold and blush pinks. There was a thick, soft dressing gown and a pair of slippers set aside on a little chair, and a long treatment table with fluffy towels spread over it.

Gretta, the lady escorting me, told me to undress and slip under a towel when I was ready. She said she'd be back momentarily. I felt so self-conscious. I removed my clothes, folded them neatly and put them on a little shelf. Then I climbed onto the treatment table and lay down, completely naked apart from the towel. Gretta and another lovely young lady gently knocked on the door and entered the room. Talk about being out of my comfort zone ...

While Gretta set up a wax pot and sorted out strips of calico, the other lady, Petra, took hold of one of my feet, applied warm oil and gave it a massage. This was mind-blowing. Her nimble fingers hit so many sore points, but it was a good pain. My stress and discomfort melted away with each stroke and caress of her soft, warm, magical hands. When she'd finished, she wrapped my foot in a warmed towel. Then she set to work on the other one.

By now, I felt totally relaxed. Gretta rolled my towel up to my navel and slightly parted my legs. I felt warm wax being applied to my lady garden, and I have to admit it felt nice and wasn't painful the way I'd expected it to be. It smelled divine too, as she smoothed it on expertly with her wooden spatula.

Then – "What the ever-loving ...? Ouuuch!"

Holy mackerel! My foot shot up in shock as Gretta applied the strip of calico material, smoothing it down, then ripping it from my body and decimating my lady garden in one fell swoop. Unfortunately, as my foot shot up, I clocked poor Petra square on the nose and blood spurted instantly. I was mortified. Ever the professional, Petra just grabbed a towel and excused herself from the room.

Gretta got me to lie back down while she finished the job. At least this time I knew what to expect. I couldn't believe women went through this to be pampered. Why?

Finally, three hours later, I'd been massaged, I'd had a facial, a hair mask, a mani-pedi, brow wax and lamination, eyelash tint and perm, and light make-up had been applied. I sat in front of a full-length mirror and didn't recognise the sensual-looking woman staring back at me. As Gloria had warned me, I had been polished and buffed to within an inch of my life, and the make-up applied to my lips made them look full and glossy.

I was relieved Franco had decided not to cut and colour my hair. He'd said it was naturally beautiful, so simply added a few softening layers and gave it a trim. I usually went to a place called "Curl Up and Dye", where my haircut cost me five pounds. But I always worried that Stephany, the young trainee, might accidentally spit her wad of bubble gum into my hair, as she clacked her gum incessantly and would keep blowing huge bubbles.

When I glanced up, I saw poor Petra. She had what looked like tampons up her nostrils, and I felt there was a good possibility she'd soon be sporting two black eyes. I gave her a weak smile and felt rather guilty.

Franco uncinched the protective cape from my neck with a flourish like a trained bullfighter, and wrapped me in a warm, tight hug.

Gloria beamed at me. "You look stunning, my dear."

"I feel wonderful," I said. I hadn't expected to, but I did. "Thank you so much."

As if it was nothing, Gloria waved my thanks away. Then she linked arms with me and escorted me to the waiting car, and a rather stunned-looking Paul. He whisked us off and, within what seemed like minutes, we were outside Balbier's.

Susan greeted us personally at the door. She seemed lovely – warm and friendly. It wasn't at all the Pretty Woman scenario I had imagined and dreaded. Susan didn't pay any attention to the hole in my hem and tights. Nor did she comment on the hair grips on my skirt.

Once again, I was overcome by the most wonderful smell, like warm cinnamon and apple. While Gloria went through what she had in mind for me with Susan, I had a brief look round the beautiful boutique. As before at Franco's, I was offered a glass of champagne, this time with a strawberry in it, and I took it with me while I browsed the rails. It was as if each garment had been measured and spaced an exact number of inches apart from the next. There was no smell of lavender water and mothballs, as I was used to when I went on my charity shop hunts, and only one item of clothing hung from each branded, padded hanger. I certainly wouldn't have to rummage to find my size. I picked up a high-waisted pencil skirt – and felt my heart stop. There was no price tag. But before I had the chance to dwell on it, I was bundled into a changing room and passed outfit after outfit.

Among the items I tried on was an exquisite, fitted, black lace evening gown, with fine straps and a plunging deep V at the front. It moulded perfectly to my figure, although exposing more breast than I would normally dare to show. The gown was also backless and had a long split that reached from the hem and up the thigh. I loved this dress, but I'd never worn anything like it before; I'd never shown so much skin. The thought that I wouldn't be able to wear any underwear underneath left me feeling sexy, if not slightly wanton and a little naughty. I was given shoes to try on with every outfit too, as well as all the appropriate underwear.

I thought about poor old Mr Heart. I wasn't sure what would cause the coronary first – the bill for the Balbier's haul or the sight of me in this dress.

After a bite of lunch, we headed back to the office with an obscene amount of shopping bags in tow. Gloria looked shattered and said she was going home early.

I reached my desk and fired up my Mac and iPad. I was greeted with three emails from Mr Heart: a general summary of what he expected of me and a sort of official welcome to the firm; a list of functions I would be expected to attend, with strict dress-code information; and my latest to-do list. I figured, with what was left of the day, I would make a start on the list. I grabbed a coffee and opened the document. A string of forty-five tasks appeared. It soon became apparent this guy must never sleep.

There were multiple breakfast meetings to set up, with satellite links to our various counterparts around the globe. There was a charity black-tie dinner coming up, and that was just for starters. I was able to fly through some of the tasks quite quickly, such as booking his appointment for a wet shave, manicure and haircut at Franco's, collecting his dry-cleaning, and making lunch reservations at Verve for himself and his mother for her birthday on Friday afternoon. I made a mental note to ask Gloria about Mr Heart's mother: how old was she? Was she in some kind of retirement home? I wanted some background in case Mr Heart ever wanted me to buy a gift for her on his behalf. I noticed her birthday was the same day as Gloria's.

I felt a little nervous making the call to Verve as there was usually a four-week waiting list. But the Heart name worked its magic and I was able to secure the exact date and time Mr Heart had requested.

I also made a note on my iPad of other important dates, such as birthdays, anniversaries and so on. And for each person I met, I wrote myself a reminder of them – things like family or what they'd discussed or what interested them. I liked to be organised.

I'd been given a company credit card for expenses and needed to order some flowers. An idea popped into my head. When I'd visited Mike in the mail room yesterday, he'd been so excited, bursting with pride as he told me about his youngest daughter opening her own florist boutique not far from this office. So I gave them a call and set up an account. I placed two orders: one for a bouquet to be delivered to Verve for Mr Heart's mother's birthday, and the other for Julia, who worked in the main reception downstairs fielding all Mr Heart's initial calls. I'd discovered Julia was due to begin maternity leave soon, so I also purchased a gift card for Mama & Babe Baby Boutique.

I didn't leave work until 6:00 p.m. – late, but I felt guilty for having spent so much time shopping and being pampered. As soon as I got home, I dived into the shower, being careful not to spoil my hair or make-up. Then I threw on my uniform, stopping off at Mr and Mrs Shoemocker's to pick up their shopping list and prescriptions on the way to my second job.

I was exhausted but it was Tuesday night, and I always worked for Mr Rumis on a Tuesday. The Rumis family had thrown me my only lifeline when Andy died, by giving me a job. The money was just minimum wage but Rosa, Anthony's wife, used to give me a few groceries now and then and some hand-me-down clothes, and there was always a wise word or pair of willing arms to give me a hug when I needed them. I also got to indulge my passion for playing the piano. Sadly, Rosa had passed away from breast cancer a month ago, but I did all I could to help Mr Rumis and his son Tony, and we'd forged a fierce friendship. They owned a little restaurant and club two blocks from where I lived, and were like the father and brother I didn't have. Tony kept me safe at the club and never allowed anyone to crowd me or get too handsy, so I always felt secure. I used to wait tables, wash dishes and serve in the bar. Then, one day, Tony heard me singing to myself while he was prepping food in the kitchen. He asked if I'd sing in the club and told me I could make decent tips, so I thought I'd give it a go.

I was embarrassed and self-conscious at first but, when you're starving and have no money, it's amazing how you can conquer your fears – I'd only ever sung in church before or for Mr and Mrs Shoemocker. Eventually, however, it became a regular thing and I enjoyed it immensely. There was an old piano in the corner and I found it a sort of therapy. The restaurant had been struggling with the recession but having the musical entertainment drew in more customers, so Tuesday nights were always packed. I suppose we all sort of helped to save each other.

With my shift finished by 11:30 p.m., I left, dead on my feet. Tony always insisted on driving me home but tonight he seemed preoccupied. I'd caught him watching me throughout the evening. Usually, we laughed and joked and he would tease me as a sibling would, but these last few hours, he'd seemed more serious. I even got a compliment about my new makeover. I smiled but was too worn out to dwell on it.

The next morning, I felt like a million dollars once I'd slipped into my new, stylish, grey, fitted pinstripe dress, complete with new underwear, stockings and shoes. I applied light make-up and styled my hair the way Franco had shown me. I was shocked when I looked at my finished appearance in the mirror. I'm not sure whether it was the fact that the clothes actually fitted me because they'd been bought specifically for me, instead of being hand-me-downs, or that I was wearing make-up and had managed to style my usually unruly waist-length hair in a loose bun, but I couldn't seem to stop smiling. As ever, Paul was waiting for me outside with the car. I'd chosen to leave for work early, just stopping on the way to collect Mr Heart's dry cleaning.

I rode the private elevator to the tenth floor and, after depositing my handbag at my desk, I continued to Mr Heart's office to hang his dry cleaning up in his private wet room. At the same time, I was zoned out listening to messages left on my mobile phone through my earpods. That's all I could hear as I opened the wet room door – at which point, I froze.

I found myself staring, wide-eyed, at the naked full frontal of a very red-blooded male specimen. He was the epitome of masculine perfection. He had a smooth, swarthy complexion stretched over perfect bone structure, and a rough, rugged look. He must have stood a good six foot four inches in his bare feet, and had an incredibly well-defined, lean yet muscular frame. He was just rinsing the last of the soap from his hair while scrubbing his hands over his face. My eyes traced the stream of suds cascading down the spectacular chest and abs into that perfect V at his groin; the Adonis belt, I believe they call it, and with good reason. I could not avert my eyes from the largest cock I had ever seen.

Initially, he was soft and flaccid but as he became aware I was watching him, the effect was instantaneous. What I thought was impressive before became sublime. My body's traitorous response saw my nipples harden painfully, but they somehow felt incredibly sinful and erotic, rubbing against the lace cups of my new bra; I sensed my satin and lace underwear dampen uncomfortably against my freshly waxed mound. This man was beautiful, with thick, wavy, black, shoulder-length hair, and a cleft chin. The sudden temptation to join him and lick the water right off that cleft chin of his was almost overwhelming. The smell of his spicy, masculine shampoo and body wash was tantalising and invaded my senses. My goodness, things tightened in places I did not know could tighten.

As usual in any awkward situation, I flushed beetroot red. The heat climbed up my breasts and neck but I couldn't tear my eyes away.

"Who the hell are you?" The man's voice jolted me.

"I'm Darcey Robson." At least I could still remember that part. "I'm Mr Heart's PA. Who are you?"

Thankfully, he grabbed a towel, because I was rooted to the spot and couldn't move even if I'd wanted to.

"I'm Caleb Heart."

I didn't seem able to answer; only to gawp.

"Although it's a pleasure to meet you, Darcey," the man went on, overriding my silence, "I've been travelling for hours and I'd really like to shower alone. So, do you think we could make our introductions once I've got my clothes on and have a cup of coffee in hand?" He didn't seem even remotely embarrassed.

I managed to recover myself a little. "I'm so, so very sorry, Mr Heart. Of course, Mr Heart." I didn't know where to put myself. But even the mortification I felt didn't stop the rush of disappointment when he covered his beautiful, pulsing length and firm arse.

I slid from the room, utterly abashed. Oh ... My ... Good ... God ... What had I just done?

I put my hands over my burning face and a nervous laugh escaped my lips. This was great. I was going to be fired for being a pervert and a peeping tom before I'd even had the chance to establish myself in the job. I couldn't stop my cheeks and neck from burning with embarrassment and discomfiture, not just at what I'd seen but at my wanton reaction – towards my boss of all people! Way to go, Darcey. How the hell was I going to work with this man? So much for thinking he'd be a thinning-haired, middle-aged bore. I almost wished he was.

As I set the coffee machine going and made a mint tea to take down to Julia, the elevator pinged and in walked Gloria.

"Morning, Darcey. I tried to ring you but my phone lost signal. I just wanted to let you know Mr Heart will be in the office at some point today."

Gloria took one look at my face and knew something was wrong. I was still puce and had to relive my mortification as I told her what had happened. She laughed so hard I honestly thought she was going to have a fit. While she was still beside herself, I took a call, then went to collect a parcel from reception. I was thankful for the distraction and the opportunity to beat a hasty retreat.

Julia greeted me from behind the reception desk and handed me the parcel, as I set the mint tea down next to her. I thought she looked tired and uncomfortable, but she only had a week or so to go before starting her maternity leave. She told me I looked fabulous, with a definite pep in my step, and asked who'd put it there.

"Was it Dylan from planning?" she asked. "Because he's been asking about you."

I didn't even know who this Dylan guy was. He had been grilling everyone about me apparently, making what he thought were discreet enquiries. I tried to change the subject.

"Oh, come on," she pushed. "I'm about to have a baby. I need to live vicariously through someone."

Reluctantly, I spilt the beans. Like Gloria, Julia exploded with laughter. I was slightly concerned the prolonged outburst wouldn't throw her into early labour there and then. As I left her, I still couldn't get that vision of male perfection out of my mind, and I flushed all the more. The feel of my damp panties was also a reminder likely to stay with me for the rest of the day. I noticed numerous people staring at me once I reached the lift, but I figured it was because I was still seven shades of purple.

I headed to the mailroom to run the last of my errands. No sooner was I through the door when Mike spotted me.

"Hey, Darcey. Thanks for putting business my daughter's way."

"Don't mention it." If I thought this was going to be a quick visit, I was mistaken.

Mike peered at me. "What's happened? Looks like someone's ruffled your feathers." And he put the kettle on.

Here we go again, I thought. As I finished telling him about my encounter, he was howling with laughter, tears streaming down his face. I could only hope Mr Heart would view the situation in the same way.

"Looking as you do," Mike managed to respond eventually, "I don't think Mr Heart would have minded the interruption."

Although I was only just getting to know him, Mike had a way of making me feel at ease.

As we finished our coffee, Joe, a young mail room guy, came over and asked me if I fancied going out with him and a group of the mail room staff for a meal and to a club next Tuesday night. He said they had reservations for Rumis, the Italians. I told him I couldn't go on a Tuesday because I had a second job. I'd only just met the guy but he proceeded to ask me a lot of questions in rapid succession – so much so that I started to feel a little wary: where did I live? Was I seeing anyone? What shifts was I working? Where did I like to hang out after work? How long did I plan on working here?

I was relieved when Mike swooped in and cut him off.

"Cool ya jets, son. Stop interrogating the poor girl," he said.

I thought Joe did look a little abashed. As I said my goodbyes, I made a mental note to ask Tony to make him and his friends a special dessert when they turned up, but not to give out any of my personal information. No doubt I'd see them. I might even be waiting at their table.

I was dreading the inevitable meeting with Mr Heart. I could feel my pulse thrumming and my heart beating staccato. I'd resembled a beetroot all morning. Every time I thought about what I'd done, I cringed and flushed all over again. My mind continued to wander back to his physical reaction after he'd noticed me blatantly ogling him, like a child at a sweetshop window. As I stepped out of the elevator, I could hear Gloria still laughing in his office.

I was so ashamed and knew I would never live this down, but I was also shocked at my visceral reaction to the sight of him. I'd become instantly turned on; my body had hummed with the need to touch and be touched. My clit had throbbed, my nipples ached and I'd had butterflies in my stomach. I'd never experienced that sort of instant attraction to anyone; not even to Andy. My next confession with Father Mark would be interesting, to say the least.

I sat at my desk and thought about how unprofessionally I'd handled the situation – and how desperately I needed this job. My mind was about to go down its rabbit hole again when Gloria came out of the office, smiling, followed by Mr Heart himself. I wanted the room to swallow me up. I could hardly bring myself to make eye contact with him, although he was now fully dressed, and I squirmed under his brooding gaze.

Gloria made the informal introductions but my stomach churned. I felt as though the devil had lit a fire under my feet. I shook Mr Heart's hand, discreetly wiping mine on my dress first. My body and blood still pulsated to a torrid beat as I gazed into the darkest, most intense chocolate eyes

I had ever seen. His still slightly damp hair and five o'clock shadow only added to his sex appeal. He could probably feel the heat emanating from my face and chest, as you could no doubt have roasted marshmallows on my cheeks. He smelt so good – good enough to eat! I knew that every time I smelled his bodywash and aftershave, I would be transported to that shower and a vision of him, gloriously naked, with his huge, thick cock and spectacularly firm butt that I could bounce a pound coin off. I hastily made my apologies as I was due in a meeting. I had never welcomed an accounts projecting and forecasting session with so much relish.

As the meeting ended, I struck up a conversation with Frank, who had been head of accounts at Heart Industries for fifty years. I'd only been asked to attend to take notes for Mr Heart, as he would be on a conference call with some overseas investors. However, Frank had been kind enough to introduce himself to me and show me to the meeting room. He had pulled out my chair and told me about all the changes he'd seen over the years under Mr Heart Senior, and now under Caleb Heart.

I knew Heart Industries was a huge global concern but I hadn't appreciated just quite how big it actually was, and how many different divisions there were. The company bought out failing businesses, stripping them apart and often selling off the most profitable areas. They then redeveloped the remaining land. Frank explained that some companies were retained and brought back to profitability through new management and modernisation.

The firm also developed various new technologies and had military contracts, but that side of the business was all completely confidential. They had their own construction, publishing, printing and marketing branches, so everything was handled in-house, which made sense.

To top all this, Heart Industries gave a lot back to the communities they served. They looked after their staff too. They had numerous charitable endeavours, where they partnered with other investors to create a safe haven for ex-servicemen and women, providing help, support and employment. They'd also built schools in remote villages overseas, and wells to provide clean drinking water to the settlements. The list went on. They were true humanitarian champions, so far removed from the likes of Rodger Abington and his enterprises. Abington was only out for himself.

Frank spoke so warmly of his time in the company. You could tell he had a soft spot for the Heart family and was an integral part of the building and the internal workings. As he walked me back to the lifts, he told me he was retiring on Thursday this week. He said his wife was claiming her husband back and he was looking forward to taking a fly-fishing holiday and seeing more of his grandkids. He then insisted on carrying all the accounts files up to my floor for me.

Gloria looked up when the elevator doors pinged open, and strode over to welcome Frank in a friendly embrace. I offered to make coffee, although I knew I would now need to offer some to Mr Heart too. I knocked on his door and waited until I was asked to enter before pushing on the handle.

"Sorry to disturb you but would you like a coffee?"

The smouldering eyes dragged themselves away from the document he was reading to fix themselves directly on me. He seemed to scan my whole body for a moment, as if he could see through my clothing. There went my traitorous nipples again, which had a direct link to my throbbing clit. I just seemed to be a bundle of dampness around this man.

"Yes, white no sugar, thank you."

I simply nodded, as I appeared once again to have swallowed my tongue in his presence and lost the power of speech.

Every day, as Gloria had told me, we took delivery of a selection of fresh sandwiches, muffins and fruit. Gloria grabbed her and Frank's coffees, together with a couple of deli sandwiches and muffins. I figured Mr Heart hadn't eaten yet, so I added a sandwich, muffin and apple to his tray. I knocked on his door and again waited till he told me to enter. He looked up, surprised to see me with a tray.

"Darcey, would you mind having a working lunch today?" he asked.

"Sure."

"Just grab yourself a sandwich and join me."

I still felt embarrassed – not just over walking in on his shower but also by the thought that I would happily have put my body between two slices of bread for him and slathered myself in mayo. Damp underwear was going to be a regular occurrence from now on, I feared.

We got down to business, hashing out the next week's itinerary and finalising details for the functions we were to attend together, and I gave him the highlights from the accounts meeting. As I sat on the other side of his desk, making notes on my laptop, we had a surprisingly easy conversation. There was no further mention of what had transpired earlier and, for that, I was eternally grateful.

I continued to take detailed notes and we discussed the accounts projecting and forecasting meeting. I also made a few observations of my own and gave my opinion, when asked, based on all I had read the previous day. Mr Heart seemed to be studying me, and a little of the tension left the room. I remembered to ask if there was anything planned for Frank's retirement. I didn't know what company protocol was for gifts and so on.

"What have you got in mind?"

"I know he likes fly fishing," I said. "I thought it would be nice to get him a little gift to do with that."

He gave me the most bone-melting smile and told me to get Frank something appropriate.

After our meeting was concluded, I stood up to leave and Mr Heart opened a drawer. He took out what looked like his own personal wallet and handed me a pile of notes.

When I glanced at him questioningly, he simply said, "Frank's present."

I was about to walk out of his office when he spoke again. "I normally only shower in my office after a run or workout. But next time, I'll be sure to sing loud enough for you to hear me."

For the umpteenth time that day, I flushed crimson and couldn't look the man in the eye.

"Thanks for the pre-warning," I spluttered and closed his door.

Chapter Three

Caleb:

As the door closed behind her, I blew out a breath I didn't even know I was holding. After two whole months stuck in the back of beyond working with a bunch of rough-and-ready contractors, Miss Darcey Robson was not what I was expecting. It was no wonder I'd had the reaction I did. I'd had to smile when I saw the look on her face during her impromptu little peep show. She flushed the cutest shade of pink as those huge doe-eyes of hers lowered. I was so busy drinking in the vision blushing beautifully before me that it took my brain longer than I would have liked to snag the towel.

There's an almost virginal, innocent quality about her. I watched as her nipples beaded into tight points under her tailored dress, and imagined what it would be like to drag her into the shower with me and strip her naked; take one of those perky, large nipples into my mouth and suck, then spin her round to face the wall, hands braced, leg raised, driving harder and deeper into her from behind up against the wall, until we both exploded with a shuddering release. I wanted to feel my hands and mouth on those tempting tits and tight arse, while entwining my fingers in her beautiful, long, dark tresses and pulling till she groaned in ecstasy.

I could see what all the fuss was about. There had been a bit of a buzz around the office and her name had come up in more than one conversation. Our Miss Darcey Robson certainly had been causing a stir. If my own body's reaction was anything to go by, half the guys in the company would be like dogs in heat. What was my mother thinking? While I could truly see the appeal, I had no intention of going there. I was rather proud of my confirmed bachelor status and had no wish to change it anytime soon.

Sitting at my desk, I found myself looking at the projections, forecasts and accounts for the latest construction works. I'd only asked Darcey's opinion to provoke a reaction so that I could watch her blush. I hadn't expected an intelligent, insightful spin on a problem that had repeatedly plagued one of our sites in particular. It was rare that I was truly impressed. Miss Robson seemed to be something of an enigma.

I worked long into the night and, no matter which way I manipulated the figures, she was right. Her throwaway comments were bang on the money. I ran the scenario she suggested and forecasted a twenty per cent saving with increased productivity. This idea of hers could potentially save hundreds of thousands of pounds but, most importantly, it could get the project back on track and within budget constraints. I needed to know if Darcey's insight and astute business acumen was a fluke or if it could be replicated with other projects. This excited me and I looked forward to finding out.

Losing all track of time, I didn't look up from my desk until 3:30 a.m. There was no point going home now, so I thought I might as well crash on my pull-out bed. I decided to grab a shower first and, as I entered the wet room, memories of the morning filled my head. I was almost sure I could still smell her perfume lingering in the air. The hot water cascaded down my body and I lathered the soap in my palms. Then, with cock in hand, I found myself pumping my shaft while resting my other hand against the cool, tiled wall. I reached my release with all the enthusiasm of a horny teenager.

Christ, I was in trouble if this was the reaction she solicited from a mere memory.

Darcey:

Paul rang me to see what time I wanted to leave this evening. For all that I was still feeling guilty about the full morning I'd spent at the salon and the money it must have cost the firm, I couldn't stay late today. I had to collect groceries and prescriptions for Mr and Mrs Shoemocker and was going to cook them a nice meal.

I helped Mrs Shoemocker get her husband ready for bed. He wasn't having a good day today. I held his wife's hand while she sobbed. My chest tightened like a vice and it felt as though I could barely swallow around the lump in my throat. Her love for him shone like a brilliant beacon. I hoped he would find his way back to her again. His periods of lucid thought were becoming fewer and fewer.

I sang softly as she tenderly brushed his hair. It was in that moment that I knew what true love was all about. It wasn't all hearts and flowers; it was about sharing your very soul and becoming one entity, so that when one hurt, you both hurt. I suggested getting some outside help, but Mrs Shoemocker wouldn't hear of it. My heart broke for the pair of them when she said she'd made her promises in front of almighty God many years ago when she'd declared she would love him "in sickness and health till death us do part". Silent tears streamed down my cheeks because, ohh ... to be loved like that.

As I greeted Paul at the car the next morning, I was looking forward to getting to work bright and early. It was officially Frank's last day today: retiring after fifty loyal years of working for the same firm. I was excited because I'd arranged for a special cake to be made. I'd mentioned to Debbie, one of the typists I'd met in the lower office, that I needed to buy a cake. She'd told me her mum owned a bakery on the other side of town and she could take care of it. We'd come up with a design and her mum had sent me a picture of the finished item. It looked fabulous.

When I'd taken the present money from Mr Heart the other day, it wasn't until I got back to my desk that I realised he'd given me five hundred pounds in fifty-pound notes. I did a little research and found an outdoor pursuits shop specialising in fly fishing equipment. After negotiating a fantastic deal, I was able to buy a new rod, reel and fishing box.

When I went down to the accounts office later that afternoon, I mentioned Mr Heart's generosity and said we needed everyone in meeting room number four at 1:00 p.m. on Thursday. I also said it was top secret. To my surprise, everyone started to chip in and soon I had a retirement fund for Frank. I was touched by all the kind stories, good wishes and the sheer generosity of his co-workers and friends. In the end, the fund almost matched the generous donation from

Mr Heart. So the rest of the money bought a weekend fly fishing retreat, and a spa treatment for Frank's wife. I also arranged for her to be collected by Paul and brought to the office, so she could see first-hand how well her husband was thought of. I ordered an additional bouquet of flowers from Mike's daughter and the scene was set.

When I reached my desk that Thursday morning, I found a stack of files that Mr Heart wanted me to read through and familiarise myself with. I loved the challenge! I set the coffee machine going and took in the deliveries. It was then that I noticed Mr Heart's office door wasn't closed, and I could see his jacket still draped over the back of his chair. I approached with caution and gave a gentle knock. No answer. On opening the blinds, I found Mr Heart fast asleep. He looked more relaxed, more carefree than I'd seen him before; not the serious, brooding CEO of the last few days.

I left the room to make him a cup of coffee, and grabbed a croissant and a glass of fresh orange juice. I figured he must have been burning the midnight oil. When I returned, a wisp of hair had fallen over his eye and, before I knew what I was doing, I was on my knees in front of him, gently brushing it away.

He woke and looked rather startled. I gave him the breakfast tray, then left his office, glancing back just in time to catch a slight smile playing on his lips.

Once Mr Heart was dressed and ready, he popped his head out of his office. I reminded him about his appointment at Franco's at 10:30 a.m. and let him know that Paul would be waiting downstairs in the town car at 10:00 a.m. I could tell by the sheepish look on his face that it must have slipped his mind.

"And don't forget your dinner plans at Verve tonight for your mother's birthday. I took the liberty of ordering flowers for you, which will be delivered to the restaurant this evening."

"Have you checked out the files I left on your desk?" he asked.

I had a stack of correspondence to answer but, while I was photocopying all the manuals for the current job sites, I'd begun to have a look at them.

I nodded. "I've almost finished going through them."

"Good. I want you up to speed as soon as possible so we can discuss the findings."

I liked my new job but Mr Heart was proving to be a hard taskmaster. I got the feeling he wasn't that keen on my suggestions from yesterday. Or maybe he didn't think I was up to the task, especially after the way I'd handled myself over the whole shower incident.

I sat down with a couple of the files that were troubling me. After reviewing all the information, two things had become glaringly apparent: three of the current projects were significantly over budget, and they seemed to use fluctuating quantities of cable. This was even though they were the same size build as some of the others and nothing was flagged up about any specific building regulations or difficulties on site. The costs were spiralling and the delays were having a knock-on effect on the rest of the build.

I explained what I'd found to Gloria. She seemed shocked that I'd discovered this correlation between the inconsistencies, especially as one of Heart's most loyal site managers was involved. I needed more information and more space to work undisturbed, so Gloria told me to use Mr Heart's office while he was out. Gloria then went to check personnel records to see if there had been any new foremen taken on in each of the problem projects or if there had been major staffing issues.

I spread the files on the floor and a pattern began to emerge. I would have to confirm a few suspicions I had, as I could find no signs of theft. But then again, I was no accountant and none of it made sense. I needed to speak to the best man for this job – and he was only employed with the firm until 1:00 p.m. It was ironic really that I needed Frank. I gave him a call to explain my findings and he asked me to come right down.

We sat in his office with all the costings sheets. Frank explained he'd already checked for fraud but the stock levels didn't support that theory. He broke the file down into sections and told me that, once each department was finished with their part of the file, then it was put back. But at no time did any one department have the file in its entirety. The little spark in his eyes told me more than he could ever say in words, and I knew why the man had done the same job for fifty years. He was like a dog with a bone; clearly, it was a male pride thing.

Multiple cups of coffee later, Gloria joined us, and the muddied waters began to clear as we merged all that we knew to be fact.

I didn't believe it was theft or that there had been any malicious intent. When I voiced my theory to Gloria and Frank, they began to laugh at how simple it could be. I figured no theft had taken place because the stock levels supported the current quantities of cable on various sites. What I noticed, however, was that certain sites were ordering vast quantities of the wrong colour cable. When the stock take had been done and the inventory taken, the quantities were right but they weren't stored at the specific sites they had been ordered for. There were also additional and unnecessary freight charges for redistribution. When Gloria added her piece of the puzzle with the personnel information, it appeared that one man alone had been in charge of the ordering.

The company had changed suppliers halfway through many of the builds, adding to the confusion, but that was because the firm they'd been using to supply the cables kept sending the wrong colours needed for the various stages of construction. I didn't pretend to understand the intricacies of wire gauge and its use, but I figured the problem could be something as simple as colour blindness. So Gloria went back to personnel to see if the foreman had ever been tested for this.

I'd discovered that the manufacturer had changed the way the cables were ordered and labelled to meet with new government legislation for health and safety. The reason why some project managers weren't ordering cables of a certain colour was that there seemed to be a surplus at some sites. So, instead of ordering more stock, they simply arranged to have the overflow stock sent via freight.

I really hoped my idea was right because Gloria seemed to know the guy involved personally and held him in high esteem. She arranged an immediate eye exam for the foreman as a matter of the utmost priority and said she would inform me of the outcome as soon as it was known.

Following our discussions, I made my way back to Mr Heart's office. As I did so, I remembered that, in my excitement, I'd left the files strewn over the floor.

I was about to walk through the office door when I was greeted with: "What the fuck do you think you're playing at?"

I was slightly shocked, and Mr Heart then lashed me with a torrent of abuse, not giving me the opportunity to respond. I guess I deserved it to some extent because I should have tidied the room before I left to go downstairs.

The colour rose in my face and chest at the admonition and tears sprang to my eyes. But I refused to cry, and just kept reminding myself how much I needed this job. I picked up all the files and put them back in order, placing them neatly on my desk. I then decided it would be better for both of us if I took my lunch break, which would hopefully allow Mr Heart time to cool off. It was already noon and I was aware I had Frank's presentation at 1:00 p.m. I grabbed my bag and left, feeling dejected and seriously deflated.

Soon afterwards, I found myself in the postroom with Mike. We sat eating our lunch and Mike produced a small bar of chocolate from his bag and offered it to me.

"Chocolate mends everything," he said. "It's the only weapon in a man's arsenal."

I unwrapped it and began to suck the life out of each cube, savouring every morsel as it melted on my tongue.

"You have to understand," Mike added, "I lived in a house full of women. With a wife and three daughters, over the years it's been survival of the fittest. Even the guinea pig and the dog were female. So I kept a hidden stash of chocolate, because it mends broken hearts, sorts out PMT, which was 'the wife's department', makes a fabulous bribe, soothes irate tempers, and gains forgiveness in the most dire of circumstances."

Even though his wife had sadly passed and his daughters had moved out, Mike still kept a supply of chocolate because he never knew when he might get a surprise visit from one of his girls or his granddaughters.

I smiled. "There is one thing that should always accompany chocolate, though."

Mike held his arms open. The man was a genius and I stepped into his fatherly embrace.

When I checked the time, I realised I'd have to hurry if I was going to make it to Frank's retirement presentation. But a very excited Gloria intercepted me before I reached the meeting room.

"I've been looking for you all over. Where on earth have you been?" she gushed. "Your theory about colour blindness was spot on. We're now rolling out testing for all staff as part of the medical. Darcey, do you have any idea how much money and time you have just saved Heart Industries?"

"No. But I know how much trouble I'm in with Mr Heart."

Gloria was about to reply when Mr Heart and Frank appeared.

Frank's face lit up when he saw me. "Has Gloria told you about the test results?"

"Yes," I said. "It's good news."

Frank turned to Mr Heart and proclaimed me an analytical genius. I felt I was dying with mortification yet again, and the praise didn't stop the rest of way to the meeting room. Both

Frank and Gloria waxed lyrical about my findings. When Mr Heart's eye caught mine, he gave me a deeply apologetic look.

I was glad Frank had just opened the meeting room door. The screams and hollers, along with the raucous chorus of "For He's a Jolly Good Fellow", rang out and put paid to the current conversation. Frank gazed at his friends and colleagues, looking slightly glassy-eyed. His wife stood waiting for him, tears running down her cheeks. Mr Heart took control of the proceedings and presented Frank with his gifts and cake, while his wife received her fabulous bouquet and gift certificate. I noticed she read the card attached and, just as Frank wound up his genuinely heart-felt speech, she read it again, this time aloud:

"After a fifty-year loan, we are returning your husband to you. Enjoy your retirement together, for behind every great man is an even greater woman. Thank you for all you have given this firm. Kind regards, Mr Caleb Heart and staff."

As I left the room, I heard people praising Mr Heart for his thoughtful and generous gifts.

My iPad flashed with a reminder that I was expected to attend a charity benefit that evening with Mr Heart. How could I have forgotten? I'd been looking forward to it but now I was terrified in case I made any more mistakes. I didn't want to give Mr Heart a reason to let me go.

I tidied my workstation and ran a whole host of errands that would keep me away from my desk for the rest of the day. I fired off a quick email to Mr Heart, justifying where I'd been and what I'd been doing, and informing him I would meet him in the lobby of the hotel at 7:00 p.m. prompt. I didn't bother Paul as I figured Mr Heart would be using the car this evening. I'd grab myself an Uber.

I had a hair and make-up appointment booked with Franco; it was my intention to be showered and massaged at the salon to try to smooth out the stress of the day before going home to slip into my gown for the evening. Franco gave me a sleek, shiny up-do that made me feel like a 50s pin-up model. The man was hilarious and stunning. His truly beautiful face must have been chiselled by the gods, and he was a demon with a make-up brush and a pair of scissors. That was his true gift to the world. He made me feel relaxed and seemed to know what I needed before I did. Thank goodness the man was gay. He'd seen way more of my body than was decent and, for once, I didn't care. As I sat at the make-up station, deeply engrossed in our gossip, he grasped my front-fastening bra and unclipped it. I let out a little squeak, but he laughed and told me he had to contour and powder the girls to look their best. By the time he'd finished, this ugly duckling felt like a swan.

As I walked into my little bedsit later, I looked and felt sensual and sexy. My skin was soft, glowing and dewy looking. I couldn't help caressing my legs as they were so smooth, and I could still smell the subtle scent of the pure essential oils I'd been massaged with.

I loved the dress Susan and Gloria had picked out, but I did feel a little naked, even though it was cap-sleeved and mid-calf length. It was a scarlet, silky creation, cut low at the front and designed to hug every curve, with a cowl scoop-back that stopped just above my butt cheeks – meaning I couldn't wear anything underneath. As soon as I stepped into it, the fabric clung to my thighs, slid over my waist, and caressed my large nipples. The stockings felt sheer on my legs and the lace tops gripped my thighs deliciously. And, ohh, my goodness ... the stilettos. They were my one true weakness – black, with a strip of the same colour red material as the dress woven through them, and finished with an elaborate bow on the side and a cluster diamanté brooch. This outfit had cost more than two months' wages.

I could feel the butterflies in my stomach begin to flutter again. What if Mr Heart hadn't calmed down? What then? Looking round my little bedsit, I knew how important it was that I keep this job. Still, although my furniture was old and mismatched, at least my home was scrupulously clean. I looked after what little I had.

As I added the finishing touches to my outfit, there was a gentle knock at the door. I cursed, hoping whoever it was wouldn't make me late. Pulling the door open, I found myself staring at a huge bouquet and the largest bar of milk chocolate I'd ever seen.

My palms grew warm; my breath caught in my throat and I lost the power of speech. There in front of me was the very debonair Mr Heart himself in a sexy-as-hell black tuxedo; broad shoulders narrowing to a slim waist, with a crisp, white shirt and black bow tie.

I noticed he didn't look too happy so my heart instantly sank.

"Would you like to come in?" All I could think was that something must be wrong because I was supposed to meet him in the hotel lobby.

He managed to make me feel even more uncomfortable as he blatantly scrutinised my appearance.

I hesitated. "Do I need to change my outfit?"

"No." That was it by way of explanation. He seemed to gather himself and asked me to turn round. "You look perfectly fine."

Being braced for the worst, all I could utter was, "Oh."

Not exactly what a girl dreamed of hearing.

Looking into those intense chocolate eyes, I thought I saw something other than the usual brooding frustration and anger. For a fleeting moment, I thought I saw lust. It was quickly replaced with embarrassment and he glanced down.

"These are for you." He presented me with the chocolate and flowers and I somehow knew Mike must have had a word in his ear.

Before I could stop myself, I said, "Do I get the hug that comes with the chocolate?"

He looked a little taken aback and the tips of his ears turned red ... and was that a blush? Then his facial expression softened and suddenly I was enveloped in a surprisingly comfortable and welcome hug. The feel of a pair of strong, masculine arms wrapped tightly around me, and the scent of his body wash and aftershave – sandalwood with a hint of spice – filled me with a sense of belonging and calm. I melted into his embrace.

Neither one of us seemed in a rush to break the contact. As he held me close, he whispered an apology into my hair for his behaviour earlier. This mercurial man was so frustrating. How could he make me feel so many emotions in one day?

"I thought you were going to fire me."

"What an earth gave you that idea?"

"Your ... outburst." I flushed and hid my face against his chest.

Caleb used a finger to gently raise my chin, and my gaze up to his. "In less than one week, you've managed to do what five teams of top professionals have failed to establish in months."

"I guess I just hit lucky," I said.

He let go of me, took a step back, and his cool, steely demeanour seemed in place once more.

I picked up the necklace I needed to finish my outfit, then handed it to him and asked him to help me fasten it. As I turned round, he caressed the side of my neck with his huge palm, moving one of my wayward tendrils of hair so it didn't get caught in the clasp. I could swear I heard him take a deep breath. Did he honestly just sniff me? Every nerve ending within me thrummed with desire. The anxious butterflies in my stomach became excited and I felt drunk with his heady scent and warm touch.

Caleb:

This little vixen was going to be the death of me. What the hell was she wearing? Her tits were glorious; like soft, rounded pillows presented in a scarlet-red satin case for my pleasure. I needed to see the back of that gown but I felt as though I'd swallowed my tongue. Then – Jesus, when she turned, I could see her long, swan neck, entire spine and creamy, flawless skin. The dress draped over the globes of her arse cheeks and all I wanted to do was lick down that slender neck and sink my teeth into that peachy firmness.

I inhaled her intoxicating smell and felt my cock stir to life instantly, and incredibly painfully against the confines of my zipper. I had to adjust myself when she wasn't looking – I was so hard I could have hammered nails. It dawned on me that I couldn't let her leave my side tonight. Many of the regular sharks who'd be at this function would come circling. I knew a lot of those dirty, lecherous old bastards and they'd be getting nowhere near Darcey if I had anything to do with it.

My reaction to my personal assistant now made me feel even more like a dog as I remembered the look I'd put on her face earlier when I'd lost my shit after walking into my office. Seeing her eyes shine with tears, I'd immediately regretted it. It wasn't her fault. I was just frustrated after the conference call with both my brothers and Darcey bore the brunt of it.

I then felt even worse when my mother and Frank told me about the discovery she'd made. They were so animated and excited – I'm sure they both thought she could walk on water. And the thing is, that was part of the reason I was so pissed. I'd had my best business analysts looking into it for months; they'd approached the situation from every angle, or so I'd thought. No, I couldn't afford to mess this up because I had a feeling I was only beginning to scratch the surface of Miss Robson's talents. I needed to start thinking with the head on my shoulders and remember she was my assistant.

The flowers and chocolate had been Mike's idea. He wasn't too happy when I told him what had happened. Darcey seemed to be a firm favourite of his already. The little minx was weaving her spell over everyone, including me.

With my hand firmly on the base of her back, I guided her out of her tiny apartment to the waiting car.

Darcey:

When we arrived at the charity benefit, Mr Heart climbed out of the car first and held his hand out to me. I felt like a starlet on the red carpet. We had pre-drinks and Mr Heart took great pains to introduce me to all the key players in the room. He never broke the physical contact between us, keeping his open palm on my lower back the entire time. The feel of his large, warm, slightly calloused hand caressing my skin sent a rush of moisture between my thighs. I couldn't help erotic thoughts of where else I'd like to feel those hands. Normally, I would take exception to being herded like a sheep. But, whether it was the openness of his caress or his possessive, dominant display, he seemed to ensure other male guests did no more than look, for which I was eternally grateful.

Then it happened.

We passed a table, and I heard him and smelled his cloying aftershave before I saw his smug, slimy face: Mr Abington, alongside his jackass of a son, Trevor. He stopped Mr Heart by offering his hand to shake. A cold shiver ran up my spine. Thanks to this creep, I had struggled to get a new job after walking out of his office. The pair of them, father and son, had made my skin crawl with their constant lewd innuendos and inappropriate, "accidental" touches. That's to say nothing of Mr Abington's shady business dealings – and the fact that I couldn't abide either of them.

Mr Heart shook the offered hand. "Rodger. Trevor." He gave a slight nod of his head.

"You're a lucky bastard, Caleb," Mr Abington said. "Just how did you get that Pearson deal sewn up before we even got wind of it to place a bid ourselves?"

Mr Heart smiled. "As you said, Rodger, just luck."

I noticed Mr Abington glaring at me, while Trevor looked me up and down as though I was naked, the sleaze.

Then Mr Abington spoke to me. "Ah, Diane. How nice to run into you again. I see you've fallen on your feet."

What the hell was that supposed to mean? He knew my name wasn't Diane.

"We had her for a spell but had to let her go," he continued, looking at Mr Heart.

"Well, Rodger, it appears my luck just keeps growing," Mr Heart replied, quick as a whip. "Darcey here has been a spectacular find. So thank you for that."

I flushed ten shades of pink, but my smile and face lit up like a Christmas tree, while father and son were rendered speechless.

"Excuse us, gentlemen," Mr Heart finished, and guided us past their table.

As we were announced and shown to our seats for the evening, he leaned towards me and whispered in my ear, "Please call me Caleb."

Abington:

I loathed these infernal fucking events. Only half an hour in and I was already bored rigid. Business discussions floated about, serving as a thin veil over the self-indulgent boasts of entitled, pretentious pricks who thought they were the next Titans of commerce. These overambitious arseholes just loved to brag about their latest endeavours. No doubt my fuckwit of a son would have his dick stuck in some hole by the end of the night – whether it be male or female was of little consequence to me. I'd already made my mind up to leave right after the meal had been served. I'd have gleaned all I needed to know by then. Why prolong the tedium?

I was aware of some sort of commotion at the far end of the room. Then I saw what had caused it: like Moses parting the fucking sea, people dropped back to make room for Caleb Heart. They seemed to fall over themselves to be in his presence, fawning at his feet. The cocky bastard infuriated me. Just like his father before him, he was a thorn in my side. He almost always seemed to get in first on so many of the deals I wanted to make and the firms I wanted to buy. I'd never been able to work out how the fucker did it, even when I'd had surveillance on him.

Then I saw her. Darcey Robson. The only woman capable of getting my cock hard over the last few years, and the one who got away. Tonight she looked like a wet dream and seriously fuckable. What I wouldn't have given to tie that flawless flesh up and whip her till her creamy skin turned the same delectable shade of red as her dress. I was still furious over the fact that she'd dared to leave my employ before I'd had the opportunity to get balls-deep in her cunt.

So, now she was working for Caleb Heart. Someone somewhere had seriously fucked up. Why hadn't my informants told me about this? When had Heart Industries employed her? And how? I'd made damn sure Darcey Robson wouldn't get another job. I figured she'd have to come to me eventually, begging for her old position back. And, being the benevolent man I am, naturally, I'd have agreed. Then she'd have become my fuck toy until I got bored with her.

But this now ... this was a fucking problem. The nosey little bitch had had access to all my files while she was working for me. And now she was employed by the Hearts. Coincidence? Hardly. I noticed the way Caleb kept his hands on her at all times. There was something going on there and I didn't like it. She was mine first. This night had just got fucking worse. The gloves needed to come off. I wanted what was rightfully mine and I'd make sure I got it by any means necessary.

Darcey:

We sat down to a magnificent three-course meal. There was an itinerary for the evening's festivities, with a pianist playing while we ate, followed by dancing, then the raffles, auctions and finally a firework display. I was so excited.

To one side of me sat a jovial old gentleman, Jed, and his wife Noreen. I soon discovered they owned one of the largest UK-based shipping firms. They were genuinely warm and interesting to talk to. Noreen made fun at her husband's expense – it was their wedding anniversary and, for the last fifteen years, he'd always had to work. She then got on to the subject of music, telling me about the attentive, dashing, young Jed, who used to take her dancing.

"He never takes me dancing anymore, Darcey," she said with a mischievous smile. "He's too long in the tooth."

We ate our meal and the conversation flowed freely around the table. But after dessert was served, a member of staff approached Caleb and passed him a message.

Caleb stood. "Apologies, folks, please do excuse me. There's an urgent matter that needs my attention."

The band struck up and started to play "Only You" by the Platters, and Jed held his hand out to me for a dance. Noreen laughed, urging me up.

Jed led me to the dance floor and turned out to be a wonderful partner, light on his feet. We laughed and chatted as we twirled around the room. I could see he'd been a rather handsome man in his day. He was very distinguished-looking and, with the way he spoke about his wife and kids, came across as a really loving, family man. He told me Noreen's favourite songs were "I Put a Spell on You" and "Baby Just Cares for Me". That was how they'd met – at a dance.

As we made our way back to the table, there was a bit of a commotion on stage. The lead singer of the group had turned chalk-white and crumpled to the floor. After a moment or two, a rather red-faced hotel manager bustled over to the mic and made his apologies. And that's when inspiration struck.

Without stopping to think about what I was doing, I made my way to the stage and had a word with the manager. Seconds later, he was introducing me to the band – and it was only at this point that I began to wonder what the hell had got into me! But it was too late to back out now.

I settled myself at the piano, took the microphone and made an announcement. "Ladies and gentlemen, may I please have your attention for a moment? I'd like to give a very personal gift to a special couple who are celebrating their wedding anniversary today."

I smiled and saluted Jed and Noreen, then invited them to take to the floor. They stood up, flushed but delighted, as I began to sing and play "Baby Just Cares for Me". Other couples soon joined them on the dance floor and afterwards,

I received a round of applause and everyone started to shout for more. So I continued with, "I Put a Spell on You", finishing just in time to see the band's lead singer, now recovered, make her way back to the stage.

I sat down at our table again to see Jed holding Noreen's hand, while she had tears of happiness in her eyes. When I turned my head, I realised Caleb was standing next to me.

"I'm sorry, Darcey, but we need to leave. Something's come up."

Noreen and Jed embraced me in a hug as I stood, and they both kissed my cheek. Caleb raised an eyebrow at me, but I simply smiled. As we made to exit the hotel, various people stopped us and said how wonderful I'd been and what a lovely thing to do. I could feel the heat flush my face and chest as usual. Then, when we reached the foyer, the manager rushed over and thanked me profusely, presenting me with a bottle of Taittinger champagne for saving the day. I gave Caleb a sheepish glance, to see him looking perplexed and not best pleased at all.

"Well," he muttered, "you seem to have made quite the impression with everyone."

We climbed into the limo and I felt a little disappointed that we couldn't have stayed longer to see the fireworks. But I figured something important must have happened to make Caleb want to leave so soon.

He seemed to read my thoughts. "I've had a call from our chief foreman in Jakarta. The workforce is threatening to walk off site. This'll have a knock-on effect over all the other projects."

"Can't the foreman resolve it?"

Caleb shook his head. "It's a bit more complicated than that. Somehow the plans got switched. The team haven't been using the revised set."

"So what happens now?"

"I've spoken to my brothers – Adam looks after the architectural side of the firm, and Daniel deals with all our legal. We're going to meet up in Jakarta. I need to get back to the office so I'll drop you at your place."

"I'll come with you," I said. "I can help get everything together you're going to need for the trip."

By the look on Caleb's face, he wanted to decline my offer, but I could see he was also resigned to the fact it would be quicker with the two of us. I suggested we swing by my bedsit first so I could change.

I threw on a pair of sweats and an overlarge hoodie, pulled out all the hairpins in my fancy up-do and secured my hair in a messy bun on top of my head. I was good to go in eight minutes. We made it back to the office in under half an hour and I put on a large pot of coffee and set to work.

Caleb dived into his wet room and came out wearing a pair of sweats slung low on his hips, with a fitted t-shirt. How the hell was I supposed to think straight with him looking like that? Then it dawned on me: he was going away again. And I felt a little bereft. I couldn't believe I was having feelings like this after such a short time – and for my boss, for goodness' sake. I needed to get a grip. I wasn't even a blip on his radar.

We worked late into the night. The last thing I remember was labelling his files and cross-checking them against the costings' reports.

Chapter Four

Caleb:

Jesus, I was in trouble. As Darcey lay curled on the sofa, sound asleep, all I wanted to do was bury my face in her sweet-smelling hair, lick the smooth arch of her long, graceful neck, nip her small earlobes, and kiss her lush, tempting mouth. I'd almost swallowed my tongue when she opened the door to me tonight. I couldn't ever remember reacting to a woman so extremely. I felt as if I was losing my mind. I'd spent all my time with her in a state of painful and bloody embarrassing arousal. I had this overwhelming need to protect her but I didn't have the first clue why.

I knew I'd acted like a real arsehole today and I hated myself for it, but I couldn't seem to help myself. Darcey had made me look good and, like a real bastard, I'd taken all the credit and praise for her efforts. I noticed she'd slipped out of Frank's presentation at the first opportunity and gone back to slaving away at the workload I'd heaped on her.

My mother had loved the flowers that were delivered during our meal at Verve. Then, as I'd entered the building the other day, Julia, who worked on the main reception, had come waddling over to me, thanking me for the Mama & Babe vouchers I'd sent and the kind words I'd written in her card. I felt embarrassed by the attention but knew instantly who was responsible. Darcey made me seem like a better man than I was.

I couldn't escape her either. Everyone complimented me on what a wonderful find she was; how astute; how beautiful. If it hadn't been for Mike having a word in my ear, I'd have made an even bigger arse of myself.

As we'd walked into the hotel tonight, all eyes had been on Darcey. That dress she had on had me adjusting myself in the trouser department more than once. I wasn't wrong about the sharks circling either. Guiding her around the room, the feel of her silky-soft skin against my hand as I caressed her bare back, I found myself scowling at some of the dirty old bastards salivating over her. It was enough to turn my stomach. I felt like a dog pissing on his territory, but I made enough of a show to make my point.

Now, I felt selfish once again because I should have insisted on dropping her back home. Truth is, I was reluctant to let her go. Knowing I'd be flying out for God knows how long, I just wanted her with me for a little more time. This beautiful, gracious and astute woman had just saved Heart Industries a little over two million pounds in her first few weeks, which must be some sort of company record; she wasn't crowing about it or demanding a pay rise either.

We worked into the early hours together, pulling all the files and documentation that would be needed. While I packed my bag, she fell into a deep sleep on the sofa.

Darcey:

I jumped myself awake when I heard Caleb drop the lid on his case and zip it up. During my impromptu cat nap, I'd managed to drool on the soft leather couch and could feel the imprint of the cushion seam on my face. Nice.

It was 3:00 a.m. and I was dead on my feet. We entered the private lift and I was surprised when Caleb said he would drive me home. As soon as we stepped into the garage, my teeth began to chatter of their own accord. It was freezing. But then I felt his warm jacket being placed around my shoulders. It smelled of him: sandalwood and spice, and it felt so comforting.

He ushered me into a sleek, silver Aston Martin and, the next thing I knew, he was gently shaking me awake, as we'd arrived at my bedsit. He thanked me profusely for everything; told me I could have the day off tomorrow – or today, whatever!

I handed his jacket back and felt its loss in more ways than one. I honestly thought he was going to kiss me goodnight, but he simply tucked a lock of loose hair behind my ear. I have to admit even my tired brain felt disappointed. I gave one last wave goodbye, locked the front door, then staggered to my bed. And I knew no more.

I didn't wake till 9:00 a.m., which was a record for me. Even though I'd only been working for Heart Industries for a few weeks, I found a notification on my phone telling me my salary had been paid into the bank. When I opened the app to check my balance, I was shocked to see the payment was for £5000. Thinking there must be some mistake, I rang Gloria.

"No mistake," she said. "It's a bonus for a job well done." She also asked me to lunch and said she'd send Paul to collect me.

I felt I'd won the job lottery and I couldn't stop smiling. I could now afford to pay all my bills, buy food, and even splurge on a washing machine so there'd be no more trips to the local launderette – whoop-whoop, and I fist-pumped the air. I then channelled my inner Celine, jumping into the shower and singing "My Heart Will Go On" into my bottle of shower gel. I donned a smart pencil skirt, with a fitted blouse and matching jacket, and added a French twist to my hair and some light make-up.

Before I knew it, there was a knock on the door and Paul was standing waiting for me, with his trademark broad smile.

Gloria:

I was still reeling from the events of the last forty-eight hours. What with Darcey's discovery of the mixed-up cabling orders, my son's message at some ungodly time this morning, and the phone call I'd received from my old friend, Noreen, I knew I'd chosen well. This girl was the best thing to happen to Heart Industries in a long time; and especially to Caleb. As I sat in the back of the town car waiting for her, I felt rather smug. My machinations regarding my Caleb were working out better than I could possibly have wished for. Darcey had him all disconcerted and discombobulated but in the best possible way.

I still couldn't help but laugh at the shower debacle, but I was truly delighted by the reactions of them both; their faces had been a picture. And at least Darcey got to appreciate all that hard work Caleb put into looking after himself. I might be biased because he's my boy, but Caleb was no slouch. He was a truly beautiful man inside and out, just like his father had been. Sure, sometimes he took life and business a little too seriously and needed to learn to let his hair down. As his mother, I knew he could come off a little detached and sharp. But his bark was worse than his bite.

When Darcey slid into the car, a broad smile lit her face and she launched herself at me, catching me off guard with a hug. Being the mother of not one but three boys, hugs had got thin on the ground as they'd got older; I usually had to demand them as my motherly right. This warm, genuine young lady was an absolute tonic.

Noreen had taken great delight in filling me in on the charity night's events. She and Jed were besotted with her too. Apparently, Darcey had saved the entire evening and her voice was like an angel's. Noreen had even gone as far as to ask if she had a sister she could pair with her eldest son, James, as she didn't think Caleb would be giving Darcey up anytime soon. And what a striking couple they'd made. Until he was called away, Caleb hadn't taken his eyes (or his hand) off her all night as he'd guided her around the room.

"Neither of us is getting any younger," Noreen had added. "We need some grandbabies while we're still fit enough to run after them."

I relaxed back into the car seat and Darcey thanked me again and again, telling me how she could now buy a washing machine. The joy was written all over her face.

Darcey:

I was thrilled as we pulled up outside The Garden Café. I'd never been able to afford to come here. The food was supposed to be outstanding.

On the journey, Gloria and I had discussed the charity gala. She'd seemed surprised to hear about me singing and playing the piano, so I told her about the songs I sang to the Shoemockers and why I did it, and about singing at Rumis.

I opened up about my past a little too. I even found myself talking about Andy; how he'd been my rock and first love, but had sadly been killed on active duty in Afghanistan.

"I was brought up as a military brat," I told her, "moving from base to base with my strict Spanish Catholic father. He was a marine. My mother died when I was little and I don't really remember that much about her; just the odd thing. My dad did his best, but parent of the year he was not. He eventually died of lung cancer when I was eighteen." I shrugged. "I've been looking out for myself ever since."

The food at the café was truly delicious, but my jovial mood had subsided a little and, for some reason, I couldn't help feeling a bit melancholy. I decided to cheer myself up with a dessert of triple chocolate – a three-tier mud cake, with a chocolate marbled curl and a warm white-chocolate pouring sauce. The cake was decadent and rich in my mouth; a total taste explosion. Gloria laughed at my expression and I realised I'd moaned in ecstasy out loud. I don't know how I managed to eat the whole thing, but I even debated licking the delicate little plate.

We finished our cups of coffee and Gloria paid the bill. I'd need to start working out if I continued to eat like this.

Gloria wanted to go to Franco's for a manicure, but I mentioned I'd promised to call in to see if Mr and Mrs Shoemocker needed anything. I was a little taken aback when she asked if she could accompany me but I thought it was a great idea. Mr Shoemocker still wasn't too good and poor Mrs Shoemocker didn't get out to speak to many other people. I thought it would be nice for her.

Paul, who'd been waiting outside, had us at my building in no time. I went to head for the Shoemockers, but stopped. There was an odd smell in the hallway. What was that? Burning?

As I stepped further in, to my horror, I was greeted with thick, black, acrid smoke rolling out from under the Shoemockers' door.

No …

I screamed at Paul to call the fire brigade, then tried to open the door. The handle was hot; the door locked. I had a key to their apartment and fumbled to find it. Paul stormed past me and grabbed it. I glanced behind me to see Gloria on the phone, then, as Paul pushed me out of the way, I ran up the stairs to the other apartments and started to bang on doors, yelling, "Fire!" Thankfully, most people were out of the building at this time of day – but why the hell hadn't the smoke alarms gone off?

One guy came running past me in just his boxer shorts. I didn't really know him other than to say a passing hi, as I think he worked the permanent night shift at the hospital. I hammered on the last apartment door but nothing. No response.

As I made my way back downstairs, I could hear sirens in the distance. The smoke and heat became more intense. I was almost at the bottom but I couldn't see anymore and I couldn't stop coughing. My throat and nose were burning and my eyes stung and streamed from the smoke inhalation. I began to feel disorientated, whether from the mad dash and screaming or the smoke I didn't know, but I was only vaguely aware of a huge, meaty pair of arms throwing a blanket over me and hoisting me over a shoulder.

Next thing I knew, I was lying on the pavement outside my building. I heard Gloria say my name and looked up to find those meaty arms had belonged to Paul. He'd placed me down gently before slumping to the floor himself. Then pandemonium broke out as police, multiple fire crews and two ambulances turned up.

I moved my head and saw the man in boxers, an oxygen mask on his face and wrapped in a foil blanket, being triaged in the street. Paul had burns to his arm, hands and one side of his leg, and was being stretchered to the back of the waiting ambulance. The street was a flurry of activity. Everything seemed to run in slow motion; sounds were muted. Looking towards the building, I could see it was well ablaze. Glass had shattered in windows and flames licked around the frames.

Then everything went black ...

I came to in the ambulance. Gloria held my hand and I had an oxygen mask on my face.

Gloria was a mess; filthy and dishevelled. I asked about Paul and she told me he had burns but would be fine and was being treated for smoke inhalation. When I asked about the Shoemockers, she just shook her head and her eyes filled with tears.

Gloria:

At the hospital, they sedated Darcey, as she was suffering from shock, smoke inhalation and minor burns. Paul had been triaged in the cubicle next door and was in a bit of a bad way too. Medical teams dashed in and out, monitoring vitals, dressing burns and checking oxygen. Paul had pulled an old lady from the burning apartment, but she'd looked lifeless.

I tried to call Caleb, Adam and Daniel. Not one of them picked up, so frustratingly I was forced to leave messages. I called the office and spoke to Debbie. I needed her to find out who Paul's next of kin was. I also wanted her to keep trying to get through to the boys for me. As there was then nothing more I could do at the hospital, I took a black cab back to Darcey's old apartment building.

Everything was cordoned off when I got there and, by now, the blaze seemed to be under control. But what a mess. The whole building had been destroyed and there was water draining away, gushing black sludge down the street drains. Between the fire and the water, I doubted anything would be salvageable. People milled around; bystanders hung about, watching. All the neighbouring residents had been moved out of their properties for their own safety, while fire crews checked the other buildings for damage.

I managed to get the attention of a young police officer. I said I'd made the call to the emergency services and asked about the Shoemockers and if anything from Darcey's bedsit could be saved. I was ushered through the tape, where a senior police officer and the fire chief listened to my account of events. That's when I saw a private ambulance I hadn't noticed before. Two firemen exited the building carrying a body in a black bag. And a cry caught in my throat.

Poor Darcey. Her poor, dear friends.

Reporters had shown up, taking photographs. The police officer I'd been speaking to kindly gave me a lift to the station to make a formal statement, then eventually took me home.

Caleb:

I'd just switched off my alarm and rolled back over in bed when I happened to glance at my mobile screen. I seemed to have multiple messages from both my mother and the office. If it was anything serious, I was sure Darcey would have been in touch. As I'd given her the day off after the charity event, I'd resisted the urge to call her, not wishing to sound like a teenage girl phoning to see how her day was going.

I was roughly seven hours ahead of the UK so it would be somewhere around midnight back home. My brain was just starting to wake up when someone began to bang – actually bang – at my door. As it turned out, it was multiple someones. When I opened up, both Adam and Daniel barged straight past me into my room.

"Hey, where's the fucking fire?" I snapped.

"So you know?" Adam asked.

"Know what?"

"About the fire!"

I glared at him. "What fucking fire?"

They both started talking at once and Adam thrust his phone at me. It was my mum and she sounded upset.

"How soon can you get the plane refuelled and be back home, Caleb?"

"Why? What's happened?"

My mother filled me in and I felt sick to the pit of my stomach. Darcey and Paul had been hurt. Mum hadn't been able to track down Paul's next of kin so I said I'd take care of it. Paul worked for the company as a close protection detail and driver for my family. We'd all served together as brothers-in-arms in the Marines before we'd made it out after our last tour. Adam, Daniel and I had gone into the family business and Paul, whom I'd always thought of as another brother, came to work for us and ran our personal security.

I honestly thought the guy was made of Kevlar; bullets just seemed to ricochet off his arse. Talk about a cat with nine lives. We'd come through more tough scrapes than most without a hair on his pretty head being harmed. Now he'd been injured rescuing my girl, which sounded about right ...

Hang on a minute ... When had I started thinking of the little minx as mine? Jesus, I knew. Exactly the moment my eyes had met hers in that bloody shower, that's when. Darcey had become my first waking thought and the last thing I thought of when I went to sleep. She even starred in my best dreams.

I was still holding the phone and talking to my mother as I started shoving things back in my case. My brothers were both on their mobiles too – one organising the plane and the other making arrangements for Paul's care.

Darcey:

I woke up and my head was pounding. My throat, nose and chest hurt. I realised I was in hospital as I had a cannula in my arm, and I was hooked up to multiple drips.

A nurse came into my room to take my temperature. "How are you feeling? You did a very brave thing the other day, but it almost cost you your life."

I'd had a reaction to whatever pain medication the paramedic had given me; my sats had dropped to dangerous levels and I was also suffering from smoke inhalation. I'd blacked out on the stairs, splitting my head open and giving myself a concussion, just as Paul had found me. My memory of events was patchy: I remembered him hoisting me over his shoulder, then nothing more until I was outside; then once again in the ambulance – then now.

The gaps in between weren't hard to fill in, though. My waist-length hair must have come undone at some point. I noticed it had been singed short to about shoulder-length on just one side. I seemed to have other minor cuts, bruises and burns, but nothing too serious, and I tested my limbs while I lay in the bed to ensure everything worked and I could move. My head had a huge white bandage around it. Still, other than feeling as though I'd been hit with a Mac truck, I was okay.

The nurse said I still had a high temperature and needed to rest. She encouraged me to take small sips of iced water.

Then, all at once, my brain seemed to switch off its self-preservation mode and my thoughts flew to Paul and Mr and Mrs Shoemocker.

"How is Paul? Where is he?" I rasped. My voice hardly worked. "The Shoemockers?"

The nurse said Paul was in intensive care but was making good progress. Unfortunately, she didn't know about the Shoemockers. I inquired if my handbag had been brought in with me. I remembered leaving it in the car as I went inside the building. The nurse pointed to the chair. I asked if she could fetch my mobile and if it was okay to make a few calls to let people know I was safe.

It wasn't until I looked at the screen that I realised I'd been in hospital for a couple of days. I had no missed calls from Caleb; not that I'd expected any really – the guy was my boss, for Pete's sake. But I did have multiple calls from Mike, Mr Rumis and Tony, to name but a few. I called Mr Rumis and he began to cry and curse up a blue streak in Italian. I was fluent in Italian and Spanish, thanks to my father's career, but I still struggled to understand him as he was talking so quickly. I reassured him I was on the mend, but said I may not be able to sing or work for a while and that I'd keep him posted.

There was a gentle knock at my door and in walked Gloria. She seemed to have aged since I'd last seen her. Her eyes were puffy and there were dark circles underneath. She appeared exhausted. As she took one look at me, awake and sitting up in bed, we both started to cry. She lowered the bed guard on one side, sat down and cuddled me as close as she could without hurting me. I truly welcomed the contact. The enormity of the situation was hitting home and I began to sob uncontrollably.

Gloria:

I held on to Darcey and my heart broke for her all over again. I'd hardly had any sleep since the fire and was functioning on caffeine alone. Paul was suffering from burns, acute respiratory distress syndrome and respiratory failure. He was still in intensive care but showing signs of improvement. We had been so lucky.

The fire chief and police officers needed to speak to Darcey. They were still investigating the cause of the blaze but initial signs pointed to an electric kettle being placed on a lit gas stove burner and left there.

Darcey had lost everything; all her worldly possessions were gone, if not ravaged by the fire, destroyed by the water. Any mementoes of her parents were gone. Nothing was salvageable. All she had left in the world was a small carry case she had kept at the office. I'd stopped off at a department store before my visit today and bought her some toiletries, pyjamas, slippers and a dressing-gown. She was very grateful and appreciative, but about the things she'd lost, she simply said, "It's just stuff. Belongings can be replaced. I've done it before."

Then she began to cry. Her shoulders heaved for the devastating loss of her poor, dear friends and neighbours. She knew she wouldn't be here to tell the tale herself if it hadn't been for Paul, and I had a feeling she felt serious guilt over that too.

The fire had made the evening news. TV crews and reporters had all been clamouring to get the story.

I switched off her mobile phone for the time being. Then someone knocked on her hospital room door and her friend Tony walked in. Leaving the two of them to catch up, I went to see how Paul was doing. I took a detour via the hospital coffee shop, where I tried to call Caleb once again.

Caleb:

I honestly couldn't remember getting off the company plane; didn't remember leaving the airport or even the ride to the hospital. I was on autopilot. All I wanted was to get back to Darcey and to see for myself how Paul was doing. Almost sixteen hours in the air gives you time to think and get your priorities in order. I'd almost lost them both. Daniel was already looking into the legal side of things for Darcey's friends who'd died in the blaze; Adam had been trying to contact Paul's gran, who was his only family.

I was also worried about my mum. I knew she wouldn't have slept much and was spending her time at the hospital, looking after Darcey and keeping an eye on Paul, for which I was eternally grateful. Daniel had flown back with me but he went straight to the office. We'd decided Adam needed to stay in Jakarta for now.

I walked into the hospital's main reception and asked which room Darcey was in. I just needed to see her; just needed to hold my girl. I'd never believed in the notion of love at first sight. I thought it was rubbish perpetuated by dating agencies, social media and the retail sector as they tried to make a few quid from desperately lonely people. I had to admit, though, that that first meeting in the shower had changed my mind. I knew Darcey felt the same way I did. There was electricity. A definite spark between us.

I needed to make this official. Darcey would be mine because life was just too short to waste time.

The elevators in the hospital took forever and the corridors were like rabbit warrens. When I finally found her ward, a young nurse pointed me in the direction of her room. I rounded the corner, flew through the door and—

What the fuck!

A guy was sitting on Darcey's bed, cuddling her and kissing her cheek and head. Who the hell was he? And more to the point, who was he to Darcey? My girl was crying in his arms, her face tear-swollen, her nose red. I wanted to tear him away from her. I mean, had I read things wrong? I didn't think I had. She'd never mentioned a boyfriend.

Darcey and the guy looked up. I got a weak smile off my girl.

"Hey," she said. "What are you doing here?"

The man just stared at me, with as many questions in his eyes as I had in mine.

When Darcey introduced him, her voice was hoarse. "This is my good friend, Tony. Tony, this is my boss, Mr Caleb Heart."

Tony was about the same height and build as I was, with a swarthy look about him. To piss me off even further, he caressed the side of Darcey's face with the back of his hand and kissed her head once more, before announcing he'd better get back. I was just glad he'd taken his lips and hands off her as I was holding on to my sanity by a thread. He seemed to have come laden with chocolates, plastic containers with some sort of food in it, get-well balloons and cards. I watched him pick up his jacket, phone and keys, then he made to leave – but not before giving Darcey another kiss on the cheek. I didn't like the fact that he was clearly trying to send me a message and stake his claim.

I walked around the bed and gave her a sudden kiss of my own, which shocked both her and me. I knew it was pathetic but I'd made up my mind she was mine. When I looked up, I saw the guy exit the room, thank God. I immediately wanted to ask what she was thinking letting some bloke paw at her in hospital, and who he was to her. On the flight home, I'd thought about my entire interaction with her, from the point of first meeting. And I'd realised how much of an arse I'd been to her. All because I didn't want to admit I had feelings for her. I was actually now feeling possessive and jealous; and I was so far out of my comfort zone with this.

Once we were alone, I placed my hands on either side of Darcey's face and kissed her like a starving man. She melted into me and kissed me back, her tongue licking and sucking my top lip then gently nipping it with her teeth. This was the most sensual thing I had experienced with my clothes on and, in that moment, I was content.

A knock on the door meant I reluctantly had to take my mouth from Darcey's to look up. My mother stood in the doorway, beaming at me. Busted! Strangely, she didn't pass comment and just embraced me in a hug. I loved my mother dearly but her timing was awful. She pulled up a chair and proceeded to fill us in on Paul's progress.

Chapter Five

Darcey:

I could feel my eyes drooping as we talked. I know it's the height of bad manners but, no matter how much I loved having Gloria and Caleb's company, I must have dozed off at some point and they'd decided to leave. When I woke, the room was empty and the sun had long gone, replaced by the glow of a streetlight outside.

I was feeling much better. I asked the nurse if I could visit Paul and she said it would be fine as long as I was in a wheelchair, so she called me a porter. I sat next to Paul's bed and tears sprang to my eyes. Crying was all I seemed to do these days. But I guess with good reason.

Paul had first-degree burns to his face and third-degree burns to his right arm and leg, so he was completely bandaged. Gloria told me he'd had synthetic skin grafts to his arm and leg and they'd been worried about infection. It was a shock seeing all the machines and drips; the oxygen mask firmly in place. I wouldn't be here if it weren't for this brave, kind man and his heroic actions. I felt so damn guilty that I'd got away lightly compared to him.

I talked to him, even though he seemed unresponsive. Strangely, I found the gentle sounds of the beeping machines soothing. I spoke to him about everything, thanking him profusely for what he'd done. I hadn't realised Paul and Caleb were so close. I thought Paul was just an employee like me, but Gloria told me how the boys had served together.

Many of the staff, including Mike in the post room, were ex-services. Mike had served with Caleb's dad. The firm also employed family members of those who'd served, and who were still currently serving their country. They had a support group set up for staff whose partners were on active duty. There was a special fund, too, for the partners who needed additional help, and a company therapist was available. It explained why everyone was so loyal to the Hearts and why the firm had such a family feel. The more I found out about them, the more I thought how aptly they were named. I'd fallen in love with Caleb, even though I knew it could never go anywhere and was pointless. But your heart loves who it loves. Sometimes, you don't get to choose.

I told Paul about the shower debacle; it still made me smile and blush. I told him about my first visit to Franco's and my personal grooming hell. I said I must love Caleb as I'd agreed to have my pubic hair torn from my body just so I could look good on his arm while representing the company. Laughing, I also told him about Caleb being an arse to me at times, but added the man had some kind of magnetic pull. I noticed the Stepford wives in the foyer walk slightly taller when he strode past; I saw the effect he had in the entire typing pool but he never seemed to notice. I figured there would be a few damp chairs.

Once I'd started talking, it seemed I couldn't stop. I told Paul about my dad; about growing up on various military bases and about my strict Catholic upbringing. I talked about

Tony and Mr Rumis. I explained I'd learned to play the piano as I was a latchkey kid and I hated the silence in the house. My father only allowed me to play classical music or hymns at home but, when he was out, I would play all sorts of things – "The music of the devil," he used to say, because it led to sin.

My father didn't like me having friends in the house, but I used to go to church to clean there, and the priest taught me to play the piano and allowed me to practise. I still loved the smell of a Catholic church and the distinctive aroma of lemon and beeswax furniture polish. It was like a balm to my heart.

I realised, as I chatted, that it sounded as though I'd had a sad life, but I hadn't. I'd never needed companionship. I was quite self-sufficient even as a child. I'd never had the guiding hand of a mother, but my dad did have "friends" who would try to take me under their wing from time to time. One lady, Louisa, had lasted longer than most. She was Italian, like my mother. We only spoke in Italian or Spanish at home.

Even in my early teenage years, a boyfriend would have been out of the question, as my studies always had to come first. I never dated or visited the cinema. I wasn't completely naive and guileless, though. I had access to the internet and the freedom of a library card, thank goodness. I always carried a book with me wherever I went. And while I did study hard, I also used to love to curl up with a spicy, hot and steamy bodice-ripper of a book. My father would have had a fit if he'd known what I was reading. But as they say, as long as a lady carries a book with her, she will always have company – and a weapon.

I went on to explain to Paul how I'd met Andy's family at church not long after he'd returned from his first tour of duty. My father had already become ill and Andy's family used to help me out occasionally with his care. They were all devout Catholics too and were fourth-generation military. Andy and I started dating just before I turned eighteen. We were inseparable but, being of such a strong faith there was no sex before marriage. So, we kissed, held hands and made plans for the future. We had it all mapped out. I was going to finish my education, get engaged, then eventually marry and raise a family.

Only that was a pipe dream and had never happened. Life got in the way. First, there was the death of my father. Then Andy. I described how he'd been ambushed in a village he was protecting. The thing is, he wasn't even supposed to have been on patrol that day.

I hadn't been to church since.

Then I got on to the Shoemockers: how we'd become friends and how they'd taught me the true meaning of the word "love". I knew my father had loved me in his own way, but I wanted to find what the Shoemockers had.

Once again, the tears welled in my eyes. There would be no more cooking or rolling the rug up for them to dance. I was just thankful that at least they'd got to go together.

The machines began to beep erratically and a nurse dashed in and started to fiddle with the drips. I thought maybe it was time to go, but instead of coming away from Paul feeling sad, I felt hope. It was as though a weight had been lifted off my chest for the first time in a long while.

Paul:

Darcey began talking to me almost as soon as she entered my room. But I'd been given some pretty efficacious pain meds and it was too much of an effort to even open my eyes. My lids felt so heavy and my body was languorous. So I lay there and just listened.

I loved the sound and tone of her voice, even though today she was a little husky. Probably from the smoke. But she was always so upbeat and excited about everything. When I heard the break in that voice, I knew she was crying. I tried to force my eyes open but to no avail. She kept thanking me for what I'd done. I'd have done it all over again given the chance.

This lady was special and selfless. Instead of getting out of the building like I'd told her to, she'd rushed headlong up the stairs to make sure everyone else was evacuated. I'd tried to stop her, but she was too quick. I knew from the conversation in the car that there were two people trapped in the apartment. It was well and truly ablaze when I entered. The whole space was full of smoke. I buried my mouth and nose in the crook of my arm and went into what looked like a sitting area. The flames were licking up the walls and across the ceiling, and the kitchen was just a fireball. The heat was intense.

I could make out a figure slumped in an armchair – a woman, I thought. I grabbed hold of her and threw her over my shoulder. This wasn't the first time I'd been in a situation like this. I'd once got caught in a burning building in Iraq. All I could think at that moment was that it was essential to get these people out, and I went into autopilot. I was a marine once more.

The woman wasn't responsive but if she was to have even a fighting chance, I needed to get her out. I ran from the building, but my chest, eyes and throat were screaming out in pain. Regardless, I knew Darcey was still in there, as well as at least one other person.

There was still no sign of the fire service, but I knew Gloria had called them. I tried to enter the apartment once more but the inferno got the better of me. My arm and leg took the brunt as some furniture fell against my side while I was trying to find Mr Shoemocker. I could barely see anything by now but I knew I had to get Darcey to safety. Thrusting my arms out to protect myself, I realised my clothes were alight. I grabbed a blanket that was over the sofa, which, thankfully, hadn't caught fire yet, and used it to douse the flames. Then I made my way back to the hallway.

Through the smoke, I saw a figure collapse to the ground. I heard a thwack as she must have hit her head. I knew it was Darcey and I threw the blanket over her – the fire had now spread into the hallway. And somehow, I got us out. Gloria was screaming for us both but I could hardly see or breathe. I laid Darcey down as gently as I could ... And that's it. I don't remember anything more. When I came round, I was here in the hospital.

I listened as Darcey talked about her life and upbringing. It all sounded so sad. How had she grown up to be such an amazing lady? I knew Gloria was smitten with her, as was just about everyone who met her. Mike had caught me up on all the goings-on so I already knew about the shower incident. He said Caleb was a goner even if he didn't know it yet. We decided to have a little bet on how long it would be before those two got together.

I liked Darcey for Caleb; I knew she'd be good for him. I also knew Gloria would move heaven and earth to make it happen. It was no secret she wanted grandbabies and lots of them. Even I didn't escape her machinations. Although I wasn't an actual son, I was still one of her boys, so I often got quizzed about whether I'd met any nice girls yet and when I was going to settle down. Yeah. Darcey would do them all the power of good.

Caleb:

I went back to the office when Darcey fell asleep. My poor little minx had been battling to keep her eyes open. I'd wanted to sit with her a while longer but my mum had dragged me away, saying we should let her rest.

I gave Mum a lift home. She told me Darcey had lost everything she owned. Apparently, none of the smoke alarms had gone off. If the fire had happened at night, Darcey could have been in there asleep. Even as I took in what she said, I'd already made up my mind about something.

I owned and lived in a huge converted penthouse not far from the office. I had more than enough room. While I had plenty of women, I never brought them back to my loft. I very rarely saw the same woman twice and, on the odd occasion I did, I made it very clear I didn't do relationships. I was honest about that from the outset. I'd never lived with a woman; I'd never felt the need to tie my future to anyone. Until now.

The thought of having someone else's shit all over my place messed with my head a little, but I had a feeling Darcey would be different – don't ask me why. I'd give her one of the spare bedrooms for now; let her settle in before I moved her into my room with me.

I knew my mother had already spoken to Susan at Balbier's about ordering an entirely new wardrobe for Darcey, and I told her to have all the new clothes sent to my loft. I expected some sort of comment, especially as she'd caught me red-handed kissing the girl senseless tonight in the hospital; but nothing at all.

When we got to her house, I saw my mum to her door and kissed her goodnight.

It was only as I was walking back to the car that she called out, "Take it slow and don't mess this up. I love you. Goodnight."

Rather taken aback, I headed for the office. I rode the lift and, as I exited the elevator, I noticed movement in the kitchen area. My brother, Daniel, was sprawled over the white leather couches and, as usual, he'd raided my fridge, and had a can of pop as well as a coffee on the table next to him. He looked all set for a gruelling night's work. His laptop rested on his legs, and files were strewn across the coffee table.

I asked, "Why don't you work in your own office?"

"Because you have the best-stocked fridges," he replied, and shoved the remains of a deli sandwich in his mouth.

Daniel had made some progress in the matters he was looking into for me. The Shoemockers had no living relatives, but there was a will and Darcey was named as the sole beneficiary. Also, her excuse for a landlord had apparently cut many corners, not just with the smoke alarms, and Daniel was on to that too. Darcey's insurance company were also playing ball. Hopefully, she'd get a settlement soon.

We held a conference call with Adam. Sadly, there was no good news from his side. It looked as though things had been purposely sabotaged and we decided to step up security across all our sites. I wanted to fly back over but I couldn't leave Darcey and Paul just yet. For the first time in my life, I felt torn. My brothers noticed and gave me shit about my new PA. I played it down; made out it wasn't personal but the fact she was brilliant at her job – a real find. Look how much money she'd already saved the firm. They seemed to swallow it and our meeting continued long into the night.

Darcey:

I asked one of the nurses when I'd be able to leave. I was informed that, if my blood tests came back as satisfactory today, I might be able to go once the doctors had done their rounds. I'd have to have someone with me though, due to my concussion, and I'd still be taking strong medication.

I thought I'd ask Gloria if I could stay with her, just for a few days until I got things sorted. I was so thankful I'd been given that bonus. Now I'd have to find a new apartment, pay all the deposits up front, buy furniture and replace all my clothes and personal belongings. It wouldn't cover everything but it would be a good start. I only hoped I'd get my deposit back from the landlord and at least I had house contents insurance. It wasn't a lot but every bit would help. I'd manage; I always did. I just needed to get back to work because, if I didn't have a job, I wouldn't be able to afford anything.

I still didn't know what had happened with Tony and Caleb. I think Caleb must have been very relieved to see I was okay and that's why he'd kissed me so hard. I'd thoroughly enjoyed it, though. My body must have betrayed my feelings for him the moment his lips touched mine.

As thoughts swirled in my head, once again I could feel myself succumbing to bone-crushing tiredness. But I knew I had things to organise. I needed to see what, if anything, was left of my previous life.

Caleb:

I ended up sleeping at the office. I still felt jet-lagged and couldn't be bothered to drive home. I had everything I needed here anyway. Daniel and I had filled Adam in on Paul's progress. Paul was my driver but his main job, along with Simon, was to head up the whole of Heart security. It was a real blow that he'd been injured; we all took it badly.

Paul hand-picked his teams. Many of them were made up of guys we'd served with. They were a unique bunch of individuals with some pretty specialist skills between them. The best of the best. We knew and trusted them like brothers; they worked as one, like a well-oiled machine, and got things done. The teams had dealt with everything, from pirates intercepting our equipment in the Gulf of Aden and Southeast Asia to attacks on our business interests in London. We'd received some death threats over the years and there had been several kidnap attempts. That was why Paul – and Simon, who was his right hand – were my family's close protection. I wouldn't entrust them to anyone else. Simon had a smaller, separate loft next to mine and he was based predominantly in the UK, specifically here in London. Paul lived in an apartment in the grounds of my mother's property. The only people with access to my family's residences were

Simon and Paul. They were regularly swept for bugs and we had panic rooms installed as well as full CCTV systems. We took the safety of those we loved very seriously.

We operated from a tripped-out security suite based deep within the Heart Industries building in the lower basement. It wasn't common knowledge and it was restricted access. Recently, we'd had an issue with a clever cyber-attack, but had managed to put paid to it quite swiftly. Paul had been putting together specialist covert ops teams to be deployed to each of our main sites that were experiencing sabotage issues.

I called the hospital to check on his and Darcey's progress and planned to visit as soon as I could get away. I just had a few loose ends to tie up in the office first.

Simon had made arrangements for groceries to be delivered to me, fresh flowers and a whole host of other girly shit, along with the clothes from Susan's, so that Darcey would feel right at home. I'd also asked him to collect Franco and take him to my place, as my mother had said Darcey would need her hair cut to hide the fact it had been singed in the fire. Simon organised everything on a day-to-day basis but I hardly ever saw him. No one entered or left my place without him knowing, and he would check the penthouse after they'd gone. It didn't feel intrusive as the man was like a ghost. I'd have to let Darcey know, though. So far, she'd only met Paul. And now she was associated with me and was basically mine, she could never take a taxi alone again and would be assigned a close protection detail too.

When I'd rung the hospital earlier, the nurse had mentioned they were just waiting on test results and the doctors coming round. If all was well, Darcey could be discharged, providing she had someone to stay with her. I thought I'd go and pick her up myself as Simon had his hands full with everything else. When I called my mother to tell her of my plans, she was already on her way to the hospital. Not surprisingly, she thought it was a fabulous idea. I figured she could prepare Darcey instead of me just springing it on her.

I finally got to leave the office much later than I would have liked. My temporary PA had managed to photocopy the wrong presentation packs for my meeting, cock up my schedule, and I'd caught her FaceTiming her friend when she was supposed to be collecting my guests from reception. It made me appreciate Darcey all the more.

I blew out a breath of frustration as I stepped from my elevator and entered the garage. Jumping into my SUV, I called my mum to let her know I was on the way. I was grateful she'd convinced Darcey that staying at mine was a great idea and that I hardly ever used the loft anyway. But, as I drove off, I had the distinct feeling that, if Darcey was in my penthouse loft, I'd be there a lot more.

Darcey:

Gloria knocked on my door. Her face lit up when I told her I'd been given the all-clear to leave, provided I had someone to look after me.

"About that, dear..." she began. And she told me everything. I was to stay in Caleb's spare room for as long as I wanted, rent-free. He was rarely home anyway, so I'd be doing him a favour.

I couldn't believe my luck. I thought it a little strange at first that my boss, of all people, would go to such lengths for his PA – but then again, the man didn't seem to sleep so he'd probably love the fact that I'd be on hand day and night. As long as I still got two days off a week, I figured it would give me a chance to save some money. I hoped I could ride into work with him too, to save on travelling costs.

When Gloria told me where the penthouse loft was, I felt excited. It was in a trendy district just a stone's throw from the office. The area was so lovely and safe, I could probably even walk to work on fine-weather days.

The porter came with a wheelchair for me and the nurses had my prescriptions sorted. I had swollen vocal cords from the smoke inhalation and I prayed it wouldn't leave any permanent damage; only time would tell. A lot of the bruising had gone down, and they'd removed the bandage from my head, and the cannula. I looked a mess, though. I'd debated cutting my hair to neaten it up a bit – Paul had thrown me over his shoulder to get us out of the building and the flames must have caught it as we'd fled past Mr and Mrs Shoemocker's apartment. Now it was frazzled and lopsided. For now, I'd settled for plaiting it back off my face.

Caleb was waiting for us at the hospital entrance. The fresh air smelled wonderful outside, especially as it had been raining. There was a rose garden next to the entrance and I could smell the heady scent of the roses in full bloom too, as they tantalised my nose. It made me smile. My sense of smell was something else I'd feared might have been permanently affected.

Without hesitating, Caleb kissed me on the lips, right there in front of his mother. Then he took my bag from the porter and placed it in the boot of the SUV. I didn't know what to make of it. I was stunned into silence.

Gloria:

Caleb's penthouse loft was in what used to be an old warehouse, with a concierge and security officer as you walked in. There were always beautiful flower displays on the desk and in the two elevators, one of which was solely for Caleb and Simon's use. The other served the rest of the residents in the building and didn't go to the top floor. This would be much safer for Darcey.

Caleb dropped us off at the front of the building and I introduced her to the guys who worked the desk. They scanned Darcey's handprint, then each finger separately. I explained to her this was so she could access the lift. Caleb joined us, having parked the car, and we rode the elevator together to the top floor. There was another small foyer with a single door off to the left-hand side, where Simon lived. The two large double doors in front of us led to Caleb's loft.

The place had been sympathetically restored with a nod to its former industrial use. There was a large log burner, which had been lit, and a lot of open brickwork. To the left was a huge, open kitchen – a chef's dream – which was honestly wasted on Caleb. Then there was a wide-screen TV, a roomy, leather, L-shaped couch, a glass balcony, and a staircase that took you to the bedrooms upstairs. The space was light and bright. Over to the right was a dining area and an office.

Caleb carried Darcey's bag upstairs, and Simon arrived shortly afterwards with Franco and his team. Thankfully, the fridge was fully stocked, so I made sandwiches and teas and coffees for everyone. Darcey flung her arms around me when she discovered her new clothes.

I stayed for a while, then Simon took me home. The last few days had started to catch up with me and I was exhausted.

Darcey:

As I was enveloped in a hug from Franco, he began to cry. Speaking in quick-fire Italian, he said words to the effect of, "My beautiful girl, how bad you look! But I will make you better – truly beautiful as before." He kept going on about my poor hair. I responded in Italian, telling him how wonderful he was and that if anyone could sort me out, it was him.

Franco instantly stopped crying. He looked at me in shock and awe. "You speak Italian?"

I replied in Italian, confirming that I spoke it fluently, and I told him about my upbringing. I said I spoke Spanish too.

Franco sat me in a chair at the dining-room table and proceeded to wield his scissors like a knight going into battle. He took great care as he combed because of the stitches in my head. When I'd been to the salon, he'd refused to cut my hair but, thanks to the fire, I soon sported a beautiful, sophisticated cut a little longer than shoulder length. I was given a shoulder and neck massage, a mani-pedi and a facial, too, and I had to admit it all felt wonderful.

We chatted about Tony and Mr Rumis and it turned out that Franco knew the club well. I couldn't understand how we hadn't met before I'd started working for Heart Industries.

Later, when everyone had left, a serene sense of calm fell over the place. It felt strange, though, being alone with Caleb here; with my boss. It seemed so personal.

The penthouse was a spectacular space and the bedroom Caleb had shown me earlier was breathtaking. It was elegant, sophisticated and stylish, with a fine, white, gauzy drape covering the huge double window that led out onto a wraparound glass and steel balcony. The bedding was a pretty vintage pink and the bed was so soft when I tried it that I sank into it. There was a stunning bathroom with a magnificent tub, a luxurious-looking shower and a double vanity sink. And it was stocked with everything I could possibly need. I also had a walk-in wardrobe. Gloria had replaced all the clothes I'd lost and added to them, from business attire and casual clothes to sports and loungewear. I discovered row upon row of clothing for every occasion.

As I stood in the middle of the room, I tried to take it all in. My life had changed beyond recognition – again. How on earth could I begin to pay back all the Hearts' kindness? Even if I worked for nothing, it wouldn't be enough.

Chapter Six

Caleb:

I stood in the kitchen and watched Darcey descend the glass staircase. I had to smile to myself. She looked so cuddly and adorable in a pair of fine-knitted pyjamas; clean, fresh-faced, her hair pulled up in a messy knot on top of her head, with fuzzy socks on her feet. She made a beeline for me. I'd made myself a coffee and realised I didn't know if she even drank coffee, let alone how she liked it. I wanted to know everything about her. I wanted to be her everything.

"Is it okay if I make a coffee?" Her question was tentative.

I smiled again. "I want you to treat the place as your own. You don't have to ask my permission about anything."

The coffee machine was the same model as the one in my office. I noticed she picked up a French vanilla pod and topped her coffee with cream, not milk. When she took a sip, she got a little cream on her top lip. And suddenly, it was all I could focus on. It taunted me. I wanted to lick it off, then devour her mouth, knowing she would taste of French vanilla.

But I knew if I started, it wouldn't stop there. I could picture Darcey, sitting atop my granite kitchen counter with a foot on each stool, while I sucked her clit and drenched, throbbing pussy, thrusting in first one finger then a second to stretch her and lick her to ecstasy and orgasm. As she threw back her head, I would lay her out like my own personal buffet and feast on her till she exploded on my tongue.

I was lost in my fantasies when I heard my name and realised she had been speaking to me. By now, my cock was straining so forcefully against my zipper, I was sure I'd be left with an imprint. I had to move and open the fridge to be able to discreetly rearrange myself. I felt like a child caught with my hand in the cookie jar again.

Darcey asked if I was hungry and I had to admit I could definitely eat something besides her. When I looked in the fridge, I wondered why it was filled with groceries: meat, vegetables and so on. I never cooked for myself. I usually had meals prepared ready for me to just microwave. Not being much of a chef and rarely here, I didn't see the point in stocking up with fresh food. This must have been on my mother's instruction.

I placed the cream that was on the counter back in the fridge and Darcey said she would rustle us up something to eat. Call me a caveman, but instantly images of her barefoot, pregnant and all mine sprang to mind. I liked her in my space, but I couldn't seem to focus with her too close, looking so cute and smelling so good. I decided I needed a shower and a little release of my own.

Darcey:

Caleb looked so relaxed and carefree in the penthouse; not at all intimidating, demanding and brooding as he was in the office. The man was an enigma. I hoped he wasn't regretting his decision to let me stay. I'd tried to speak to him but he seemed to be in a world of his own. I also got the distinct impression he didn't entertain many guests in his private home.

He'd taken his coffee upstairs and announced he was going for a shower, so I thought I'd make a meal for us both. The fridge was brimming with fresh produce. I found mince and all the ingredients for a spaghetti bolognese. I liked to cook with music on so I hit the playlist on my phone and sang quietly as I worked, testing out my voice. I found a fresh baguette and made some garlic basil butter, topping the slices off with a little grated cheese.

The aromas from the food made me think about Mr and Mrs Shoemocker, and tears sprang to my eyes. No more cooking lessons. I enjoyed preparing meals but couldn't afford to do it for myself. Besides, there never seemed any point in cooking just for one.

I was about to drain the spaghetti when I looked up and saw Caleb. He was wearing only a pair of low-slung lounge pants and had bare feet. My lady bits did a little happy dance as I drank him in; the man was cut. Not hugely muscular but fit and incredibly well-defined, with just the right smattering of chest hair. His skin was bronzed and smooth. He must have used the same body wash as he kept at the office because he smelled divine. I noticed he had a T-shirt in his hand, and felt a frisson of disappointment. He reached up and I watched as he flexed his beautiful torso and arms to put the shirt over his head.

Realising I was staring, I switched off my playlist and turned back to the task in hand. Caleb took over draining the pasta and we moved around the kitchen together with a seemingly practised ease. I stirred the sauce and took the garlic cheese bread out of the oven. By this time, Caleb had taken out two pasta dishes and was opening a bottle of wine. As I plated everything up, strains of soft music began to play in the background.

We ate at the kitchen island, chatting and drinking our wine. Caleb snaffled the last piece of bread to mop up the sauce around his plate. We then demolished the tiramisus I had created. As the flavour explosion hit my palate, I couldn't help wondering how it would taste if I were licking the dessert off his defined torso. I figured the thought wasn't perverted. I'd simply be doing my bit to save the planet by washing fewer dishes if I used Caleb's torso instead of crockery.

With everything cleared away, we fell onto the sofa and Caleb flicked through the channels on the TV. There was a throw blanket over the arm of the chair and I threw it across my legs. Next thing I knew, Caleb had grabbed my legs and placed them over his, rearranging the blanket so it covered us both.

Caleb:

I honestly couldn't remember the last time I'd enjoyed a meal or anyone's company so much. The night had been fantastic. It felt so easy and comfortable; so natural, the two of us sharing this space as though we'd been together forever. A real couple. It had taken me by surprise a little but I'd realised that's what I wanted. I decided to bite the bullet and put it out there. Say how I felt.

As Darcey snuggled closer, I told her I'd fallen in love with her; that I wanted to make this arrangement permanent. She had come to mean so much to me in a short space of time and the fire had made me see things clearly. Why wait?

I'm not quite sure what I expected from my grand declaration but it wasn't the little snuffle that followed. I looked down. Darcey was cuddled into me, fast asleep.

My phone started to ring in my pocket, so I slipped away so as not to wake her. It was Adam. I knew there must be an update. I also knew I needed to be back in Jakarta as soon as possible. I couldn't believe it – the timing was awful. But I packed a bag while Adam and I continued to speak. I didn't want to leave Darcey but I had no choice. I wrote her a note, letting her know people were on hand and she'd have a close protection detail from now on. Then I called Simon to ready the jet.

Darcey:

I woke with a slight crick in my neck, wrapped up like a burrito on the sofa in the soft, warm blanket. It took a while for my brain to catch up with the happenings of the previous night. The last few weeks had been a complete whirlwind and my life had literally been turned upside down. And now I seemed to have gone from Caleb being simply my boss to ... something more ... but I wasn't sure what. I knew where I wanted it to go but did he feel the same way?

I didn't have time to dwell on it, however. I had a lot to do today and I needed to get to work. I padded over to the kitchen, made a coffee and grabbed a croissant. Then I went upstairs to get dressed.

I was just stuffing the last of the croissant into my mouth when I got the shock of my life. A beautiful young woman in a tasteful maid's uniform appeared out of my ensuite bathroom. I almost choked, dropping the coffee cup in fright. It smashed into pieces on the hard floor.

The young woman was full of apologies. She introduced herself as Mr Heart's cleaner and began to pick up the pieces of the broken cup.

"I'm so sorry too," I said. "Silly of me. You startled me, that's all."

The girl's name was Lucy and she was very pretty. I couldn't help a pang of jealousy and wondered if she was just a cleaner for Caleb, or if there was more to it. But I had no right to be jealous. It wasn't as if Caleb and I were together. I just worked for him like she did.

I found a note from him on the bed, telling me he'd gone back to Jakarta. He must have written it right before he left. He asked me to call Simon when I was ready to go out anywhere, and said he'd fill me in on the security detail. That puzzled me. I wasn't sure why he thought I needed a security detail; I was just his PA. But I did as he asked: called Simon and informed him I'd be going into the office today.

Simon met me in the lobby a little over half an hour later and we were on our way.

Gloria:

I was shocked when I looked up to see Darcey walk through the door at 8:00 a.m. I hadn't expected her in today, or even for the next few weeks. She poured me a coffee and said she'd rather be at work to take her mind off things. I was truly grateful. We'd already gone through two temps, as Caleb had fired them both. Meanwhile, the work continued to mount and I was struggling to manage.

By 10:00 a.m., you'd never have known Darcey had been absent. Caleb's work schedule and calendar were sorted; meetings were booked and others postponed until he was back in the office. All the reports he needed had been forwarded and she'd begun to research some urgent information he'd asked for. She was nose-deep in files, patent information, plans, books and charts that were spread all over the boardroom desk. I slipped in with a sandwich and soft drink around 1:00 p.m. Darcey thanked me but barely looked up and simply kept at it.

A while later, Daniel strolled out of the private lift with more files in his arms. He planted a kiss on my cheek and went to find Darcey. The two of them didn't emerge from the boardroom till well after 6:00 p.m. I couldn't help thinking what a striking-looking couple they made, although I still felt she was more suited to Caleb. Either way, any of my boys would be lucky to have the love of this little firecracker.

I'd seen the longing glances Caleb threw Darcey's way when she wasn't looking. He was always aware of her in a packed room; they seemed to move together in sync, the tension between them palpable. I just hoped he'd be back from Jakarta soon.

Darcey, meanwhile, seemed oblivious to all the attention she was attracting. We were getting many more visitors to the executive floor now. Not only was she a beautiful young woman, she was also intelligent, thoughtful and kind. I noticed Mike, Simon and a few of the other security detail seemed to have eyes on her all the time as she went about her day. At least one of the security team was in the office with us at all times. They would work away on the small desk tucked in the corner, and I'd been instructed to let them handle the mail in the morning.

I never questioned it when my boys organised any security; they were just keeping us safe. Darcey was none the wiser or, if she'd noticed, she didn't mention anything. I don't think anyone could have got within five feet of her without being intercepted by the team. I wasn't sure if that meant something was going on or if it was just Caleb's way of protecting his own interests.

Darcey:

Daniel was good company, though nothing like his brother. He was quick to laugh and always seemed to have a ready smile. I noticed he was impeccably dressed and groomed, as well as being well built, in an incredibly fit sort of way. He looked as though he could certainly handle himself if the need arose. But I got the sense he just didn't take life too seriously. He was a handsome-looking man too, yet I felt absolutely no attraction towards him. I almost wished I did as he was so sweet.

We worked well together, shifting between sharing ideas and a companionable silence. Neither of us felt the need for idle chatter and we were able to get through most of the tasks on Caleb and Adam's lists.

Daniel planned to visit Paul once we'd finished so I asked if I could tag along. He said that wasn't a problem and he could drop me home afterwards. Caleb seemed to have given him strict instructions too that I was to have a security detail at all times.

We walked into Paul's hospital room to find he wasn't in his bed. The sheets were rumpled and his charts were still in place, so we took a seat and waited. Before long, he was wheeled through the door. I was happy to see he looked so much better. The large bandages had been removed and the skin, while still appearing raw, was healing. He'd also been given treatment for his lungs.

He and Daniel began to talk about security issues, until we could see Paul starting to tire. Then Daniel drove me back to the loft.

"Shall I make us something to eat?" I asked.

"Sounds good. And ..." he hesitated. "I need to talk to you about some legal stuff to do with the fire."

At the kitchen island, he opened his briefcase and took out a sheaf of papers. As I set about preparing a meal, he went through the details of my contents insurance, the case against the landlord for negligence, and the arrangements for Mr and Mrs Shoemocker's funeral.

I felt my eyes sting with tears again. The Shoemockers had no one but me; and my heart broke for them even more.

Once the food was cooking, I nipped upstairs to change out of my work clothes. Then we ate; we talked.

"How come none of you are married?" I asked.

Daniel shrugged. "We were in the forces together. We didn't have a lot of opportunity to get into long-term relationships. Caleb did come close a few years ago but, thankfully, it didn't work out."

Thankfully? What did that mean? I was bursting with curiosity but didn't feel I could pry.

"What about you?" Daniel asked. "Why aren't you married – or at least engaged?"

I told him about Andy and saw immediate understanding in his face.

"I lost people too," he said. "Friends. In similar circumstances."

It was only when Daniel left later to have a phone call with his brothers that I realised how truly bone-weary I felt. I made sure everything was clean and tidy and decided to take a long soak in the tub. I ran the water, adding some luxurious bubble bath I'd found. It smelled divine and heady; like a high-end perfume, clean and sweet. The tub was huge and deep and, as I sank into the bubbles, I felt I was washing all my heartache away.

I missed Caleb, though. I wondered why things hadn't worked out with his girlfriend; why Daniel seemed to feel Caleb had had a lucky escape. Then my mind wandered to all the security arrangements. Just how safe were Caleb and his brothers at the moment? I knew there had been trouble at the site and they believed it had been targeted and sabotaged. But what did that mean for them?

I'd not long been in bed when my phone rang. I grabbed it and was excited to see it was Caleb, FaceTiming me. I hit the accept button, and his beautiful face filled the screen. He seemed tired and he hadn't shaved. His hair looked as though he'd run his hands through it too many times. I wished I could run my fingers through those thick locks too. He appeared thoroughly tousled yet delicious.

"You're in bed," he began. "I'm disturbing you – I'm sorry."

"No." I shook my head. "You can call me whenever you need to."

He smiled. "Thanks for getting all the files sent over so quickly. I really appreciate it."

"Daniel and I visited Paul this evening," I told him. "He looked much better."

"That's great to hear," he said. "And I hope Daniel took you home afterwards and saw you right to the apartment."

"Oh, he did. Actually, I cooked dinner for us and we hung out here for a bit."

Was it my imagination or did that seem to annoy Caleb? I thought he'd have been pleased, especially as he'd rather I wasn't left alone. Who could I be safer with than his brother?

We eventually said goodnight, but not before he'd reminded me I had to let Simon know when I was leaving in the morning, and that I must have a security detail at all times.

I gazed at him, trying to read his face. "Is everything okay?"

"Yes, of course. It's just a precautionary measure. Goodnight, Darcey."

I fell into a deep, sound sleep, filled with beautiful brothers and sexy bosses. And I wondered just what that facial stubble would feel like rubbing between my thighs ...

Caleb:

FaceTiming my girl, I thought she'd never looked more beautiful. Her face was make-up free; her hair was down and fanned out over the pillow. She had rosy cheeks and sleepy eyes and she just looked adorable.

But when she mentioned she'd cooked for her and Daniel, I felt I'd taken a blow to the stomach – I'd not long finished speaking with Daniel and he hadn't mentioned a damn thing. So – what? Did she have feelings for him? I told myself he was simply doing as I'd asked and looking out for her. I'd asked him to work from the office to keep an eye on her and Mum.

Only now, I felt uneasy. Daniel was good-looking, a genuinely nice guy, but he also had a reputation where women were concerned. He'd never had a serious relationship in his life. Darcey deserved more than to be another one of his conquests. The thing was, though, I knew she was special. If anyone could curb Daniel's womanising ways, it would be her.

I couldn't believe I felt jealous of my own baby brother! I just needed to get this shit sorted out so I could go home.

Gloria:

I stepped out of the elevator to see Darcey was already sitting at her desk. Caleb had become a slave driver. He seemed to have forgotten she was still recovering from the fire, and had her working all hours. The more Darcey did, the more he seemed to heap on her. I'd have to have a word with him.

Simon was at the corner desk, working away on his laptop, and I heard him take a call.

"I have to pop to the security suite," he told me. "You and Darcey don't have any plans to leave the office anytime soon?"

Darcey looked up and shook her head.

"No," I said. "We'll be here."

I went to make coffee when I heard the lift ping. A young man in a baseball cap, presumably from the mail room, stepped out. He must have been new as I hadn't seen him before. Instead of putting the mail on Simon's desk, he strode across the floor and handed it to Darcey. I noticed he didn't speak. In fact, he barely looked up, and then he left.

As I carried a tray of coffee and warm croissants to my desk, I glanced at Darcey.

Her face had turned ashen and her hands were shaking. In front of her was a manila envelope and she'd pulled out some photographs.

"Darcey? What is it?"

Her doe-shaped eyes flicked towards me and she pushed the photographs across her desk.

I stared at them in horror. They were pictures of her taken through the window of her old bedsit. Some of them were pretty close to the knuckle: images of her in just a skimpy thong with no bra; others with only a towel wrapped around her body. There were pictures of the fire too – Darcey sitting on the ground, covered in ash with her head bleeding, and being lifted into the ambulance. Some of the images showed her with me and also with Caleb; others when she'd been riding the tube.

What the hell ...?

I pressed the emergency pager clipped to my skirt.

As the lift pinged again and the doors opened, this time, it was Simon who stepped out.

I pointed to the photographs on Darcey's desk. "Someone just delivered these. I thought he must be from the mail room but I'd never seen him before."

Eyes alert, Simon pulled a pair of latex gloves from his back pocket and snapped them on. Then he grabbed the photographs from the desk. He picked up the envelope, too, and looked inside. There was a typed note Darcey had missed: We are watching. As I watched Darcey read it, I thought she was going to vomit.

Simon didn't waste any time. He barked out commands into his radio. He asked a slew of questions about who had delivered the mail. Darcey was too distracted to be of much help. I sat with my arm around her and I felt sickened. Who could be so vile? So brazen?

Before we knew it, there were multiple members of the security team on the floor around us. On a tablet, Simon pulled up some footage of the young man who had dropped off the package. I confirmed it was him. There was a flurry of activity. Then Simon said he wanted Darcey to go home.

"Why don't you come and stay with me?" I offered. "You look shakey."

She shook her head. "No. Thank you, but no. I'll be fine in the loft. Simon's only across the hall."

Simon whisked her out of the office and drove her home himself.

Simon:

Shit! How did this creep get past us? Mike had already raised the alarm when one of the mail room workers, Joe, had reported losing his security pass.

This wasn't the first security incident we'd had in the building recently either. Someone had tried to hack some of our personnel files from inside the building, including Darcey's, but they'd tripped the extra layer of security measures we had in place. Truth be known, though, they should never have been able to get that far in the first place. Was this an inside job? I couldn't imagine it, only we had to look at all the possibilities. Joe seemed harmless enough, but I felt a little more digging into his background was necessary, especially when Mike mentioned his interest in Darcey.

Caleb was going to lose his shit when he found out. The man was head over heels for Darcey and had been becoming more antsy the longer he was apart from her. He wouldn't be home anytime soon, though. We seemed to be fending off multiple attacks from various fronts and locations across the company. I had the full team working flat out in the incident room within the basement of Heart Industries. Many of the department heads were ex-forces too. They'd been briefed and placed on high alert; as a team, I knew we had a unique skill set between us. It was only a matter of time before we got our first break.

Still, we should have been ready for this. The reason Caleb had installed Darcey in his penthouse loft wasn't just because he had a thing for her, but because Mike's team in the mail room had intercepted a photograph and note quite by accident. It was for Darcey but had been opened in error. The picture was of Darcey and Caleb at the charity event they'd attended together a few weeks ago. The word bitch had been scrawled across Darcey's face in red marker pen and each letter had been scratched and scored through with something sharp.

I'd investigated Darcey's personal history, finances and family. This was sensitive so I'd been careful to do the searches myself. With the firm, it was different. No matter how ethically the Hearts conducted their business, it was inevitable they'd make enemies due to the line of work they were in. But Darcey had lived like a nun – not so much as a parking ticket. So why would someone want to hurt her? It didn't make sense.

As I drove Darcey back to the loft, she took a phone call from someone called Tony. They made plans to meet the next day for coffee. From my background checks, I knew this was the son of the guy she worked for. He wasn't a choir boy, but he didn't pose an immediate threat either. From what I could gather, Darcey had no clue he was interested in her and nothing had ever happened between them.

My main focus was to find out who this guy was who'd delivered the photographs today. He'd been very aware of the CCTV cameras and had kept his baseball cap tipped down. He hadn't seemed to make eye contact with anyone and he'd done nothing to draw attention to himself. Had he acted alone? Had someone sent him?

I wasn't looking forward to reporting back to Caleb.

Abington:

I was sick of the fucking Hearts holding all the cards. It was time to stack the deck in my own favour. I had constant surveillance on them now. I also needed them distracted and away from Darcey. I wanted her to feel scared and unsafe. She'd come back to me. I'd make sure of it.

The Heart Industries sites in Jakarta were also causing me distribution problems. This was a good opportunity to kill two birds with one stone.

I called Harry. He's an unscrupulous son of a bitch, who'd do anything for the right price.

"Frighten the shit out of her," I instructed him. "I need the timeline sped up."

I knew this would cost me dear but it'd be worth every penny. The Hearts would be so busy putting out fires on every front, they wouldn't know what had hit them. I'd teach them to screw with me. Then I could sit back and watch the carnage unfold.

Caleb:

I felt drained. There was one issue after another and they just kept coming. Someone was sabotaging our sites. Permits had been cancelled, equipment had gone missing and damage had occurred that no one could explain.

I'd flown out to Jakarta with a team I trusted implicitly. It was made up of my special ops buddies. We'd run many unconventional missions together during my time in the services and we still operated as a close unit. Everyone had their own speciality and we'd set to work like a well-oiled machine. I had a group working on local intelligence, a few of the guys had joined the work crews, and I was based at the offices on site. I also had a floating crew setting covert cameras and the like. At least the cost to us had only been financial and no one had been hurt, even when the equipment had clearly been vandalised. But I had every faith in my team. We'd catch those responsible and they would pay.

My phone rang and I took a call from Simon. He told me about a delivery Darcey had had at the office. Photographs. Intrusive, invasive, very personal images.

I felt sick to my stomach. He must have known I'd hit the roof. But he assured me he'd doubled her security detail and tightened all security at the Heart Industries building. He was also giving daily briefings to keep everyone who needed to know abreast of what was going on. Even so, that delivery creep shouldn't have been able to get within feet of Darcey, let alone hand-deliver her a package.

I put the phone down and all I could think was, I shouldn't be here. I should be in London, protecting my girl.

I was dragged from my thoughts by a frantic banging on my door. When I yanked it open, Ali all but fell into the room. The guy was pale and sweating.

"Ali? What?"

"It's Lloyd," he murmured. "Lloyd's been shot. He's dead."

Chapter Seven

Adam:

Over the years, I'd lost many friends and brothers-in-arms. But Lloyd's death hit me hard. I'd watched him bleed out in front of me. I could still see him, sprawled in the sand, his lifeblood staining the earth beneath him.

He had been working the perimeter of the site, fitting covert cameras and checking the feed. Lloyd, the epitome of resilience and camaraderie, met his end while diligently securing our perimeter. A single bullet silenced his laughter and dreams of fatherhood, leaving behind a shattered future for his unborn child and devoted, loving wife.

Killed outright with a bullet to the back of the head.

Lloyd had been one hell of a soldier and friend. And he'd been about to become a dad for the first time. This hard-as-nails guy, built like a Mack Truck, had been reduced to mush whenever he'd spoken of his beautiful wife and soon-to-arrive baby.

Caleb was as shocked as I was. He said he'd send Daniel, Mum and Darcey to break the news to poor Julia. Julia worked for Heart Industries in London on the main reception and had only just started her maternity leave. This would have been Lloyd's last job before he'd flown back home for the birth. What had gone wrong? The man was no rookie. He was a time-served, hardened veteran. No one could have sneaked up on him. How could this have happened?

I felt devastated for Daniel – my brother, Lloyd's confidant and closest friend, who now bore the weight of sorrow and responsibility as he prepared to deliver the crushing news to Julia that would forever change her life. Daniel and Lloyd had been really good friends. They were the closest in age of the three of us and Daniel would eat at their house at least once a week. He'd even been asked to be godfather to the new baby. He looked out for Julia when Lloyd was away on a job. I didn't envy him having to knock on her door with this.

I slipped into military mode; calm, detached, methodical. I had to be. Shit had just got real. This was now an all-out war.

Daniel:

What God-awful time was it? I was going to fucking kill Caleb. Since he'd been separated from Darcey, he'd been acting like a bear with a sore head, barking out orders day and night. I glared at my phone, blurry-eyed, as the incessant ringing dragged me from my sleep.

Caleb got straight to the point. "Lloyd's dead."

I felt sucker-punched. All the air seemed to leave my lungs.

I was due to fly out any day now and relieve Lloyd so he could make it back to be with Julia for the birth of their child. We'd shared the same speciality in the forces. We'd worked side by side for years. I'd been there the night he'd met Julia; been his best man when they'd got married, and would soon be godfather to their new addition.

"What do you mean, dead? How can he be dead?" Even as I said the word, I didn't know how to make myself believe it.

Marines aren't supposed to cry. But as I hung up the phone, I balled my fists into my eyes. I couldn't hold back the emotions and a wail tore itself from deep in my chest.

I don't know how long I sat there. Eventually, I heaved myself up and put on a pot of strong coffee. With a mugful steaming in front of me, I became laser-focused. I made a list of everything that would have to be taken care of. Julia would need me more than ever. Lloyd had always made me promise to look out for her when he was deployed. She was his world. Even though it felt as if someone had cut my heart out, I would be there to get his girl through this.

I called Adam. His voice broke as we spoke; the emotion was raw. He talked about getting Lloyd's body home; about the action they were taking. Adam and Caleb, while they could smile prettily and scrubbed up well in a suit, weren't the men to cross. Especially when the welfare of those they cared for was on the line.

The last thing Adam said to me was, "We'll get them. We'll make those fuckers pay."

Darcey:

Gloria and I hadn't been at work long when the lift pinged. Daniel stepped out. It looked as though he hadn't slept a wink. He wasn't dressed for work. He was in old, worn jeans, boots and a sweater.

Before I could open my mouth, Gloria beat me to it. "What's wrong? What's happened?" Her words hung heavy in the air, thick with dread.

Daniel's haunted gaze met hers as he implored us to sit, his own anguish palpable. The news he delivered landed like a hammer blow: Lloyd, Julia's beloved husband, was gone. Gloria sucked in a breath and her complexion drained of colour, while a wave of nausea churned in my gut. Daniel enveloped us in a desperate embrace, offering what little solace he could amid the crushing weight of grief.

"Julia doesn't know. We have to go and see her. We have to tell her."

Julia. That poor, poor girl. Her baby was due any day now. A baby who would never know their daddy.

As we made our way to Julia's home, Simon joined our sombre procession, his presence a silent testament to the gravity of the situation. Julia's hopeful smile faltered on seeing our pained expressions, her world shattering with Daniel's words. In an instant, her joy turned to anguish as she crumpled under the weight of her grief, clutching her burgeoning belly in a futile attempt to shield her unborn child from the devastation.

Daniel and Simon caught her before she hit the floor. The echoes of her wails pierced the air, each cry a dagger to the heart. I could barely see through my own tears as we guided her to the sanctuary of her home, her agony etched into every line of her face.

Then, "No, no ... God, please no ..." She said the words, over and over.

Gloria and Daniel sat on either side of her and simply held her, lending her their strength.

I glanced around their living room. On a side table were multiple beautiful, framed pictures of her and Lloyd's life together: their engagement, wedding, honeymoon. I moved in a daze to the kitchen, needing to be useful. While I put the kettle on to make a pot of tea, Simon collared their dog, a solid, steel-grey pit bull called Hendricks, to take him for a walk around the block. I could hear Julia's wracking sobs as Daniel explained what had happened; what the plans were to bring Lloyd home.

As the hours stretched on, Julia's tears subsided, leaving behind a hollow shell of the woman she'd been only a short while before. With a heavy heart, I realised that nothing would ever be the same again.

Simon said he'd drive us back as Daniel was going to stay with her.

"I can't go back to work," Gloria said. "Drop me off at home."

Her voice was so quiet. I knew she was made of strong stuff but this had really done a number on her.

All I wanted now was to speak to Caleb. I needed to know he was okay.

Caleb:

I hadn't slept a wink. I went down to the site and helped the guys trawl through the hours of surveillance footage. When my phone rang, I grabbed it without looking at the screen and barked, "Yep!"

It was Darcey. And I felt I could finally take a breath. I had never been so glad to hear from her.

She was crying. I could hear it in her voice. It slayed me. I just wanted to hold her; smell her; kiss her. She said they'd spoken to Julia. She described how awful it was.

"We have some leads," I told her. "The guys are following them up. But there's a lot going on here. I've found discrepancies and things have happened on site."

Darcey had cross-referenced all the staff who'd been flown out, and Simon and the team had looked into everyone's backgrounds and bank accounts. We were also investigating those we'd employed in Jakarta.

As our conversation ended, Darcey said, "Caleb, please be careful and come home safe."

I wanted to believe there was genuine concern behind her words; concern for me, Caleb, rather than just for Mr Heart, her boss.

Darcey:

I finished up for the day but something kept niggling at me – the discrepancies Caleb had talked about. The company seemed to be getting attacked on multiple fronts, both at home and abroad. No sooner had we put one fire out than two others sprang up in different locations.

I had a knack for numbers and was a creative thinker. I wanted to see all the data together. We had to be missing something vital. I needed to fly out and help. I knew Caleb wouldn't be happy about it but I couldn't just sit here when I was sure I could make a difference.

I wanted to visit Paul in hospital, so Simon said he would accompany me. On our way, he got a call from Daniel. Julia had been rushed into hospital with pre-eclampsia, most probably brought on by distress and shock. She'd begun vomiting and her hands and feet had swollen. Simon told him we were already on our way. I decided not to ring Gloria till we had more news.

We burst through the doors of the hospital and hurried to the main reception desk. Julia had been rushed to the delivery suite. Simon had called Paul on the way in and, as we waited in the seating area, he met us in his wheelchair.

Paul knew exactly what had been going on. Recovering or not, this man was abreast of everything. He thought it would be a good idea for me to join Caleb.

"Not that Caleb will be on board with it," he added. "If you do this, we don't tell him till wheels up."

"And you'll need to be prepared," said Simon. "The accommodation is a little basic. Everyone's in huge tents and are all sleeping on site now to guard the compounds."

We sat, drinking hospital coffee, until Daniel came bursting through the double doors in scrubs, with the biggest smile on his face and tears in his eyes. Julia had delivered a healthy 8lb baby girl. She'd named her Hope and they were both doing well. Thank goodness for some good news at last.

Paul:

As Daniel took Darcey through to visit Julia and baby Hope, I told Simon I'd be getting out in a day or two. I was on the mend and had already been working from my hospital room. I knew it would still be a slow recovery, but I needed to get back to the control room HQ. I felt I was climbing the walls in here.

I was beginning to think the attack on Darcey wasn't isolated. Somehow it was linked to what was going on in

Jakarta. Until I found a connection, I told Simon I thought she'd probably be safer out there with Caleb, Adam and the crew. I doubted Caleb would let her leave his side. We'd recovered the stolen mail room uniform, baseball cap and pass card that had been used to gain access to Darcey in the Heart Industries building. They'd been shoved in a public waste bin outside a tube station. Our forensic team was going over them. We'd been tracing CCTV footage too.

Caleb would likely kick Simon's and my arses over this, but it might also calm him down. I knew he was out of his mind with worry over Darcey's safety. Having her close would go a long way to resolving that. The two of them made quite a formidable team. I knew from background checks on Darcey that she was a little spitfire. Her military father had taught her hand-to-hand combat. She also used to do mixed martial arts and was no slouch at them according to my sources. I thought she'd be just fine if we did a little brush-up session or two and got her kitted out properly.

Darcey was far from being a spoiled princess. And she was good for Caleb. He needed someone strong by his side and, if he wasn't worried so much about her, he could focus on other things.

I had concerns about Gloria too. I thought she'd looked tired when she came to visit me. As I lived in a cottage in the grounds of her home, once I was out of here, I'd be able to keep more of a close eye on her. Truth be told, she couldn't keep putting her surgery off.

Mike and I spoke almost daily. He'd been staying at mine while I'd been in hospital, keeping an eye on Gloria and driving her when Simon couldn't. He'd also been feeding and walking my dog, Rooney. With his wife now gone, I knew Mike had a twinkle in his eye for Gloria, so it hadn't been a hardship for him to look out for her.

When Simon and Darcey left, I called Gloria to bring her up to date. I gave her the good news about Julia and baby Hope; told her I was thinking it might be a good idea for Darcey to join Caleb. Gloria was astute and understood my reasoning. She was also desperate for one of her boys – her own sons or extended family – to make her a granny, which I was sure helped her agree to my proposal. I knew baby Hope would be a tonic. Gloria had adored Lloyd and loved Julia too. It felt good to be able to share some exciting, positive news with her.

Darcey:

I fell into bed and was asleep within moments. Now I knew I was flying out to join Caleb, I felt a renewed focus. I was nervous though. Simon and Paul had worked out a rough schedule for me, and Simon said he and a couple of the team would help me brush up on my combat skills. I had no idea what I'd be heading into.

I woke at 6:00 a.m. and was in the office by 8:00 a.m. Daniel had beaten me in and he beamed as he told me about baby Hope and Julia's progress.

He had other news for me too. "Mr and Mrs Shoemocker – they're bodies have been released."

I instantly felt guilty. With everything else that had happened recently, I'd had to put them to the back of my mind.

"They had a pre-paid funeral plan and had chosen their plot in advance," Daniel said. "They organised it some years ago because the graveyard where they wanted to be laid to rest was filling up. They wanted to be buried together."

I half smiled. More to myself than to Daniel. "That doesn't surprise me."

"Obviously we need to arrange the funeral date. There'll also be a will reading but that can wait till you're back in the country."

By now, my insurance company had paid out on my contents policy so I really had no reason to remain living in Caleb's loft. I had the funds and needed to start looking for a new place to rent. Daniel had also sued the landlord of the building on my behalf, so I was expecting a decent settlement from that too, as well as getting back the original bond I'd paid when I signed my lease. That would be more than enough to find a new place. Yet somehow, I didn't feel any excitement about the idea. Instead, I felt a little bereft at the thought of no longer being with Caleb in such an intimate setting.

I loved being in his private space. The whole loft smelled of him. I never felt lonely as I knew that, ultimately, he would be coming back here. It was weird. Having looked out for myself for years, loneliness wasn't something I generally experienced. But I did at the thought of not being with him like this. Caleb seemed to have seeped into my pores, my very being – which was utterly ridiculous as he was just my boss, who had been kind enough to offer me somewhere to stay when I needed it.

I was still daydreaming when the lift pinged and in walked Gloria. She clutched gift bags and baby balloons and, for the first time in a while, I thought she looked more like her old self. She was so excited and Daniel soon took her off to the hospital to meet the new baby.

I went to the mail room to see Mike and tell him about my plans to fly out to meet Caleb. To my surprise, he already knew. I'd brought my gym bag with me – I thought getting in a workout would help me prepare for the trip. Mike said he and Simon would join me to brush up on my hand-to-hand combat skills.

Towards the end of the day, the guys took me through my paces in the gym. I wasn't quite sure what they expected but my dad had taught me well. He wanted me to be able to protect myself if ever I was attacked. Neither of them went softly on me and Mike was quick for an older guy. His skills were impressive. I couldn't help feeling a certain satisfaction when I clocked Simon with a roundhouse kick and took him to the mat.

By the time we'd finished, I was breathing hard. Sweat trickled down my back, breasts and temples, but it was exhilarating. I knew I'd be sore in the morning, though, as I'd hit the mat more than once.

I went to Caleb's bathroom for a shower. Locking the door, I slipped out of my sweaty workout clothes and placed my washbag on the shelf. As the streams of hot water cascaded over me, I remembered the last time I'd been in this room. The heat still crept to my cheeks at the thought. I reached for my shampoo – then changed my mind and chose Caleb's instead.

I began to wash my hair, and that smell that was uniquely him drove me insane. It evoked all kinds of naughty memories and thoughts. I missed him and the smell made me horny. I wondered what it would feel like for Caleb to tangle his large hands in my hair and pull gently while washing my locks. Oh, my ... I used his shower gel and washed along my arms and across my breasts. My nipples were hard and erect and, as I ran my hands over them, I felt a need to rub my clit in firm small circles too.

While the shower got steamy, so did my libido. I used the fingers of one hand to rub my clit, gently pinching and rolling my nipples slowly with the fingers of the other. My orgasm crashed over me as I imagined it was Caleb's hands driving my pleasure.

I could no longer hide the fact that I was in love with my boss.

When I was ready to leave for the day, I found Simon. He handed me what looked like tactical gear in my size, complete with a helmet.

"When you get back to the loft, you need to pack a bag," he said. "By any chance, did your father round out your education with firearms?"

I grinned. "Well, obviously! And I kept my skills sharp at the firing range until I lost my last job."

We made our way home. I dived into the loft and grabbed my holdall.

Caleb:

I'd tried calling Darcey several times. We'd spoken every day but the last time I'd been able to catch her had been 7:00

a.m. yesterday. I'd talked to Mum and she'd told me all about Julia and Hope. I'd also spoken to Daniel and Paul. No one had mentioned Darcey other than to say she'd been busy and I must have missed her. I was going out of my mind. I didn't want to ask too many questions and give my hand away. I just wanted to see her and speak to her for myself.

Pulling up the video surveillance in my apartment, I saw she'd packed a bag. I figured she must be going to stay with Julia, as Mum had said she was out of hospital. It was selfish of me, I know, but I'd taken to watching her move around my space and I got comfort in that; knowing I could see my girl whenever I wanted. Not in a creepy way – there were only cameras on the lower floor – but it eased my anxiety. I wasn't due to fly back for a few days yet. We had Lloyd's funeral coming up, and I wanted to be there for Darcey when she went to the Shoemockers' funeral too. My girl had a lot of heartbreak to deal with.

My phone rang. I looked at it hopefully. But it was Adam, asking me to meet him at HQ.

"We're making progress," he said. "We've tracked down a man we believe could have been responsible for sabotaging one of our big rigs on site. The guys checked and he was wired a substantial sum just before, and then just after the damage occurred. Benjamin's going to have a little chat with him."

I smiled. A little chat with Benjamin meant he would soon be singing like a songbird.

"We're also trying to trace the source of the money," Adam went on. "But it's been routed through various offshore accounts."

"You'll find it," I said. "I've got every confidence in the team."

The murder of a close friend and brother has a way of focusing the mind and motivating you like nothing else. We'd employed the best of the best on this. We ate together, and Benjamin briefed us on what he'd learned.

I went back to my digs to get a shower and a shave. Lying on my bed for five, I tried to process everything we'd found out. But instead of being able to answer questions, I found I had even more. Still, at least there had been no more sabotage of our equipment on site; all seemed to have gone quiet for now.

Another one of our teams was working on a lead thrown up by the surveillance footage in connection with Lloyd's death. I kept going over and over things, wondering what I'd missed.

Eventually, I dozed off. I hadn't been sleeping well and I was exhausted. It was just coming to the end of the wet season. When it rained here, it really rained. The sound must have lulled me to sleep.

I woke when my phone rang. Bill was bringing in the supplies, equipment and additional manpower we needed via Soekarno-Hatta International Airport. I'd intended to go with him. He was calling to let me know he had a little something special for me and would drop it off. I figured my mother must have sent me some kind of care package.

Adam:

Daniel and Simon must have known what they were doing, but Darcey was the last person I expected to see roll up in the supply trucks. We'd spoken on conference calls and I knew she was smart. What I hadn't expected was when Simon filled me in on her background.

"I don't have time to fucking babysit," I told him, and he laughed.

"Darcey's no damsel in distress," Simon said, "and I strongly advise against treating her like one. She made me eat mat when I was sparring with her."

Now that piqued my interest. The woman would have to be made of strong stuff to put up with Caleb's ornery arse, because he was getting worse.

Darcey handed me a whole host of files. We spread them out and started to create a timeline. The supplies had all been unpacked but we discovered we were one tent and one bed short. Darcey was about to check again when there was a commotion.

I heard him before I saw him. Caleb came storming into the HQ.

Chapter Eight

Caleb:

What the ever-loving …? Why the hell was Darcey here? And why was she wearing cammies? We all wore them when we were deployed overseas but seeing her dressed like that had me instantly hard. There were more than a few pairs of eyes taking in her arse as she bent over the desk too.

Adam began to speak but I wasn't in the mood to listen. Grabbing Darcey by her wrist, I dragged her out of there. She was quickly losing her shit but I needed to speak to her in private.

As soon as I got her into my tent, the girl became almost feral.

"What the fuck, Caleb?!" She broke my grasp on her wrist.

Right now I wanted to pummel Simon and my brothers. What were they thinking, sending her out here? They had no right to put her in harm's way.

Darcey raged at me. "How dare you treat me like that! Who the hell do you think you are?"

"You've no business being here! I'll treat you however the hell I want!" I was furious; relieved; horny. As I yelled, all I really wanted to do was kiss the living daylights out of her.

She went to leave. The next thing I knew, I had her backed up against the large central pole in the tent. I kissed her hard, my mouth devouring hers in an all-consuming frenzy. After an initial shocked reaction, she melted into me. And we both became frantic.

My hands roamed all over her body; up her shirt. She didn't try to stop me. Her hands stroked my abs, then gripped my hair. I pulled down the cups of her bra, violently, unceremoniously, in utter desperation, and began laving her nipple with my mouth while squeezing the other in my palm. Darcey let out a guttural moan.

As I moved us to my bed, she wrapped her legs around me. It made me crazed. We became a frenzied blur of flaming passion, limbs and need.

I lay, stark naked, my cock jutting out ramrod straight and throbbing. There was already pre-cum leaking from my tip. Darcey was fucking waxed down there, apart from a neat little strip of hair. The woman had my mouth salivating. I wanted to own her; to taste every part of her. She was wearing some sort of mesh, see-through panties. She looked incredible laid out on my bed, her long tresses billowed around her. She was like an avenging angel.

I had fantasised about this moment. But my fantasies never came close to this.

I had to taste her first and make sure she was wet for me. I slipped my fingers past the flimsy fabric and found her opening. The scrap of material was drenched with the juices from her pussy. She was dripping wet with the need for me.

I peeled the scrap of material down her hips. Slow down ... I needed to take a moment or I'd blow my load like a pre-teen.

I slid down the bed and parted her legs; sucked her clit while adding first one digit, then two, curling them inside her to hit just the right sweet spot. Fuck me, she was tight and, oh, my God, she tasted so sweet on my tongue.

Darcey:

To say I was livid was an understatement. I figured Caleb might be a little shocked to see me, but for him to go all neanderthal on me and haul me out of HQ in front of everyone was a step too far. He had a tight hold on me all the way to his private tent and, once we were there, I screamed at him.

Next thing I knew, we were up against the pole. His mouth was on me; my hands had a mind of their own, groping, caressing, stroking every part of his hard body. I gave in and my anger was replaced with a frantic urgency and need. My hand brushed across his cock. He was thick, hot and huge. He was already leaking pre-cum. All I wanted to do was take him into my mouth and taste him.

He slid his hands into my panties and added first one finger, then two into my channel, stretching me and exploring my clit. Every thought in my head disappeared. He settled between my legs and began to lick and suck me. I didn't have time to feel embarrassed. He set a punishing rhythm and I just did what felt right. I began to grind against his face while I grasped his hair. And I moaned in pleasure as I found my release on his tongue.

Caleb became even more frantic, if that were possible. He slid up my body, licking, kissing and sucking me everywhere. Eventually, he grasped my head firmly and started to kiss me passionately, his tongue licking over the seam of my lips, demanding entry. He invaded my mouth at the same time as his steel-hard cock nudged against my opening and our bodies aligned. He was so hard and I was so wet that the tip slid in of its own accord without any help. I could taste myself on him. The large mushroom head of his cock stretched me and temporarily stole my breath as he pushed all the way in, balls-deep, in one smooth motion.

Caleb had his mouth on mine. I stilled for a moment as I felt the sharp stab of pain and burning, which soon subsided. His eyes went wide as saucers. Then I started to move. I don't know if they were my moans or his, but we moved together in a relentless rhythm. He never tore his mouth away from mine the whole time he was pumping into me, kissing me deeply; loving me.

I didn't know I could feel so full. Without warning, a second orgasm wracked my body and I milked his cock for all it was worth, just as Caleb bellowed, joining me, thrusting hard and deep at the same time.

At last, we lay quiet. Caleb cuddled me closer, remaining inside me. I'd always thought men were supposed to go instantly soft but it didn't feel as though Caleb had. He kissed first my nose, then my forehead, and I nuzzled my face into his neck. We fell asleep like that.

When I woke, he was stroking my hair. The bed was a mess. I was mortified to see blood on the sheet, as well as a huge wet patch. I went to look away in embarrassment but Caleb caught my chin to stop me.

"Was I too rough?"

I shook my head. I'd loved every minute of it.

"I hope you're not sore," he said.

I had to admit I was, but I was definitely down for a repeat. I truly hadn't thought sex could be like that.

He told me he loved it that he was my first. He said the thought of anyone else fucking my pussy would have driven him mad.

Taking my hand, he led me over to the crude shower in his tent. He took a soft washcloth and proceeded to wash me reverently and thoroughly. I began to get turned on again as he brushed the cloth over my swollen, aching clit and erect nipples. I dropped to my knees and took his cock in my hand. I couldn't fit him all in my mouth, not even close, but I sucked and licked, getting to know his taste.

After a beat, Caleb let out a guttural moan. "If you don't want me spilling down your throat, you'd better pull away ..."

I wanted to taste him fully, and swallowed wave after wave of his hot cum.

Caleb:

I pulled Darcey up from her knees and we began to kiss once more. I could taste myself on her lips and it was so hot. I can't remember when the shower got turned off. I picked her up and sat her on my table, spreading her legs, resting one foot on each of the two chairs. Then I began to suck and wring an orgasm out of her. I figured she might be sore after last night, but I was a selfish bastard and wanted her honey on my tongue again.

Darcey fell back on the table to her elbows, fully stretched out in front of me like an absolute vision. I sucked her rosy nipples to peaks and, as I leaned forward to kiss her, the head of my cock nudged her entrance of its own volition. Once again, our bodies aligned and she was drenched.

I looked into her eyes. No words were spoken; she just gave a little coquettish smile. This time, I pushed inside her slowly and made love to her while worshipping her body. I was home. This was all I'd wanted for so long.

I flipped her over so her chest lay on the table. Her arse was presented to me in the air and I moulded my entire torso over her back, wrapping my arms tightly around her; cradling her breasts into my palms from behind. I pushed in and out of her so deeply, pulling and rocking her backwards, impaling her onto my steel-hard cock. Her moans of pleasure tipped me over the edge. I came so violently that my hot seed splashed deep inside her and I felt my legs tremble.

Stripping the sheet off the bed, I grabbed another and spread it out. Then I lay Darcey down. It looked as though I'd fucked her into a coma. I knew that feeling too. She'd felt so tight around me, I thought I might pass out. Darcey Robson was mine.

Darcey:

Once my sex fog had cleared, I woke to find Caleb gone and his side of the small bed cold. My luggage had been brought to his tent. I dressed quickly, then spotted a note on the table. As I sat down to read it, I felt deliciously sore.

Then it hit me. We hadn't used protection! What the hell had we both been thinking? Actually, we hadn't been thinking at all – that was the problem. I thought I knew better than that, though.

The note read: "Back soon. Make yourself at home. Coffee in the pot."

I poured myself a cup of coffee and snagged a croissant too. By the time I'd washed my face and put a brush through my hair, Caleb had returned.

He walked up behind me and cuddled me close, moulding his body against my back and kissing my neck.

I turned round in his arms. "Caleb, we need to talk about this."

Caleb simply growled and said, "You're mine!"

Coming from any other man, that would have pissed me off. Coming from Caleb – I had to agree with him. I was his, and spoiled now, I was sure, for any other man.

But I had to say it. "We didn't use protection."

Caleb shrugged. "I'm clean and get tested regularly. And we both know you are, so there's no problem."

Was he deliberately missing the point? "What about pregnancy?"

He shut me up with a bone-melting kiss. I had a feeling we'd be late to HQ ...

Caleb:

I hated getting up and leaving Darcey. She was sound asleep and looked adorable. I'd had trouble sleeping since I'd arrived here but last night I slept like a log. When I woke, I felt refreshed for the first time in weeks.

I saw Adam and told him Darcey had jet lag, so I was letting her sleep it off a bit. Adam just smiled and nodded. I took her case to my tent – I wasn't letting her go anywhere.

Then I scooped up the sheet I'd taken from the bed. I felt like crowing and keeping it when I first saw the blood; the proof of her innocence. But I got rid of it before she woke. I didn't want her to be embarrassed.

I felt like beating my chest. I honestly didn't know what had come over me. I'd never felt like this about another individual, and I'd had my fair share of women over the years. I did come close once. But the way I felt about Darcey only proved I was right to call things off when I did.

It wasn't until Darcey mentioned we hadn't used protection that it even crossed my mind. I'd never had unprotected sex, apart from with Charlotte. I knew right then that I'd never use anything again, though. Last night had felt too amazing. Mind-blowing, actually. I didn't want there to be any barriers between me and Darcey. If we got pregnant, so be it. Darcey wasn't going anywhere and I was shocked to find I quite liked the thought of her being my baby momma. Growing round and swollen with my son or daughter. I wanted and needed her in more ways than I could describe.

Adam:

Simon and Daniel weren't wrong about the effect Darcey being close to him would have on Caleb. When they eventually came waltzing into HQ, they both wore that same look – like the sheets should be on fire. Caleb was calm and laser-focused, but he never let Darcey get more than two feet away from him. He touched and caressed her at every given moment, even while being fully engaged in the conversation.

The pair worked in perfect sync around each other. It was impressive to watch. Caleb all but peed on Darcey to mark his territory in front of the crew. The man was a complete goner. The mighty Caleb had finally fallen and was well and truly off the market. I was pleased for them both. My mother, Simon, Paul and Daniel all adored Darcey. She'd even won Mike over.

I continued to work on the timeline she and I had started yesterday. The money transfers had been filtered from one offshore account to another and were proving tricky to trace, but not impossible. We tracked down three of the local employees we'd hired over the different sites, who were responsible for the sabotage and theft of our machinery. Unfortunately, someone had beaten us to it.

The men sat slumped around the card table they'd been playing at. All three of them had been shot in the head, execution style. Whoever was behind this had serious money and influence and didn't want us in this territory. The two key questions now were who and why?

Gloria:

I visited Julia and baby Hope again today. My Daniel was staying with her and working from there so he could help out. He was off walking the dog when I turned up.

I offered to take Hope for a walk in her pram. Julia looked so washed out and tired. I thought it would give her the chance for a bath and to catch up on some sleep. I bundled the little cherub into her pram, packed a bag with expressed bottles of milk, and off we went.

With Hope in tow, I met up with the girls – Noreen, whose family were in shipping, and Doris, my old friend who ran the

Office Angels recruitment agency. I loved it that we had baby Hope to fuss over, but it was under such sad circumstances.

"And how is Darcey?" Doris asked.

I had to smile. "Adam says my plan is going swimmingly. I said I had no clue what he was talking about, but he told me not to get ideas where he was concerned."

We all laughed. If only he knew. The three of us had raised wonderful, independent, successful children. We were incredibly proud of what they'd achieved, but not one of them was married yet or had children of their own. And we were all desperate for grandbabies.

"Well, I've told Charlotte," Doris said, "that if she slips up and falls pregnant, it won't be an issue. I can watch the baby when she goes back to work."

We burst out laughing again. Charlotte, Doris's daughter, had been engaged for two years now, but there was still no wedding date set, no matter how many bridal magazines her mother bought for her. My own family, both by blood and extended, simply had no clue. I just wanted to see them settled down and happy.

Hope had fallen fast asleep in my arms. I'd always thought Daniel carried a torch for Julia, but he'd actually had a hand in her getting together with Lloyd. I'm so glad that happened. Lloyd was a lovely man and they'd been very happy together. I hoped, when enough time had passed, Julia might find love like that again. I personally never had, and I knew first-hand how empty life could feel, traversing the ups and downs alone.

Noreen's eyes twinkled. "My son carries condoms in his wallet. If he doesn't get a move on, I'm going to start poking holes in them!"

"By the way, I meant to say," said Doris, "I had a visit from Mr Abington's latest PA. She's desperately looking for another job and asked me to keep an eye out. She said Mr Abington had been expecting to bid on a big contract but Caleb had sealed the deal privately before it was ever offered out for bids. Apparently, he was raging and screaming about it like a madman."

I shook my head in sympathy. That wretched, odious man had something of a reputation with his female staff. His son was supposedly even worse.

"Could you imagine if Caleb had actually married his daughter, Gloria?" Doris added. "If you ask me, he had one heck of a lucky escape."

"You're telling me," agreed Noreen. "She was a devious, cold bitch of a woman."

The whole family were vile. I told Doris to send the PA my way. Darcey had become more than a PA and my boys kept heaping more and more work on her. I needed someone reliable for the normal filing and reports, and to liaise with Darcey about Caleb's calendar. When Darcey was out of action, we'd tried a couple of temps but they hadn't worked out. I was also conscious I'd be having my knee surgery at some stage, and I needed the right fit for the office.

Daniel:

Mum texted me to say she was on her way back with Hope. There had to be a security detail for every member of our family all the time. One of the guys would have had eyes on her the whole afternoon. I told her I'd unlocked the door and she should just let herself in, as Julia was out for the count and I didn't want her to get woken up.

Eventually, I heard the latch and Mum appeared with the pram. I was so grateful to her; she was an incredible lady. She looked after all of us, taking everything in stride.

Hope was fast asleep, so I put the kettle on while Mum started making a chicken pasta dish. The aroma made my mouth water.

Not only was she a terrific cook, Mum was also astute. She said I looked tired, which I was. I'd been working round the clock on issues for Darcey, as well as arranging everything for Lloyd's funeral and helping look into some leads for Caleb. Julia was trying to hold it together as best she could, but it was clear she needed a helping hand.

I still couldn't get my head round the fact that Lloyd was gone. He would have been an amazing dad. I missed my friend to the point it hurt. This was the least I could do.

Julia had been waking with night terrors. She would often shout out in her sleep. But she insisted on breastfeeding because that's what she and Lloyd had decided. I felt useless through the night as she had to do every feed herself, although I had taken to winding and changing Hope afterwards, so Julia could go back to sleep. Most nights we just ended up crashing on the sofa and never made it into our beds.

Julia:

I woke with a start. How long had I been asleep? The house was silent.

I walked into the living room in a panic and found Daniel stretched out across my sofa, out for the count. My tiny baby girl was sprawled on his broad chest and a blanket covered both of them.

Gloria had left me a note. Not only had this kind lady given me some time for a bath and some sleep, she had also cooked dinner. The smell had my stomach growling. As I walked into the kitchen, I saw she'd put a load of washing on, had ironed a pile of clothes, and all the baby bottles had been cleaned and were in the steriliser ready to use. The delicious smell was coming from a pasta dish in the warmer.

I started to cry. I couldn't help it. Just as I grabbed a tissue, Daniel walked in with an alert, wide-awake Hope in his arms. He looked so tired, but I honestly didn't know how I'd have managed without him. We were united in our grief and our love for Lloyd, so I knew he understood what I was going through.

I took hold of my sweet baby girl and hugged her close. I missed Lloyd so badly. I looked a mess, the house was upside down and I couldn't believe I was planning the love of my life's funeral. It didn't feel real. I was still waiting for him to waltz through the door.

Daniel said we needed to talk about final arrangements, as Lloyd's body was due to be flown home from Jakarta tomorrow.

"Will I be able to see him?" I asked.

Daniel's eyes were so full of sadness. "I don't think that's a good idea," he said. "The bullet did a lot of damage."

I nodded. What else could I do?

They'd tracked down the men responsible for the sabotage. The shooter had turned up too; badly beaten and dead, with a bullet between his eyes. But I didn't feel relieved; I just felt numb.

The guys were like brothers. They had all wanted to attend the funeral but a few teams had to remain in Jakarta to ensure everything stayed on track with the job. Lloyd was a Marine, first and foremost. Many of the guys had sent me private messages and had popped in to be with me when Daniel had to go into the office. I would be forever grateful. The funeral would be hellish, but I knew Lloyd's friends would give him full honours and the send-off he deserved. Hope had so many good people in her life. I had to be thankful for that.

Adam:

Darcey, Caleb and I had a video conference with Daniel. It was weird as hell seeing my younger poser of a brother, pacing Julia's living room in the early hours of the morning while rocking and winding Hope, a cloth spattered with baby spit-up draped over his shoulder. He never broke stride, even when Hope let out the biggest belch.

Daniel mentioned Mum had met with Doris and Noreen. Our families were close as friends and we did a lot of business together too. Noreen's husband, Jed and eldest son, James handled the majority of our shipping, and Daniel had gone to university with Doris's daughter. They'd both studied law. We also used Doris's Office Angels for all our recruitment.

"The thing that's interesting," Daniel said, "is that Abington's current PA has been to Office Angels on the lookout for a new job. Apparently he threw a fit over not getting the chance to bid on that project."

Caleb laughed out loud. "Not my fault he's a sore loser."

And all at once, it became glaringly obvious. Abington was the common denominator in all our problems.

Darcey had had a run-in with him and had quit. Since then, she knew he'd blocked her employment, pulling strings to ensure she couldn't find a new position. Darcey was also one of the employees the hackers had attempted to go after, plus there had been the creepy stalker incident. On top of that, Abington was raging over the contract he felt Caleb had stolen. Caleb had almost married his daughter, too, until the plans fell through. The list of grudges Abington might have against Heart Industries went on.

But grudges were one thing. We needed actual proof. We were still trying to follow the money trail. Abington had the money and the motive, and the guy was dirty and underhanded. There had been rumours a few years ago about his son too – guns, drugs, trafficking – and to be honest, I wouldn't have put any of it past him.

"Now – Lloyd," I said. I really didn't want to get on to this. "James and Jed have arranged for his body to be placed in a specialised container that will travel in the cargo hold of the aeroplane. When the plane lands, the funeral director will take care of getting the container to the funeral home. I've been dealing with the Consulate since Lloyd's death. We'll return home together for the funeral, with quite a few of our special ops teams."

We ended the call in a sombre mood.

Caleb:

Darcey sat on my knee during the video conference at HQ. When the penny dropped about Abington, I noticed she paled a little. Recent events had taken their toll on us all. I wanted to ensure the guy was put away for life and his business ruined.

Seeing Daniel step up the way he had made me feel a sense of pride in my little brother. He looked a natural. Hope was so tiny but he handled her expertly. I rested my hand on Darcey's belly. I had to admit, I quite liked the idea of having a baby; something I never thought I'd want. With the fact I couldn't keep my hands off Darcey, it could already be a real possibility.

Darcey never left my side. I thought it would drive me crazy always having someone in my personal space, but she was remarkable. I know Adam had a lot of time for her. Her foresight had been bang on the money and she tended to think around a problem, so she'd earned his respect. Reluctantly, I had to admit that sending her over here had been a wise move.

That evening, we all ate together in the mess tent and Darcey pitched in and helped out. As the guys swapped shifts, they sat round the table and one of the lads produced a harmonica. Darcey began to sing along while he played.

I went instantly hard. She had me mesmerised. I couldn't believe how beautiful her voice was. Darcey hadn't known whether or not her throat would be permanently damaged after the fire, but clearly it hadn't been. The mess tent fell silent. Everyone just stared at my girl. The lads loved her and the moment did wonders for morale. They'd all been on edge since Lloyd's death but this was a tonic for everyone.

Tomorrow would be tough. We were taking our boy back home to the UK and to his loving wife and final resting place.

Chapter Nine

Paul:

I was finally out of hospital and back home. Mike had decided to stay at mine a little longer to help me out. It would be a while before I was fully back on my feet.

We talked strategy. Mike had a wealth of knowledge. He'd been in special ops for most of his working career, until he'd made the move to Heart Industries. After the revelation from HQ, the pieces had started to fit together. However, now we knew who the main culprits were, the trick would be proving it. We needed hard evidence against the Abingtons. I was out of action physically, but we had surveillance set up at all their warehouses, docks and storage yards, as well as at the main family members' homes. Thankfully, a few of the ops teams were returning with Caleb, Adam and Darcey, so we would have even more boots on the ground.

Daniel:

The day I'd been dreading was here. Lloyd's body was finally home. As the plane touched down, Jed and James joined me. They'd taken care of everything. A Union Jack flag was placed over the container and it was escorted to the waiting hearse.

I hugged my brothers and Darcey at the airport terminal and we headed back to Heart Industries. We needed a debrief.

Paul, Simon, Mike and my mother would be there. Even Frank was dropping in.

We entered the building through the garage, parked up and went down to the lower security floor in the lift. This was mainly Simon and Paul's domain as Heads of Security. Most of our special ops and surveillance missions were planned here. It was a vast, sophisticated floor of tech and kit. We had storerooms for every gadget we could possibly need, and weapons were kept in locked and coded, solid-steel cages. There were sleeping bunks and washrooms too.

Darcey seemed to automatically slip back into her role as PA. She brought down sandwiches and other refreshments, and set the coffee machines going in the kitchen area. I truly loved her for Caleb. My brother acted completely differently around her. He seemed lighter since they'd got together; more at ease. She was his person.

The rest of the teams joined us, and the floor became a hive of activity. I took a seat at the head of the table with Caleb, Adam and Darcey. We'd raised the company threat level to a code red. Many of the heads of my departments were ex-military and special ops. They knew how to keep their eyes and ears open for any perceived threats, and were each responsible for the safety of their staff and teams.

The first tier of our meeting began with outlining the funeral plans and arrangements to honour Lloyd. Then we explained the reason for the revised threat level, what to look out for, and summarised our understanding of the situation. Ideas were put forward and discussed. The relevant staff were then excused.

Both Paul and Simon had put together special ops teams and, in the second tier of the meeting, everyone was given their assignments. Jed and James had been key to setting up surveillance at the dock. We'd heard rumours the Abingtons were into drugs, guns and trafficking. Through our informants all over the city, we understood they were expecting a big shipment, but of what, we didn't yet know.

A tech team was looking into the attempted data breaches – why specific people had been singled out and what the correlation was between them. One of them had been Darcey but others had been staff in our distribution departments, in contracts and in planning.

As the meeting drew to a close, we'd set our plans in motion.

Caleb:

The plane ride home had been excruciating. I'd sat next to Darcey as we took off and all I could smell was her hair. I held her small hand in my much larger one; let my finger stroke over the back of it. I just needed to touch her, hold her, be inside her. Darcey calmed me, grounded me, and made me bat-shit crazy all at the same time. I felt jealous if she paid too much attention to anyone else, even to my own brothers, which was insane. Most of the time, she was oblivious to the interest shown by other men.

I wished we were alone and I couldn't wait for the seatbelt sign to switch off. I'd taken to liking Darcey sitting on my knee. It kept her close, hid my straining cock from view and, when she sat those peachy little globes down, she had a delicious habit of wriggling to get comfortable. I was constantly hard around her; in a permanent state of arousal.

A flick of her hair; a shy smile; even the unique scent of her. It all drove me out of my ever-loving mind.

As soon as the seatbelt light went out, I popped the clasp and dragged her onto my lap. Instantly, I felt more settled, with Darcey moulded to my body and snuggled in my arms. Within minutes, she was fast asleep and warm against my chest. When I thought about it, I could barely remember a life before this woman. My father had loved my mother fiercely and with utter devotion. Now I understood. I'd found my person and I had no intention of letting her go.

Although I was desperate to pee, I didn't wanted to wake Darcey. But as we were only half an hour from landing, I gently stroked her cheek until she opened her eyes. Her little moan, scent and sweet kiss had me desperate to relieve myself in more ways than one.

I made my way to the bathroom. I was bursting to pee now but I had a raging hard-on, so I couldn't. I felt a bead of sweat break out on my brow. As I sat on the toilet seat and thought about the forthcoming meeting, I willed my dick to soften so I could at least empty my bladder. Once I'd finished, I flushed and made to wash my hands. But thoughts of taking Darcey in here, joining the mile-high club on this little vanity unit, took over. I grasped my shaft firmly and pumped it, spreading the bead of moisture at the tip for lubrication. I came so hard my thighs quivered. I needed to be balls-deep in my girl, and soon.

It was cold and wet as Darcey and I dived into the slick Aston Martin I had waiting for us at the airport. I merged into traffic on the motorway and turned the heating on. I also hit my playlist. I had pretty eclectic taste and the car filled with the sound of country music.

Just as I felt myself relax into the driver's seat, a little hand sneaked across and started to unbutton my belt. It seemed I wasn't the only one feeling a need.

Darcey's eyes were closed, her head tipped back against the headrest. But there was a smile on her plump, wicked lips. My length hardened painfully as she slid open my zipper and freed me from my briefs. Wrapping a warm hand round my shaft, she pumped me from root to tip, with just the right amount of pressure and pace. While I tried to concentrate on the road, I found myself smiling like a loon. I was desperate to have her hot, wet mouth wrapped around me, sucking and licking for all she was worth.

As if she'd read my mind, she leaned across and put me in her mouth. Nirvana! It was a good thing the road we were on now was quiet. I pulled over into a lay-by. She picked up the speed and momentum, and I shot hot streams of cum down her throat as I pulsed out my release. Then she reached up and kissed me with real passion. It was the hottest thing I think I had ever experienced and I could still taste myself on her lips. I was panting.

Unfortunately, we had a meeting to get to before I could return the favour, so I drove on. Besides, I wanted Darcey in a proper bed, with no time restraints.

The word "restraints" stuck in my mind. Now that did give me some wicked ideas ...

When we got to the Heart building, Darcey wanted to go up to the office first so she could load a trolley with all the day's sandwiches, muffins, pastries and fruit. We then made our way down to the security floor, or "bunker" as we called it. Darcey had never been down there. She was fascinated and couldn't believe the size of the place. I suppose it did look impressive if you were seeing it for the first time – the walls covered in monitors and the computer deck. Most employees had no clue this space was even here.

I gave her a guided tour as everyone was arriving. We passed the bunker room and I had to fight the serious temptation to slip inside with her for a quickie. As tempting as that was, though, the place was swarming and I would never expose Darcey to anyone else's eyes. We returned to the main room and took our seats at the head of the table with Adam and Daniel.

During the second tier of the meeting, Darcey helped us identify three companies she knew the Abingtons dealt with regularly. When she'd worked for them, she'd obviously been privy to invoices, shipping schedules and so on. It made us wonder if that was another reason why they'd targeted her – because she knew too much.

Darcey:

We headed to the loft, my mind reeling with everything I'd learned recently about Caleb, his brothers and Heart Industries. I now understood the need for special ops, especially after everything that had happened in Jakarta. I was worried, though. This was dangerous.

Caleb wasn't your average CEO. He was also a marine and still took part in many of the missions himself, along with Adam and Daniel. They were very hands-on and I didn't know how to feel about that. What shocked me was the number of people I thought were general office staff, who slipped into a completely different role when called upon for their unique set of skills and talents. No wonder Heart Industries was so successful.

I knew I had to bring up my living situation. I was only staying with Caleb because my place had been destroyed by the fire. Now I had my compensation and insurance money, I really needed to find somewhere of my own.

I felt so mixed up. My inner turmoil was slaying me because I didn't know what we were; we hadn't put a name to it. We hadn't talked about us. Actually, we hadn't talked much at all as we couldn't keep our hands off one another for long enough. As soon as we found ourselves alone, our clothes seemed to fall away. So ... were we dating? Was this just a mutually beneficial hook-up? I hadn't done this before and I was frightened I was making it out to be more than it was.

Caleb was the first man I'd slept with. If I was honest with myself, I was head over heels in love with him. The thought truly terrified me because I could so easily get hurt. I didn't know what things would be like now we were back home. Had it just been adrenaline? The emotion after what had happened to Lloyd? The stress of the situation? I honestly didn't know.

We arrived at Caleb's building and I entered the private lift from the garage. I caught sight of myself in the mirror on the back wall; I looked a complete mess. Caleb stepped in behind me.

As soon as the doors closed, he pushed my face into the mirror and his hands were all over me. He slid his fingers into the front of my yoga pants, moving my knickers to the side. Kicking my legs out a little wider apart, his thumb rubbed my clit deliciously. With his other hand, he pushed down the cup of my bra and gently rolled and pinched my nipple. While he kissed and licked my neck, I rode his hand, writhing against his fingers until I exploded around them as a sweet orgasm overtook me. My legs gave out, but Caleb caught me without missing a beat.

Before I knew it, he'd lifted me into his big, solid arms, and I was being carried, bridal style, across the threshold of his apartment. I don't know which magician had done it, but some Chinese food we'd ordered before leaving the Heart building had been laid out in front of the fire, which was lit. There was a bottle of wine open, with two glasses next to it. Our bags had already been dropped off and were piled beside the door.

We sat down on the rug in front of the fire and ate like two starving people. The same soft strains of country music from our earlier car journey started to play.

Once we'd eaten our fill and moved to the couch, Caleb grabbed my wrist and pulled me on top of him. I could feel how hard he was, and my nipples began to pebble. We kissed, licking, sucking and nibbling on lips and tongues. It was so sensual. Then Caleb got off the couch, picked me up again, as though I weighed nothing, and carried me up the glass staircase to his bedroom.

His bed was huge. I guess that made sense since he was such a big guy, and the room itself was very masculine, in shades of steel-grey, black and white. He lay me so reverently on his bed, and began to worship me. Climbing between my legs, he peeled off my yoga pants and tore the sides of my lace knickers away. I was soaking for him. This man turned me inside out. I could feel my nipples and clit throbbing. Next went my t-shirt and bra, until I lay completely naked on his bed.

I began to rub my own clit while I watched him devour me with his eyes. He groaned as he looked at me, and tore his polo shirt over his head. I loved his bare chest; the right amount of hair over his dusky nipples, and abs that were so well defined, he made my mouth water.

He grabbed his trousers, pushed them down his legs and threw them to the floor. Finally, like some kind of erotic male striptease, he hooked his thumbs into his briefs on either side and slid them down past his happy trail and over the firm globes of his arse. His large, steel-hard length sprang free and to attention. Like this, he looked huge, and my pussy began to pulse in anticipation.

He placed his hands on my knees and opened my thighs wide. Nestling himself between my legs, he grabbed my butt and pushed my pussy into his face, eating, sucking and licking me to another orgasm. I grasped at the sheets and the moans tore from my throat.

Then he positioned me on my side and pushed into me. As large and thick as he was, he slid into me easily since I was so wet for him. One hand crossed over and grabbed my hip firmly as the other reached for my breast, and all the while, he drove into me hard and deep. The rhythm he set was punishing.

I rolled over and sat astride him, impaling myself on his length. And I rode him. He was so deep; he filled me so completely. His hands on my breasts, rolling my sensitive nipples, we both came undone.

I suddenly felt boneless and so exhausted.

Caleb got off the bed and padded to the bathroom. I heard sounds of the tub being filled and I could smell his bubble bath. He led me by the hand and encouraged me to step into the warm, inviting, sudsy water. Then he sat behind me, coaxing me to lie back on his chest while he proceeded to sponge me clean.

When I got out of the bath, he wrapped me in a huge, warm, fluffy, white towel. I didn't know if he wanted me to go to my own room now. He soon clarified that when he led me to his bed again, pulled back the covers and tugged me down so I fell with him onto it. Then he scooped me into his chest and I used him like a warm pillow.

I was asleep within seconds.

Adam:

I was dreading giving Caleb the news. I knew he'd go batshit crazy. When I told him what I'd found out and what we'd have to do, he'd no doubt fight me on it. I called him at 6:00 a.m. and he sounded groggy when he answered.

"Caleb, we need an urgent meeting ASAP. I'm calling the whole team together."

"I'll wake Darcey," he muttered.

"No. She must be jet-lagged. Let her sleep."

"Okay. See you in the bunker in twenty minutes."

Simon and I met him at the lift and we sat round the table with the team. Simon, Paul, Mike and three squads of guys had been chosen to undertake the special ops missions yesterday. Now it was up to me to break the news.

"Some intelligence has come in," I began. "Darcey has a hit out on her."

The Abingtons were clearly worried about what Darcey might know, especially as they were aware how close she and Caleb had become.

"They still have no clue we're on to them, though," I continued. "They're so arrogant they're getting sloppy. They think they're untouchable. They've done pretty well covering their tracks so far – killing those contractors in Jakarta, hiding the money trail – but our guys are better."

Caleb looked first devastated; then furious. I gave him a moment.

Finally he asked, "So what's the plan?"

I took a breath. "We need you to be seen to be distanced from Darcey. It has to look as though she doesn't work for us anymore. With immediate effect." I paused. "Paul's arranged for her to be moved to our Ireland office; out of sight and out of mind. He's going to go with her for her safety, as well as two other guys and one of the girls on our crew."

We'd expanded our operations in Ireland and I knew Darcey would genuinely be invaluable over there with helping to get things established.

"Paul's sourced a large townhouse to rent," I added. "They'll all be able to stay at the same location, five minutes from the office. But here's the thing. Darcey can't know anything. Not the real reason she's been moved. No one can."

The colour drained from Caleb's face. Normally so practical, so in control and sure of himself, he looked almost mutinous. The guy couldn't think straight where Darcey was concerned.

"No." He shook his head vehemently. "No, that's not happening. Darcey's not going anywhere. I'll keep her safe here."

"And what if you can't?"

"I will!"

Mike grabbed him by the arm; forced him to look his way. "Listen to Adam, Caleb. We all want to keep Darcey safe. Every single one of us. But this is the only way to do that. Now, I know it's tough but you have to let us do the right thing. For the sake of our girl."

Caleb stared at Mike. There was real desperation in his eyes, but deep down, I could see he knew it was the only thing that made sense. As the reality finally sank in, he looked totally crestfallen.

Lloyd's funeral was the following day. We'd have to mobilise straight afterwards. I advised Caleb he'd have to cut communication with Darcey to the bare minimum and that it should be work-related only. Realistically, though, there should be no communication at all.

"One more thing," I finished. "You can't sleep at the loft tonight."

Darcey:

When I woke, Caleb wasn't there. I saw a glass of orange juice on the bedside table, with a single red rose lying next to it. There was a note too: "Gone to the office for an urgent meeting. See you soon. Caleb x".

Smiling to myself, I realised my muscles felt exquisitely sore. I'd been woken in the early hours to find Caleb between my thighs once more. We went for rounds three and four till first light, when we fell fast asleep in each other's arms. I couldn't imagine ever tiring of this.

Gloria called me to tell me she'd booked me in at Franco's at 9:00 a.m. today for the works, ready for the funeral tomorrow. She and Julia would join me. I dressed quickly and the car that had been sent for me took me to the Heart building. Hoping to get a sneak peek of Caleb, I knocked on his office door but he was nowhere to be found.

I felt a little deflated as I met with the girls. Julia looked as though she hadn't slept at all. Noreen had come too, so she could look after baby Hope while Julia got her treatments and hair done. When I returned to work, Simon, Paul, Adam and Daniel were in the office waiting for me.

Something felt ominous; as if they were about to give me bad news. My stomach lurched. They ushered me to the boardroom and we'd barely sat down before Adam told me I was urgently needed at the Irish office.

I wanted to laugh. This had to be a joke.

"I'm sorry ... I don't understand." I looked from Adam to the others. "My role is here."

"Our presence in Ireland is expanding," Adam replied. "You've shown us some pretty expert skills and we really need you over there."

"Well ... what does Caleb think?"

"Oh, he's all for it," said Daniel. "In fact it was his idea."

That totally took me aback. His idea? So what did the last days mean? What did last night mean if Caleb was planning to send me away?

"How long will this be for?" I managed to ask. "Is there a plan?"

The guys proceeded to give me the details, although they couldn't confirm the timescale. I couldn't take it in. The whole thing sounded like a done deal. And it seemed Caleb had signed it off without even discussing it with me.

Gloria caught me as I left the boardroom.

"It's a wonderful opportunity," she said. "Ireland is breathtaking. You'll love it."

I didn't want to seem ungrateful but how could I see it as any kind of opportunity when I'd had no say in it? My eyes stung with tears but I was determined not to cry in front of anyone. I felt as though I'd just been shelved or sucker-punched.

I tried to call Caleb. It went straight to his voicemail.

Simon:

For this to work, Darcey couldn't know what was really going on. Nor could she be seen to be having any contact with Caleb, as we knew people were watching them. I felt like a total dog deceiving her like this. When you saw the two of them together, you could feel the sexual tension radiating out from them. But it was the only way. We had to break Darcey's heart temporarily to keep her safe.

Caleb was livid. He was already climbing the walls and he wasn't even aware of everything yet. Adam had arranged for him to join the operations down at the docks' warehousing area to keep him out of the way.

Unbeknown to them both, I'd been back to the loft to pack all Darcey's things. It needed to look as though she'd never been there. Once that was done, she was told we'd moved her out of Caleb's apartment. She'd be flying to Ireland immediately after the funeral tomorrow and, until then, we'd booked her a room in an airport hotel. Her Irish counterparts had contacted her by email and they'd go over further arrangements when she arrived.

Later that day, I dropped Darcey off at the hotel and saw her to her room. I'd set up a tab and told her she could order anything she wanted on Heart Industries. No sooner had I stepped back into the corridor and shut the door than I heard her gentle sobbing.

The next day, I went to collect her for the funeral. She looked a complete knockout in a tight-fitting, black, long-sleeved dress, with a gold zip that went from the nape of her neck to the hemline just below her knees. The dress was incredibly modest but, OMG, Caleb was going to swallow his tongue. I just hoped his brothers would be able to keep him in check. Darcey's hair was wound in a loose knot at the base of her neck and she wore light make-up and a huge pair of Jackie-O sunglasses. I had a feeling I knew why that was. As we left the hotel room, she grabbed a black pashmina and wrapped it about herself.

I took Darcey's arm as we stood outside the chapel. There was a huge crowd of mourners, many wearing their medals, which identified which of the armed forces they belonged to. Some were in full uniform. It truly was a sight to behold. We moved to the front of the line, with Gloria, Mike and Paul.

The funeral procession arrived and Julia got out of the car. She was sobbing as she passed her baby to Noreen. Daniel, wearing his military medals, almost had to support this grieving young woman physically. Adam and Caleb stepped out last, dressed in identical, immaculately tailored, dark navy suits, with all their medals in place. The coffin was dressed with a Union Jack and the most beautiful spray of flowers in red, white and blue. Lloyd's service medals rested close to them on a velvet cushion just in front of the flowers.

Adam and Caleb acted as bearers, together with some of the other guys Lloyd had served with. They stepped forward, hoisted the casket onto their shoulders and walked their friend and brother-in-arms, perfectly in step with one another, into the chapel.

Caleb:

The journey to the chapel was heartbreaking. Julia's soft sobs were killing me.

Lloyd would be given full military honours, as befitting an elite Royal Marine. We'd all been based together at RM Condor in Scotland, part of 45 Commando, an amphibious commando unit that formed part of 3 Commando Brigade Royal Marines. Our elite troops conducted a range of operational tasks at home and across the globe. We had many friends spanning the service and it was humbling to see such a crowd of them here today to honour our brother as he "crossed the bar".

I caught a glimpse of Darcey in the chapel but, when we moved out to the graveside, she was nowhere to be seen. She looked stunning but seemed to glare at me as I took my place next to the guys in the pew. I didn't know what I'd done. None of this was my fault. I wanted to catch her afterwards to explain; not everything, obviously, but enough so she knew how I felt about her; that this situation was only temporary.

But she was gone.

As we made our way back to the waiting car, Adam pulled me aside.

I wanted to punch my brothers bloody when he told me what Darcey had been led to believe: that sending her to Ireland was my idea. What must she think of me? I felt sick to my stomach. No wonder she'd looked at me the way she had. I wanted to kick my own arse! And now I was being told I couldn't see or contact my girl for the foreseeable future.

Since Darcey had flown out to Jakarta, we'd never spent a night apart. Before, when I'd had a bedmate, I'd finish the deed, dispose of the condom and get out of there as quickly as possible.

But I loved waking up with Darcey in my arms each morning. This could destroy the best thing I'd ever had.

I had to talk to her. Soon. I needed to fix this.

Gloria:

I was shattered. It had been a long, incredibly draining day; heartbreaking but beautiful at the same time. I felt so proud seeing all my boys come together like this for Lloyd, and carrying his casket. As the first few bars of "Abide With Me" played, I couldn't hold back the tears. This is what we'd sung when I'd buried the love of my own life.

I looked at Julia. She resembled a hollowed-out shell, just going through the motions. I knew from experience how much harder it would get. To begin with, everyone is around you; helping, supporting. You never seem to be alone. With funeral arrangements to be made, people and businesses to be informed, the first few weeks are a hive of activity.

But when it's all over and the dust has settled – when you close the door and at last you're completely by yourself – that's when you feel it. That's when you really know what loneliness is.

I felt a tap on my arm. Mike handed me a tissue, then linked his fingers with mine and gave them a little squeeze of comfort. Darcey sat on my other side, her arm through mine. She looked stunning; like a fifties movie starlet. A far cry from the dishevelled girl who'd come to me for a job a few months back. Hiring her was possibly one of the best things I'd ever done. Not only was she brilliantly clever, astute and beautiful, but she'd enchanted my Caleb and half the firm. I'd almost given up hope of anyone ever capturing his heart.

Something was bothering her though. We hadn't had the chance to catch up properly and I thought she'd be excited about the opportunity in Ireland. It wouldn't be for long, the boys had told me; just to help establish the office over there.

But she looked sad, and it was more than for Julia, I was sure of it. I only hoped it wasn't Caleb's doing.

Chapter Ten

Darcey:

I felt so stupid; completely foolish and naive. I'd truly believed Caleb had feelings for me. He was the first man I'd ever slept with. And they say you never forget your first.

Yet I had been ejected from his apartment without warning. Dumped out of the way at an airport hotel, like his dirty little secret now he'd had his fun. How had I read the situation – how had I read Caleb – so wrong? What hurt the most was the fact that he hadn't had the balls to do it himself. Nor had he answered any of my phone calls. It was radio silence. I kept wracking my brain: what could I possibly have done wrong?

And what the hell was up with me? I couldn't stop crying. I felt sick to my stomach and couldn't help but think I'd been played. I was so embarrassed about what people must think of me. Paul, Simon and his brothers – Caleb had got all of them to do his dirty work for him. I could tell they'd felt sorry for me as they struggled to make eye contact.

Well, I would remain professional and do the job they'd sent me to do to the best of my ability. I would focus on getting the Irish office set up. Then I would look for another job. This thought brought on a whole new wave of tears, but I knew I couldn't stand the humiliation of seeing Caleb with a new conquest on his arm. It would finish me off.

I didn't bother with the hotel tab. It had crossed my mind briefly to get blind drunk and charge it to Caleb. But that wasn't me. Besides, I needed to have my head on straight for the funeral tomorrow.

I must have dozed off around three in the morning. My alarm sounded at six. I got out of bed and stumbled to the mirror, taking in my bloodshot, puffy eyes. I looked a total mess. When I called Julia, I don't know which of us sounded worse. I didn't mention any of my troubles, we just chatted. We both cried over the phone too, which helped me put my life into perspective. I only had a broken heart to contend with. Julia had lost her soulmate.

I showered, then turned on the radio to drown out my thoughts. Caleb would be at the funeral and wouldn't be able to avoid me. I wanted to make sure to remind him what he'd be missing. Fortunately, I had just the dress and an amazing pair of sky-high heels. I took my time pinning up my hair and applying my make-up. By the time I'd finished, I looked nothing like the bedraggled reflection I'd seen in the mirror earlier that morning.

There was a knock at the door. I strode over to open it with an air of confidence I most definitely did not feel.

On arrival at the chapel, Simon, who'd driven me, escorted me to the front of the building to join Gloria, Mike and Paul.

It wasn't long before the hearse pulled up. Julia stepped out, followed by the boys. And Caleb. My eyes fixed on him instantly. I couldn't help myself. He looked stunning. It was lucky the large sunglasses I'd chosen to wear hid my eyes.

I held my head high as I walked with the others into the chapel. We sat in the front left-hand pew. I was grateful to have Paul on my left and Gloria on my right. As I linked arms with her, she patted my hand.

I found myself crying before the service had even begun. Paul handed me a tissue. My tears were for poor Julia, Hope, Lloyd; even a little for myself. I felt Paul's arm around me, giving me a gentle squeeze of support, and I rested my head on his shoulder. For a moment, I didn't feel so alone.

The guys walked in slowly, in perfect step with one another. Lloyd's coffin was draped in the Union flag, with a breathtakingly beautiful spray of flowers laid across it, and his service medals nestled on a velvet cushion. You could smell the delicate scent of the freesias as the procession passed by.

Caleb caught my eye. I had just removed my glasses for the service and I felt as though he could see right through me. My hurt was so raw. I could only glare at him, then turn my head away. He sat in the front pew with the other bearers as the service began.

I somehow zoned out. It wasn't until Lloyd's friends stood up to sing that I sort of tuned back in.

It was so wrong, all of this. Opening your heart to another person just made you vulnerable. I needed to get out of there. I felt claustrophobic. I couldn't even begin to imagine how Julia felt. It looked as though she was just going through the motions too.

I said my goodbyes to everyone, but I couldn't speak to Caleb. He was carrying the coffin once again and didn't even look back. They made their way to the graveside as I headed to the waiting car in the opposite direction. I had a security detail with me. I don't quite know what sort of scene Caleb thought I'd cause, but I wouldn't do that. It proved he didn't know me at all.

I sat next to Paul in the car. There were two other, rather serious-looking guys with us, and a lady sat in the front passenger seat. I just wanted to get to Ireland to begin my new chapter and lick my wounds.

The journey felt long. When we eventually arrived, we were driven to the house where we'd be staying and Paul opened it up. It was elegant, with a modern twist. Unsurprisingly, no expense had been spared. I found my room and couldn't wait to get to work. The sooner I sorted the Irish office, the sooner I could move on with my life. I couldn't keep on crying.

Paul:

The funeral was hard on everyone. It never got any easier, saying goodbye to a brother. I hadn't actually served with Lloyd but I'd come to know him well through working for Heart Industries. I'd also got to know Julia. As we left the chapel, I put my arm around her. I felt bad not staying at the graveside, but I had to leave for Ireland with Darcey right away. She needed to be whisked off before Caleb had the chance to speak to her.

My scars felt tight and itchy under my suit. I was desperate to get changed. I'd been working on my fitness and was doing a lot better, so this time away served a dual purpose. I was to protect Darcey, advise on security and carry on with my rehabilitation. When I joined her in the back of the car, I noticed a single tear track down her cheek, before she dabbed it away as she watched Caleb's retreating figure through the window.

For the whole journey to the airport, Darcey was silent. We boarded the flight but she still seemed in a world of her own. When we touched down in Ireland, we were met and driven straight to our new townhouse, which was to be home for the next few weeks – or months. None of us had any clue how long this situation would take to resolve. Not a word was spoken in the car.

I had the keys and opened up the house. The building was situated in the old industrial quarter, now the business district. It was right next to the office and had undergone extensive renovations. Inside, it was very slick and modern. Darcey chose the room next to mine; we both had huge bedrooms, with balconies overlooking the district. We unpacked our bags and freshened up after our journey. But I could see Darcey had lost her sparkle. Her light had dimmed.

Abington:

As I sat at my desk, my mobile rang. Harry.

"Boss, I thought you'd want to know – Darcey left the funeral early. She didn't stay for the full thing."

"What do you mean, she didn't stay?" I demanded. "Where did she go?"

"A town car whisked her away as the service finished. She was flanked by a full security detail," Harry responded. "We tried to follow but lost them in the town traffic ..."

I hung up. That slippery little bitch. What was she up to? Where the fuck had she gone? And why would anyone leave a funeral early? I thought the grieving widow was a friend of hers ...

Paul:

We all made our way to the office together to check the place out. Zoe, the head concierge, gave us a tour of the building. Not quite as large as Heart Industries, it was still pretty impressive. I was to shadow Darcey and work out of the same office, reporting back to the boys.

All business, Darcey sat down and opened her file. She made a note of everyone and their specific job role. The girl was sharp as a tack and easily answered question after question, sounding confident and sure of herself. By the end of the first meeting, there were lots of head nods and comments of agreement. She had officially charmed the Irish contingent. Attending scheduled meetings with each department head to discover any issues, she seemed to hit the floor running, throwing herself into her new role.

When we left the boardroom, Zoe asked if we'd like to grab a drink after work and said she'd show us around Dublin. I fully expected Darcey to decline but she surprised me by accepting the offer. At the end of the day, we all met in the reception area. There were approximately twenty of us: me, Darcey, the other security detail, as well as Zoe, Connor, Patrick, and a few of the department heads who had attended the meetings earlier.

We went to an Italian restaurant and the food was out of this world. Darcey didn't look or act like her normal, vivacious self, and only picked at her meal, but she still chatted and smiled.

Afterwards, Zoe took us to a traditional Irish bar. The place was quaint, full of locals and incredibly busy, while the atmosphere was warm and friendly. Strangers said hello and smiled as we filed in, so we felt welcome and at ease. We managed to snag a booth in the back corner just as one party left, and grabbed spare stools from other tables to accommodate us all. There was an old piano next to our table, so we fitted the stools around this and the booth as best we could.

Darcey had a rum and coke and began to unwind a little. Then the music started: the beautiful, soft strains of a violin; a penny whistle that joined in a couple of minutes afterwards; and finally the strumming of a guitar. The tune had a haunting quality and the pub quietened down as we all listened. The playing appeared to be spontaneous, with the instruments in the hands of regulars. No one batted an eye, so I think it was safe to assume this was the norm in this pub.

As the piece ended, a new one began. After the first few bars, I recognised the song as "Molly Malone", an old Irish classic. That's when Darcey excused herself. I thought she was getting up to go to the ladies' room and I nodded to Sierra, the female security operative, to go with her. But then, Darcey surprised us by sitting down at the piano and joining in with the music. The other musicians stopped briefly, smiled at her, then began again. And as they did so, Darcey opened her mouth and began to sing.

Her voice was clear as a bell; hauntingly melodic. I was astonished. When the shock wore off, I whipped out my phone and took a quick video. She was unaware of the stir she was causing, her eyes closed, seemingly lost in the music.

The barmaid polished a glass and placed it on the piano top. Next thing I knew, people were dropping notes and coins into it.

When the song ended, the musicians asked if she knew "The World's Smallest Violin".

Darcey laughed. "As it happens, I do," she replied, and they began to play. The pub erupted into applause and punters joined in and sang along with her.

And then I noticed. All around, there were phones recording her. How could I have made such a monumental error? We were supposed to be keeping a low profile. I had to get Darcey out of there. Fast.

Abington:

My phone rang.

"Fucking Ireland?!" I boomed into it when Harry gave me the news. I was already in a piss poor mood. "What the hell is Darcey doing in Ireland?"

"I'm sending you the footage now," Harry said. "It went viral."

What the fuck ...? I stared at my phone's screen. There was Darcey, sitting at a piano living her best life – and fucking singing in a bar. What the hell was Caleb up to now? That tricky bastard never did anything without a good reason.

"Harry," I said, "you need to get over there. Now." I hated being caught off guard. "Darcey might be a hot piece of arse but I'd like her so much better if she was a dead piece of arse. The girl's nothing but a ball-ache."

"Got it." And Harry hung up.

Just how much of the dock information had she seen? Had she put any of the other pieces together? I'd hoped the death of one of those fuckers would have had them too busy chasing their tails to be looking into me.

I had to focus. I needed to tie up some loose ends in Jakarta and get my distribution flowing again. I did wonder if Darcey had been sent to scope out our docks in Ireland, as quite a few of our main shipments came through there. It was about time I called my Heart informant to see what was going on. He was a small fish but useful, as he had access to most areas within the building. A little pressure and he would sing like a songbird.

Darcey:

My contacts at the Irish office seemed pleasant enough. I wondered if they knew the real reason I'd been sent here. Connor and Patrick were a great help throughout the day and Zoe, the head concierge, was lovely. When she asked me out for a meal and a few drinks at the end of the day, my first thought was to say no and go back to my room. But I knew that wouldn't solve anything. I needed a fresh start. Today had been filled with so much sorrow and heartbreak, I had to get out of my own head. I must admit Paul looked a little taken aback when I said yes.

The food and company were great, but I had no appetite. Still, it was better than sitting in my room, crying. I forced myself to smile and joined in with the banter at the table. It seemed that my reputation had preceded me, though for all the right reasons. Everyone knew about my recent trip, my findings over the cabling, and the fact that I'd been key in implementing other financially beneficial strategies for Heart Industries in the London office. I'd apparently been sold to them as the "UK darling". They seemed genuinely interested in me and I began to relax a little.

After the meal, we moved on to a traditional Irish bar. It was so quaint-looking; like stepping into a time warp. The atmosphere was warm and welcoming, and the place had a good smell and vibe all of its own.

As my new work colleagues filled me in on office goings-on, I suddenly heard someone in the bar start to play the violin. The sound was beautiful. Other instruments joined in and the background noise dropped away. Then I heard the opening of "Molly Malone".

There was a piano by the booth where we sat. I'm still not sure what made me do it, but I got up, opened it and played along. The other musicians beamed at me and, as I started to sing, I let myself get lost in the music.

Paul:

Back at the house, Darcey took off to her room right away.

I had four calls from Caleb on my phone, as well as one from Simon and one from Adam. I'd already told Adam I'd dropped the ball, and sent him the video of Darcey singing and playing. You could clearly see other people in the background filming her. Adam said he'd been watching it when Caleb had walked into the room. Caleb had snatched his phone and watched the footage over and over. He was handling things about as well as we'd all feared he would. Normally, nothing distracted Caleb from a mission. We'd never known him to get so cut up over a woman. But Darcey was his everything. We'd known it from the first moment we'd seen them together. The sooner we could wrap this up the better; that poor girl upstairs was heartbroken.

I wasn't looking forward to calling Caleb.

He answered his phone on the first ring. "About fucking time."

I thought he sounded as though he'd been drinking. At least his brothers were with him.

Before I could say a word, he asked, "How's my girl? That fucking video sleighed me. Man, she looked and sounded so sad. And I did that to her. Fuck!"

"She's fine," I said. "I'm keeping a close eye on her."

"I had something delivered for her," Caleb went on. "It's in the sitting room."

As we talked, I wandered through to look, and there, near the window, was a huge, black grand piano. The coffee table that had stood there before was gone.

"She'll love it," I said.

He gave a brief, bitter laugh. "She'll forget all about me. She'll think I'm a complete bastard."

I couldn't deny it because, right now, that's exactly what she did think.

The next day, I told Darcey it was me who had organised delivery of the piano. I hated lying to her but she couldn't know it was from Caleb. She had to believe he didn't care about her anymore.

As the weeks passed, her singing and playing could be heard all over the house. It was beautiful. Her tastes were eclectic so we had classical music, ballads, and movie soundtracks. But they all had one thing in common: they all sounded sorrowful.

At the office, Darcey threw herself into a tough work schedule. She made friends with Zoe and a few of the other girls, and I was glad about it. Whenever they went out, Sierra, her security detail, would go with them.

I noticed she was also garnering a few admirers. But she always politely declined any advances and invitations, and never looked twice at anyone.

One of the girls mentioned that her family had a lake house and asked if we'd like to visit for a weekend getaway. I thought it would do Darcey good. Tom and Travis, part of our security detail, went on ahead to scope it out. I booked a lakeside bungalow for myself and the guys to stay in, and it was agreed Sierra would stay with Darcey and the others in the lake house next door.

Darcey:

I honestly thought I'd be getting over him by now. It had been a while. Yet the pain I felt was still just as raw; Caleb was never far from my thoughts. So, when one of the girls asked if I fancied a weekend away, I thought some time somewhere beautiful might be just what I needed.

The place turned out to be breathtaking; green and lush. Our lodge was nestled amongst huge trees right on the lake's edge. There was a pretty little dock at the front, where a wooden rowing boat was tied up. It truly was picture-perfect; like something from an old-fashioned candy box lid.

That week, a few of the staff in the office had been sick with a stomach bug. We left for the lake on Friday morning but, unfortunately, by teatime, Zoe had fallen ill and couldn't stop throwing up. Then another of the girls started. Not a great beginning to our weekend.

I decided to get out of the lodge and take the boat on the lake. I had a good book and it was a balmy sort of day. The exertion of rowing was exhilarating, and the tranquil sounds of nature were like a balm to my wounded heart. At a midpoint across the water, I lay down, propped up in the bottom of the boat, and just read for a couple of hours.

By Sunday morning, however, I'd joined the choir of people puking their guts up. I felt really rough. We were supposed to be going home but decided to stay on a few days till we all perked up; it wasn't as if we'd be going into the office like this.

A short while into the day, my tablet pinged. I'd forgotten I had it set to any alerts about Caleb. I knew I shouldn't look but, hey, I'm only human.

As I sat on the bathroom floor, having just vomited my guts up once again, tears streamed down my face. I couldn't get the images of Caleb I'd just seen out of my head. He was at a gala, looking brooding and deliciously handsome in a well-fitting tux – and with an extraordinarily beautiful blonde on his arm. Obviously, I hated her on sight. Her dress was incredible and left nothing to the imagination. It looked as though it had been painted on, and she had the widest smile on her face as she posed for photographs with Caleb.

I was still retching over the toilet, my tablet discarded on the bathroom floor, when I heard a gentle knock, and Paul entered. As if my humiliation wasn't already complete, he knelt beside me and held my hair away from the toilet bowl as I continued to dry heave. He didn't seem concerned that he'd get sick himself, or covered in my puke. When the retching finally subsided, he wiped my face with a cool, damp cloth, then picked me up like a rag doll and tucked me into bed.

Afterwards, I heard him cleaning the bathroom for me, because I hadn't quite managed to make it to the toilet in time.

Paul:

I heard Darcey vomiting, and found her crying over the toilet bowl. The poor soul looked as though she had no strength left, and I knew how tough Darcey normally was. This bug had floored her just as it had all the girls.

It was after I'd put her to bed that I noticed her tablet on the bathroom floor. I picked it up and it sprang to life. And I saw what Darcey had been looking at.

Shit ... She wasn't supposed to see this.

Adam:

I got the call from Paul and I knew there would be fallout. Caleb hadn't wanted to go through with it. It had taken us a lot of effort to convince him.

Caleb was engaged to Abington's daughter a few years ago. But Charlotte – or Lottie as she often went by – was a piece of work. Don't get me wrong, the girl was exquisite. Long, blonde hair, legs that went on forever, a body to die for and the most striking face. I totally got why Caleb had decided to tap that – quite frankly, who wouldn't?

The thing was, though, she was a venomous bitch. A complete viper only interested in her own agenda, money and influence. Sure, she looked like butter wouldn't melt but you wouldn't dare turn your back.

Caleb had been set on marrying her; until she'd got caught screwing her investment banker. A big scandal ensued as it turned out she hadn't been declaring all her business earnings to the Inland Revenue. There was a huge investigation and she narrowly missed jail time for fraud. Her banking boyfriend did actually get done for fraud. He was given a decent sentence but always claimed he was set up.

But there was no set-up around the banker and Charlotte. Caleb caught them together red-handed, punched the guy and broke his nose. He then threw Charlotte out rather publicly, yet never batted an eye or seemed remotely upset over it. I don't think he was ever truly in love with her. Charlotte, however, never gave up trying to win him back. She maintained it was all a huge mistake; an accident. Obviously she accidentally fell on the other guy's cock.

Reading the article she wrote for a lifestyle magazine still makes me want to roll my eyes. What a load of tripe. All she wanted was the money and influence Caleb and our family could afford her. Abington had been keen to promote a merger with our family too. He was supposedly scathing when Caleb rejected her and turned his back on her. And he'd been baying for Heart family blood ever since. The fact that his daughter had been caught shagging around didn't seem to register with him.

Still, the Abingtons couldn't know we were on to them and, all of a sudden, Charlotte looked useful.

We needed Caleb to take her to a gala event as his date. Sick, maybe, but what better diversion tactic to take the heat off Darcey than to stoke the possibility that Caleb wanted a reunion with Abington's daughter.

Caleb finally agreed, for the sake of his girl. Charlotte met him at his loft apartment for a drink, then they drove to the glitzy event together. As predicted, Ms Abington was shameless as she worked the red carpet.

Naturally, the media had eaten it up. The next day, they were supposedly "in love". There were rumours of a possible shotgun wedding because Charlotte was pregnant – and that was just a couple of the stories I read. Who made this crap up? It must have been a slow news day.

Of course, it was great the plan had worked so well. Only now Paul had told me Darcey had seen some of the articles online; which must have been like rubbing salt into her red-raw wounds.

Gloria:

I missed Darcey so much at work. Truth be told, I hadn't thought she'd be away this long and the office wasn't the same without her.

I eventually video-called her for a proper catch-up, but when she appeared on the screen, I was a little taken aback. We'd been texting but it was the first time I'd seen her in weeks. Darcey's face was thin, tired-looking and drawn. She said it was nothing and told me she'd caught stomach flu but I knew there had to be more to it.

When I finally asked her point blank what was wrong, she broke down and told me everything.

I was aghast at how callously Caleb had treated her. I adored each of my sons but right now I wanted to box Caleb's ears.

"Do you think I'm pathetic?" Darcey asked.

"You? No, dear. Never in a million years." Seeing her in so much distress, I was almost at a loss for words. "You didn't deserve any of this. I am utterly appalled at my son's behaviour."

Darcey seemed to turn even more pale.

"Gloria, what do you mean – your son?"

"I'm ... Caleb's mother," I said. How could she not have known? "I'm sorry – I thought you realised that."

Darcey suddenly put her hand over her mouth and said she had to dash.

And the call was over.

Caleb:

My mother's voice was usually full of warmth and comfort. Today when I picked up the phone, it sounded like a raging thunderstorm, crashing and booming with righteous indignation.

"I am beyond livid, Caleb James Heart. Utterly appalled by your actions." Each syllable was laden with fury. "How could you treat our Darcey like this? I raised you better than that."

The tirade must have lasted a good five minutes. I held the phone away from my ear and let her get the rant out of her system before I even attempted to speak. Never in my life had I been on the receiving end of such a vehement reprimand from my mother. The strength of her disappointment hung heavy in the air and bore down on me like a crushing weight.

"Why, Caleb?" she demanded at last, her voice trembling. "What possessed you to act like this?"

For a moment I was lost for words. Then, "Mum, we had no choice," I managed to choke out.

"That girl deserves better, Caleb. So, so much better. I can't even fathom what you were thinking."

"I do love her, Mum." I could hear the desperation creeping into my voice.

"I know you do." Her tone softened slightly. "But she doesn't believe that now and do you blame her? What possessed you to act like that towards her?"

In that instant, my worst fears were confirmed. As far as Darcey was concerned, I'd betrayed her.

"She must hate me," I whispered. A lump formed in my throat. "And I can't say I blame her." As the full weight of my actions was brought home to me, tears welled up in my eyes, hot and stinging.

For the first time in my life, I allowed myself to break. The tears flowed freely, unstoppable torrents of pain and regret, as I poured my heart out to my mother, the one person who had always been there for me.

"I want to marry her, Mum," I confessed. "But right now, I can't even begin to make things right."

As I wept, clinging to the fragile hope that somehow, some way, I could repair the damage I'd wrought, I realised I had never felt more lost and alone in my entire life.

Chapter Eleven

Paul:

We were back at the house in Dublin, where the air was thick with tension and sickness. Darcey was well and truly drained by the relentless grip of the stomach flu. The others who'd caught it were fine now and back at work. It had only lasted a couple of days for them. But Darcey was getting no better so, in the end, I took her to hospital.

When I carried her into A&E, she was like a limp rag. Doctors and nurses swarmed around us, whisking her away for tests, their urgency a stark reminder of the fragility of life.

Alone in a private room, she lay motionless and sound asleep. I sat in the chair next to her bed, holding her hand. It didn't seem that long ago that she'd done this for me.

A doctor eventually came in, all smiles, which I thought was strange given the apparent severity of Darcey's illness. Then, he delivered his verdict – to me, as Darcey was still sleeping. And his words pierced the quiet of the room like shards of glass, shattering any semblance of normality.

"I've organised some fluids, as this young lady is seriously dehydrated, and some anti-sickness meds," the doctor continued, having dropped his bombshell. "I'll also be adding some intravenous antibiotics. A couple of days and she should be good to go. I'll get a prescription for folic acid and vitamins sent up. And we want to do an ultrasound, but all seems well. The little tike is mighty resilient – congratulations!"

The doctor left the room and I sat back in the chair, slack-mouthed like a goldfish.

Darcey was pregnant. And she had no idea.

Darcey:

I woke up feeling slightly better than I had in a few days, and with a cannula in the back of my hand. I vaguely remembered arriving at the hospital, but mostly what I felt was a crushing tiredness.

Paul was holding my hand. He sat in a chair next to me, fast asleep, his head resting on my bed. It couldn't have been comfortable for him.

I was about to wake him when Gloria's revelation blasted into my mind. How had I not figured out sooner that she was Caleb's mum? Why had no one thought to tell me? In true, unfiltered Darcey style, during that last conversation with her, I had basically blurted out what an arsehole her son was and how badly he had treated me.

Then I thought of how we'd first met and the whole shower debacle – and I wanted to crawl into a hole with mortification because I'd shared that with Gloria too.

Paul stirred.

"Hey, you," I said. "Thanks for bringing me here."

He rubbed his eyes and yawned as he came to. Then, looking right at me, his expression changed. He seemed anxious.

"What?" I asked. "What's wrong?"

He opened his mouth to speak but didn't get the chance. At that moment, a jovial, elderly nurse came into the room, pushing a large machine.

"I'm here to do your ultrasound, honey," she said, and moved the machine next to me.

I heaved myself up to a sitting position and blinked at her.

"Do you know how many weeks along you are, darling?" the nurse asked.

My eyes widened but no sound came out of my mouth.

Paul piped up. "Er, no. We're not sure."

It was as if time stood still while my poor, fogged brain scrambled to take in what was happening.

The nurse whipped out some clear gel, which she squirted on my stomach. It didn't even register till later that she'd hiked my hospital gown up under my bust in front of Paul, and I was now lying there in a pair of cotton knickers.

The next thing I knew, she was running a weird-looking wand over my abdomen and there was a whooshing sound followed by a strong beat. Then, in a moment that defied all logic and reason, the truth was laid bare before me: not one, but two tiny heartbeats echoed through the room, their existence a testament to the unfathomable miracle that had taken place inside me.

"Twins!" the nurse said, as if the mere utterance of the word could convey the magnitude of the revelation.

As I gazed on those blurry images, a sense of wonder washed over me, eclipsing the fear and uncertainty that had plagued me moments before. For in that instant, amidst the chaos and confusion, I found a glimmer of hope – a promise of new life, of love renewed, and of a future yet unwritten.

"I would say you're just a little over four months pregnant," the nurse went on. "Nice strong heartbeats."

The machine spat out a couple of pictures.

And there they were. My twins.

Abington:

Once again, Darcey seemed to have vanished. What was the bitch up to? She hadn't been in the Irish office for days. I might have been wrong about her and Caleb; or he may have just tapped it and then shipped her out of the way once he was finished with her – who knows? I still couldn't take any chances.

Fortunately for me, Charlotte had finally wormed her way back into Caleb's good graces. I knew it was just a matter of time. My beautiful girl's like a siren and Caleb was drawn there again like a moth to flame. As much as I hated the prick, it was better to have him close, and Charlotte deserved a little payback after he'd humiliated her the way he had.

My brilliant girl would make him pay though. Of that I had no doubt.

I grabbed my mobile and dialled. "Did you get it done, Charlotte?" I asked when she picked up.

"Honestly, Dad, did you really doubt me?"

The phone clicked off and I smiled.

Daniel:

I was still staying with Julia. It was weird adjusting to life after Lloyd. I missed my friend every day; kept expecting him to walk through the door with that shit-eating grin of his all over his face. We held it together as best we could. It had been unsettling after the funeral – as though we didn't know what to do, or what to say to each other. We just knew we needed one another.

Every time I looked at Hope, I could see her daddy. Thankfully, she was a settled baby, and Julia and I had a good bedtime routine going. Julia was still breastfeeding and would express milk so I could help with nighttime feeds too.

It was coming up to her birthday and I'd been thinking about what to get for her. I'd finally decided to have the triangular, folded Union flag she'd been presented with at Lloyd's funeral mounted in a box frame, with spaces for three photographs underneath: a head-and-shoulder picture of Lloyd in his dress uniform; the two of them on their wedding day; and finally Hope when she was a newborn. I also wanted Lloyd's campaign medals displayed either side of the flag.

My mind was all over the place. There had been so much to deal with and, on top of it all, there was a lot going on with work. I was lucky, though. My mum, Doris and Noreen were a huge help. One of them would stop by pretty much every day while I was out. They treated Hope like their own grandbaby and spoiled her and Julia rotten. I was grateful but it made me re-evaluate my own life. I had never felt reluctant to undertake a mission before. Now things had changed. I was needed. Really needed. If anything happened to me, what would Hope and Julia do? You always felt a frisson of fear going on a mission; anyone who says otherwise is a liar. But I'd never had as much to lose before.

I decided to work the control room in the bunker this time around, instead of being boots on the ground. I also wanted to keep looking into the Abingtons' legal transactions. Lottie had narrowly avoided a prison sentence – how? Who had they paid to make it all disappear? And what had she been up to since then? What was her agenda?

Most of all, I wanted to find out what it was the Abingtons thought Darcey knew that would make them target her. Why had they put out a hit on her?

I'd created a timeline wall in the bunker, and all the surveillance was starting to pay off. We knew Abington was expecting a big shipment any day now. We were closing in.

Adam:

I'd hardly slept these last few weeks. I'd been on the ground in the surveillance missions. Suited up, we'd entered the water at the docks and installed cameras to capture absolutely everything; even small craft coming and going. Caleb had been crashing overnight in the bunker with various teams. He had a gruelling routine: through the day he was the CEO, ensuring he was seen at every opportunity and making it look as though it was business as usual. Then, in the evening, he would help the special ops teams.

Tonight, he was attending a charity dinner with Mum, and he knew Abington would be there too.

When Charlotte had met Caleb at his loft before the gala event, Caleb had left her on her own downstairs when he went to the bathroom. On Simon's regular sweep of the apartment after Charlotte's visit, he had found two listening devices. The only people who had access were obviously Simon, the cleaner, Caleb, Mum, Daniel and me. It didn't take a genius to work out who'd planted them. We decided to leave them in place to feed back false information and throw Abington off the trail.

I was worried about Caleb. For a good few nights, he'd gotten blind drunk. Then, suddenly, it was as if he'd had a moment of clarity. Instead of wallowing and drowning his sorrows, he'd become laser-focused in the hope of a quick end to this so he could have Darcey back. I don't know which mood was worse. He was much quieter and testier than usual; I'd never seen my brother like this before. I could tell the fact he had to have complete radio silence with her was killing him. Whether it was right or wrong, he'd got Paul to fit up a security feed in the sitting room in the Irish house. I caught him a few times just watching her play the piano. He was literally torturing himself.

Through our surveillance, our information indicated that the Abingtons' shipment would arrive soon. Everything was in place. All any of us could do was stay primed – and wait.

Darcey:

I was still reeling from my discovery. So it wasn't just stomach flu I'd had; there were two little jelly beans causing havoc inside me.

Once the anti-sickness drugs had kicked in and I was more hydrated, I began to feel (and look) much better. I still missed Caleb something fierce but now I had a new focus: I had to look after my growing babies and work on becoming a single mum of two.

I swore Paul to secrecy. He'd been truly amazing, making sure I ate, slept, and took my vitamins regularly. There was never any doubt that I would keep the babies. Other people managed. I could do this.

I went back to the office full-time. Shortly afterwards, I had to chair an important meeting with a potential investment client. As it was close by, Zoe, Vivian from accounts, Patrick, Sierra (the security detail) and I all walked to the restaurant that had been booked. Paul was on his way in the car and would meet us there.

As we made our way down the street, some total butthead, who wasn't looking where he was going, tore out of a coffee shop and collided with me.

"Aaah!" I yelped. My hands flew instantly and protectively to my belly. "Holy mother of fudge, that's cold!"

I glanced down to see I was doused in some sort of iced-chocolate, whipped-cream-and-caramel-topped beverage. It was plastered down the front of my fitted grey dress and jacket. My cherry-red shoes had miraculously escaped but, as the guy slammed into me, I went over on my ankle and ended up on my butt on the pavement. The arsehole didn't even have the decency to help me up or offer to pay for my ruined suit. He just dashed away as fast as his legs would carry him, giving me a muffled "sorry" over his shoulder.

I looked a complete gooey mess. And I was freezing. I couldn't believe it.

Sierra was beside me in a flash, laughing her arse off. She helped me up and we dodged into the coffee shop so I could try to clean up a little.

Then, as I stared at myself in the mirror in the ladies' toilets, she said, "Just switch outfits with me."

Brilliant idea. We were the same build and height, and had the same hair colour. We'd even styled our hair the same today. Sierra's dress and jacket were just a shade darker than mine and I knew they'd look good on me. In any case, I couldn't possibly attend the meeting the way I looked right now.

We swapped clothes in the toilet cubicles.

"The shoes too, Darcey," Sierra said. "You can't walk in those now you've gone over on your ankle."

I didn't want to part with my beautiful, crazy, mile-high stilettos. But I knew she was right. My ankle was swelling already and there was no way I'd be able to walk in those heels. Reluctantly, I passed them to her, and slipped my feet into her sensible, flat ballet pumps.

Sierra sponged my dress off as best she could, then we got underway again. We were running late for the meeting now but at least the others had gone ahead to greet the client.

Just in front of us, the pavement was being dug up and orange cones cordoned off the area where the workmen were busy. I walked close to the shop windows to squeeze past, and Sierra dodged to the outside edge of the pavement.

"You see, I could never balance on a kerb in those heels," I said. She laughed. "I'm not kidding – I could fall over a matchstick ..."

I trailed off. At the sound of a car driving at speed, engine revving, we both turned our heads. From out of nowhere, a large black vehicle careered towards us.

Sierra couldn't reach me across the pavement works.

"Darcey, get back!" she yelled.

It was all over in a second. At the last moment, the speeding car swerved into her. Sierra hit the bonnet, bounced off the windscreen and was flung into the road.

And the car was gone.

I was dazed. What had just happened? There were people around me on phones. Some were filming; others looked up the street as if they were trying to see where the car had gone.

And Sierra lay, unmoving, in the road.

I ran to her.

"Do you know her?" a woman asked.

I nodded.

"My husband's calling an ambulance," she said. "They'll be here soon, I'm sure they will."

"Sierra ..." I leant over her. "Sierra, can you hear me?"

There was no response. Her head was bleeding badly. I could see she was breathing; but only just.

As I crouched beside her, I pulled out my phone and called Paul.

"You stay there," he said. He sounded distraught. "You don't move, Darcey – you stay there."

I don't know how much time passed before the ambulance arrived, but it was quick. Strangely, I felt quite calm amid the flurry of activity as the paramedics tended to Sierra.

Paul arrived at the same time as the police. Sierra was now on a backboard with a brace on her neck and an oxygen mask over her face. Her hair had come undone and it fell over the sides of the stretcher. She was in a bad way. Still unconscious. Her head was bleeding profusely.

I knew the police wanted to talk to me but they'd have to wait. Once Sierra had been lifted into the ambulance, I jumped in with her. I heard Paul shout, "I'll see you at the hospital – I'm right behind you."

Then the doors slammed shut.

Paul:

I had just parked the car when I got a call from Darcey. I could hardly believe what she told me. Feeling sick to my stomach, I ran to the coffee shop. Sierra and I had become close over the last few months. I knew I had feelings for her. But, what now? Was she even alive?

I called Patrick at the restaurant as I ran. Vivian instantly wanted to cancel the meeting, but that was pointless. There was nothing any of them could do other than land this client, because Darcey had put a lot of time and effort into setting up the deal.

I got to the scene at the same time as the police. Paramedics were dealing with Sierra.

"She's still breathing," Darcey said.

I wanted to feel relieved but things didn't look good.

I filmed the scene, taking in all the local businesses with CCTV. Then I called Simon and sent him the footage. He could look for any cameras that might have caught what happened.

Darcey told me why she and Sierra had swapped clothes. From the back, the girls would have been hard to tell apart.

So that was it. The hitman wasn't after Sierra. He was after Darcey.

Our time in Ireland was over. Abington had found her.

Abington:

I had my new secretary bent, facedown, over my desk. I was balls-deep and fucking her hard when my phone rang.

I snatched it up and barked, "Yes?"

"It's done, boss."

I disconnected the call. As I slapped the girl's arse in triumph, she cried out in surprise. My day was suddenly looking up.

Paul:

I needed to get Darcey away from there. We'd been at the hospital for hours and the poor girl was still in shock. So was I. All I could do was hug her and hold her hand as we sat together in silence, waiting for news of Sierra. They'd become friends and I knew she felt responsible for what had happened today.

I was torn up, too. I felt helpless. Sierra had come to mean a lot to me in the time she'd been working with us. More than a lot. I think I loved her a little and, right now, I wasn't sure if she was going to make it.

There was a drinks machine down the corridor so I bought us two excuses for a cup of coffee. It was warm and wet but that was pretty much all you could say. Darcey cuddled in close while tears ran down her blood-smeared cheeks.

Recently, all she seemed to do was cry. There had been so much heartache and I worried about the twins. I'd been sworn to secrecy but what I wanted was to be a fly on the wall when Gloria, Noreen and Doris eventually found out. They would spoil Darcey and those babies something rotten. And when Caleb knew ... well, his face would be a picture. God help those babies if they were girls, though. Between their daddy and their uncles, no man would dare come near.

But for now, my job was to keep all three of them safe. I needed to hide Darcey somewhere off the grid. I'd already spoken to Adam; told him Darcey was handing in her notice with immediate effect. It would be processed in the usual way through the Heart HR department, but we wouldn't be telling anyone where she was going. Not even the boys. We were still convinced there was a mole working for Abington; someone passing information and trying to infiltrate Heart Industries back in London. The pictures of Darcey, the computer hacking and who knew what else – we had to be extra vigilant.

I had a place that used to belong to my parents. It was in the country in the middle of nowhere. I liked to go there for weekends sometimes and the local farmer kept an eye on it for me. It was the perfect place to keep Darcey hidden. Adam agreed this was the best plan. I'd have Tom and Travis with me. I knew I wasn't recovered enough to manage on my own quite yet. They would discreetly pack up the house in Dublin and stock up on enough provisions to last us for a few weeks.

I glanced at my watch. "I'm going to see if I can find anything out."

As I approached the nurses' station, the doctor we'd seen when we arrived appeared through the double doors.

"Is there any news? I'm ... Sierra's brother," I added, because I really needed this guy to talk to me.

"She's just out of surgery," the doctor replied, "and, quite frankly, she's lucky to be alive. She's lost her spleen, has a broken leg, arm, collar bone, pelvis, and she's got some swelling on the brain as well as bad lacerations. There are a few other things too but she's fighting."

It was a lot to take in. "Can we see her?" I pointed to Darcey down the corridor.

"For five minutes only," the doctor said. "Follow me."

I wasn't prepared for what greeted us. They had put Sierra into an induced coma to give her body a chance to heal and allow the swelling on her brain to hopefully go down. She lay there, broken. Her beautiful face was swollen and there was still dry blood caked on her skin.

I gave her a gentle kiss on the cheek and Darcey did the same. Then she was taken off to intensive care.

Somehow, it felt as though they'd wheeled my heart away with her.

Darcey:

When we left the hospital, we found Tom waiting for us in the car park in a large Discovery, with Travis riding shotgun. The 4x4 was packed full and there was one of those hard-shell cases on the roof. We jumped in and Tom sped off.

But not back to the house in Dublin.

I couldn't make it out. All of a sudden, Paul was telling me we had to disappear. He collected everyone's phones and my laptop, saying he'd post them back to the office. We had to be totally off the grid. He told me I couldn't use my credit card or any other device. I could tell he was holding something back but I didn't want to press him on it right now. Emotions were running too high. All he'd say was that the Abingtons were fearful I knew too much about their operation and that the hit-and-run might not have been an accident.

Their operation? This was scrambling my brain.

Paul must have seen he'd scared me because he gave my hand a squeeze.

"Don't worry, it's all being taken care of," he said. "We just need to lie low."

But where? I had no clue where we were going.

We'd been driving for a couple of hours and the landscape had changed from the city and suburban to the Irish countryside. We had to stop for petrol and Paul paid cash. He also grabbed us all some fish and chips as we passed through a village. We stuck predominantly to the back roads and they were pitch-black dark. Paul drove now and obviously knew where he was going. I heard the click of the indicator and we pulled off onto a side road. After another twenty minutes, we seemed to have reached our destination.

It was too dark to see much; only what the car headlights illuminated. But I could make out what was perhaps a farmhouse with outbuildings. To be honest, at this point I didn't much care where we were. I was wiped out. I just wanted to pee and go to bed. Being pregnant explained a lot – especially the need to pee all the time, the bigger boobs and the tummy bump that was now clearly visible.

It turned out Tom and Travis had cleaned out the Dublin house of all our belongings. No wonder the Discovery was packed to the gills. Paul helped me with my stuff and put me in a front bedroom. I brushed my teeth, had a hot shower, and fell into bed.

In the morning, I woke to the sound of a cockerel. A cockerel?! Where in the world was I?

I got out of bed and had to pee right away. That done, I padded to the window and looked out. What I'd thought last night was right. We seemed to be on a farm of some description. I wrapped my dressing gown around myself and followed my nose to the kitchen. My morning sickness seemed to have abate/d for now, and I was greeted with the delicious smell of bacon sizzling in a pan.

"Morning," said Paul. "How did you sleep?"

"Fine," I replied. "Just ... not long enough."

He nodded towards some fresh-cut tiger bread on a board next to the stove. "Help yourself."

I grabbed two slices and made myself a chunky bacon sandwich. It was heaven – which was more than I could say for the coffee Paul had poured me.

I took a sip and could barely swallow it. "Eew, I think the milk's gone off. I'm afraid I can't drink this."

I saw his eyes twinkle.

"I don't think it's the milk," he replied with a smile.

It took a moment to click. I'd noticed pregnancy food cravings and my tastebuds did seem to have changed – but going off coffee? That was something I hadn't bargained for.

"So, where are we?" I asked.

"This was my parents' farm," Paul said. "There are still some animals but nowhere near the numbers my dad used to have. A local farmer's son keeps an eye on things for me. Travis and Tom have gone on a recce. Have a look round. I think you'll like it."

I did like it. There were log fires in the main rooms; there were also solar panels, a generator, a wind turbine, and even a veggie patch. Everything we needed to be pretty self-sufficient.

Chapter Twelve

Caleb:

"Where the fuck is she, Adam?"

I'd been watching the security feed in the house in Dublin: there was no one living there. Had they gone back to the lake house?

Then Adam gave me the news that Darcey had handed her notice in at work. She was gone.

I was hit by feelings of despair and panic. My stomach turned somersaults.

"Gone? Gone where?" I squared up to him. "Gone where, Adam? What do you know that you're not telling me?"

Adam grabbed me by my biceps. "You don't need to know. Now, you keep your shit together, Caleb. We have to see this through so we can bring Darcey home for good."

Keep my shit together? And how the fuck was I supposed to do that? It had been hard enough when I knew where Darcey was. Now she could be anywhere.

Adam let go his grip on my arms. "We're going to get this done tonight," he said. "We'll meet all the guys at the bunker for a final debrief. Then everything's set. This is it, Caleb. This is the culmination of weeks – months – of surveillance." He stared hard into my eyes. "Don't blow this."

I held his gaze; then I gritted my teeth and nodded.

We had teams covering all the main sites: at the docks, warehouses, Abington's main home, his son's and his daughter's places. We had proof, too, that Abington had paid contractors to kill Lloyd and sabotage our job site. Daniel's speciality wasn't just the law. He was also a mean hacker, code writer and breaker. Call it a misspent youth, but the government had ended up paying him handsomely to do it as a full-time job. No information was safe from my brother, and he'd been working round the clock on this. He'd traced all Abington's offshore accounts, trying to fill in the blanks we'd been missing. There had been large money transfers to these accounts and to dummy corporations – you name it, they'd funnelled funds to it. Plus, of course, they had known links with traffickers, gun-runners and drug cartels.

By 5:30 p.m. I was positioned on the docks. A ship from Croatia called the Zvonimir was due in at 7:00 p.m. As it drew port-side, it was berthed. There was a slew of activity while the security belonging to the port authority did what they needed to do.

Our team was in position in the water, and we waited.

Then everything fell quiet. Until 9:00 p.m.

Two jet skis approached and a speed boat, which cut its engine as it got closer. The jet skis crisscrossed each other's paths until they finally came up alongside the ship. Facing out over the water, they were hidden from the view of the dock cameras.

But not from us.

The pilots were all taken out by our amphibious team, just as some men appeared on the deck with crates. Next thing I knew, the men on deck had been brought down by our guys too. Not one of them had seen it coming.

Daniel:

I'd predominantly been working from the bunker; stepping back from the ground for the sake of Julia and Hope. Today, though, I had no choice. Adam and Caleb needed me to head up a team.

I got a call from Simon.

"You ready?" he asked.

"As I'll ever be," I said.

We made our way with the teams to one of the main warehouses Abington owned. It was just registered as a storage facility but the utility records showed huge usage of electricity – five times what a normal storage facility would use. We'd long thought Abington's control centre was no longer at his house. He'd moved it when he'd got wind of possible police raids because of his daughter's tax fraud and embezzlement. And it was more than likely he'd moved it to this warehouse.

Our teams managed to enter and secure the building without too much fuss. But as they searched the premises, they found a sub-level that hadn't appeared on any plans.

We approached what looked like a largely concealed door with caution, then busted through. The space on the other side appeared to be deserted. We must have somehow triggered a silent alarm. There was a control deck in the centre of the area, much like our own set-up in the bunker, though not as sophisticated. A red and amber light blinked on and off on the deck; obviously some sort of warning system as the staff had clearly fled in a hurry.

As we took in the flashing light, three things became apparent: one, they had detected our arrival; two, the computer panels were smoking, perhaps blown and fried as a security measure; and three, there had to be another way out of here.

We heard a noise and turned towards it.

I signalled to a couple of team members to go and check it out. Then I made my way to the computer panels to look at the damage and see what might be salvageable. If I was lucky, I might find out what Abington was truly up to.

I didn't get far.

"Fuck! Get out!" A shout rang out from the main warehouse followed by muffled cries, then steady streams of rapid gunfire.

I left the panels and hurtled towards the noise.

As I entered the space, more bullets exploded, ricocheting off the metal walls and roof. I ducked down. It was carnage in there. Bodies were strewn across the floor and slumped against crates. One still twitched and moaned. But not for much longer. I saw him raise his gun, where he lay, towards one of my men. And I raised mine. The bullet left my gun chamber and entered the fucker's chest with a dull thud.

There was more shouting. An angry, greasy-looking guy stood a distance away from me, yelling at some other armed men.

"You have no clue who you're messing with! Just kill all the fuckers. Shoot them so they can't talk."

"They'll be pissed!"

"Just fucking do it!"

The men never did get to carry out their orders. No sooner had the last words left the angry guy's mouth than he took a series of bullets, one after the other. The force thrust him backwards and he fell hard, sprawled across some sacks.

In total, we killed eighteen of Abington's men. A few of our team members were injured, but nothing major.

I swung round to see what they had been guarding. And I felt sick.

Cages, approximately seven feet tall but no wider than the span of your arms, stood side by side against the walls. They held women and a couple of very young boys, practically babies. In each cage, there was a filthy blanket and a bucket. The prisoners cried, screamed, pleaded, their hands flailing through the bars.

My breath caught in my throat. The air was thick with the stench of fear and despair; it was suffocating. I looked from one gaunt face to another. Each one was twisted in anguish, and the pitiful cries echoed off the cold, metal bars.

I walked towards one cage that held a small child, but I'd hardly taken more than a few steps when he recoiled in terror, his eyes huge; horrified. He clamped his hands over his ears and started to scream and tremble.

There were at least twenty cages. The prisoners' bodies were broken and bruised from weeks, perhaps months, of abuse. They ranged in age and were filthy. One woman appeared to be so badly beaten, she couldn't stand. Another lay motionless on the floor, her life snuffed out by the cruelty of her captors. Whether she had died before our arrival or in the chaos of the gun battle, I couldn't say.

I told a couple of my men to search the guards bodies for keys. We had to get these people out. It turned my stomach to see what had been done to them. Then I radioed Adam to report back. He would call in contacts of ours in MI5, the National Crime Agency and the Ministry of Defence, as well as a few select cabinet ministers.

In the control room, my team had already sprung into action, dismantling it piece by piece. They'd also taken the video footage and equipment, as this would prove useful in identifying as many as possible who'd been involved here. What we were unravelling was a sinister web of corruption and cruelty; one that reached far beyond anything we'd imagined.

Rodger Abington had been a busy boy. But his vile tower of cards was about to come tumbling down.

Caleb:

We boarded the ship, and the teams began a sweep from top to bottom. One of our guys let the attack dogs loose. The hounds were in a frenzy of excitement, barking, snarling, jaws snapping; saliva frothed behind their razor-sharp teeth. They pinned a crew member against a wall. He was that terrified, he pissed himself.

All at once, I heard raised voices. Different languages and the sound was urgent. Then gunfire broke out. A bullet whizzed past my head and lodged into a wooden crate next to me.

My adrenaline was pumping. I broke cover and rolled across the deck to a stronger position, firing my gun as I went. A man crumpled to the ground to the right of me. My bullet had hit its mark.

Out of the corner of my eye, I saw another guy creeping up on one of my team. I didn't hesitate. I simply opened fire. Multiple rounds penetrated his body. He dropped where he stood, and the young operative he'd had in his sights gave me a silent salute of thanks.

These fuckers were coming out of the woodwork like cockroaches. Only, unlike them, we were prepared. We captured twenty men. Killed a few. But all our guys got out without injury.

There were crates on board that appeared to hold cheap ceramic ornaments, and the drugs dogs went nuts around them. When we smashed them open, we found they held plastic-wrapped packages containing a white powder. And it wasn't talc. We also found guns, and a host of other stuff the authorities would salivate over. Abington couldn't wriggle his way out of this. He was going down.

Daniel radioed in with what they'd found in the warehouses: women and children being trafficked for the sex trade; guns, drugs, explosives, tobacco and booze.

The explosives were a sweet bonus as they meant Abington could now also be held on terror charges, thanks to our contacts in counter-terrorism.

That night, we discovered why we'd been targeted in Jakarta too. Our site there was bang in the middle of their distribution routes. It was clear the Abingtons were only the beginning; a haul this size was bound to lead to other, much bigger fish. This was a sophisticated distribution web, way above the likes of the Abingtons' capabilities.

My contacts met me on the dock and we handed over.

As I left the scene, all I wanted was to find out where Darcey was and go to her. But I knew she was still far from safe. Her life would be in danger until all the loose ends were tied up. The Abingtons would no doubt scatter to the winds, baying for blood.

And, after tonight, Darcey was likely to be top of their list.

Adam:

Daniel said it was bad and he wasn't wrong.

There was a complex system of tunnels within the warehouse, and a bunker that wasn't marked on any maps. Crates were stacked up, full of engine parts, cigarettes, pouches of tobacco, bottles of spirits, a few odd ornaments and God only knew what else.

Daniel's guys had started to free the captives. One woman had to be stretchered out. From the looks of her, I wasn't sure she'd make it. Another young girl was dead in her cage. I watched as yet another emerged from behind the bars that had held her captive. She was filthy and bedraggled, yet she had an air of defiance and carried herself almost regally. Her eyes were the most piercing blue. She didn't speak a word; just nodded at the guy who'd set her free. The others cried and wailed but not this woman.

I jumped back into the 4x4 I'd driven here and headed to the bunker with Daniel and all the fried computer hard drives. The guys I'd left in charge could tie up the loose ends. We passed the authorities I'd called travelling at speed in the opposite direction, lights flashing. Since we still did the odd private job for king and country, though strictly off the books, we were pretty well connected.

Abington:

"What is it? Spit it out, man." Harry had shown up at my house uninvited, so this had better be important.

"You're not going to like it, boss."

"Just tell me!" I snapped. I wasn't going to play guessing games.

"There's been a raid at the dock. The place is swarming. They managed to blow the systems before they cleared out but the product and flesh have all been seized."

I stared at him. I could feel the blood throbbing in my temples.

"How?" I hissed.

"We don't know yet." Harry hesitated. "What we do know is that the Darcey girl is still alive. The security detail was hit instead of her. There was some sort of mix-up over what they were wearing."

"Fucking incompetent ..." I seized him by the throat. "Well, where is she?"

"That's the thing," Harry gasped. "We've lost her. She's just vanished without a trace."

"Then tell me, why don't you, what the hell I'm paying you all for!"

I squeezed his throat harder, then shoved him. He fell back against the front door. Rage boiled up inside me. This was the Hearts doing. They had to be involved somehow – I felt it in my bones. And right in the middle was that cow, Darcey. Whatever she'd seen, whatever she'd heard when she worked for me, now she seemed to be wielding it like a machete.

I glared at Harry as he straightened his collar. "I want her fucking dead, do you hear me?"

My phone rang and I snatched it up. My daughter.

"Not a good time, darling ..." I began.

"Dad, get out. Get out now!"

Then the line went dead.

Paul:

I woke at dawn, went downstairs and lit a fire in the sitting room and the kitchen. Then I took out the burner phone and called the hospital for an update on Sierra. She was still in the coma for now but her vitals were looking better, and the swelling had started to reduce. I smiled as I ended the call; even allowed myself to feel hopeful.

When we arrived a few days ago, I'd stowed the Discovery in one of the large barns. I wasn't taking any chances on it being spotted. I kept an old beetle car out there too. It hadn't been driven in a while so I figured I'd take a look. As I was tinkering with it, Darcey walked in. And I could hardly believe the change in her. She now carried a full bump that hadn't been there the night before. She was glowing too.

Since the morning sickness had subsided, she'd been eating much better and didn't look so drawn. I think the good, clean country air had helped too, and had put little apples in her cheeks where before she'd looked so pale.

"Breakfast's ready," she said. "The others are already tucking in. Oh, and, er" – she glanced down and patted her rounded tummy – "the cat's kinda out of the bag now. I've told them Caleb can't know."

I'd kept my promise. I hadn't let on about the pregnancy to anyone. But now we were all holed up together, Tom and Travis were always going to find out. This was the morning Darcey's body had finally given her away.

Darcey:

My jellybeans had been busy. I woke up a few days into my new country life to find my discreet little bump had grown overnight. There could be no hiding my pregnancy anymore. It was there, in full view at the front, and my bust was huge. I couldn't believe how suddenly this had happened. I'd already been leaving the top button undone on my trousers but now I was definitely going to need some new clothes. Virtually nothing I had would still fit me.

I sat on the window seat in my room and gazed out, trying to make sense of the chaos that seemed to be my life now. Paul had finally told me (with huge reluctance) that the Abingtons had put a hit out on me. That was a bombshell. It certainly explained why we were hiding out in Ireland. It made me wonder too – what was in Abington's business files? What did he think I'd seen?

At the same time, if it truly was the case that I'd been sent out here for protection, why hadn't Caleb tried to contact me? All Paul would say was the less I knew the better.

But I had to start thinking ahead: what would happen after this – assuming one day it would be safe for me to return to London? I'd need to find somewhere to live. I'd need a job so I could support myself and my babies. I didn't know how long we'd be here but I guessed at least it gave me some time to work things through in my head. Make a plan.

I imagined taking a trip to the local village to find a payphone; calling Caleb and letting him know he was going to be a daddy. But then I thought about how callously he'd treated me. How he'd just wanted me gone and out of his life, and how quickly he'd managed to move on with that blonde I'd seen plastered at his side. He'd never made any attempt to get in touch with me since the day I'd left his bed.

I'd spent barely any of my wages since the fire because I'd been living with Caleb. I hadn't touched the insurance money, my bonus, or the money from my landlord. That meant I should have enough to put a deposit down on a little two-bedroom flat and live worry-free for a while, if I was frugal and moved out of London. I should be able to claim maternity and child benefits. I'd have to look into it as I'd never claimed for anything before.

I knew one thing, though: I wouldn't be asking Caleb for help.

Later, Paul, Tom and Travis took me to the village so I could buy some new clothes. There were only two streets of shops but one clothes shop did have a small selection of maternity wear. Paul gave me cash, but I kept a tally of everything so I could pay him back. I also added the last £50 I had in my purse as a deposit to cover the bras that had to be ordered. I needed a selection of sizes as I figured I was only going to get bigger. The shop assistant asked for a credit card too, to keep on file till the items arrived and I'd collected them. I reiterated that I wanted to pay cash for everything and she assured me it wouldn't be used – it was just security for the order.

Gloria:

The headlines were sensational. Abington: sex trafficker, drug-runner, terrorist. The claims made for horrific reading.

I called the boys to the house. Adam, Daniel, Caleb, Simon, Mike and a few others came. I wanted to know exactly what was going on. I'd always known Abington and his son were vile, but to discover his daughter had been one of the main ring leaders in their dealings – I have to admit that shocked me utterly. She was a viper, yes, but capable of this? Charlotte truly was a cold-hearted bitch. Caleb had had one lucky escape.

My boys thought they needed to shelter me from certain things, so I didn't worry. They tended to forget I'd supported their father for all those years. There wasn't much that got past me, even now. I still occasionally wandered into the bunker and I noticed everything. The place had been a hive of activity recently.

There had always been a fierce rivalry between the Abingtons and our family. We seemed to go after many of the same acquisitions in the early days.

"Did you know your dad and Rodger got into a bidding war over two dockside properties many years ago?" I asked.

From the expression on my boys' faces, I could tell this was news to them.

"Your dad wanted to develop it, but Rodger bought it in an underhand fashion and then did nothing with it. It just lay abandoned, which didn't make sense as it was prime real estate."

"Does he still own the land?" said Caleb.

"As far as I'm aware. I certainly don't recall seeing it being sold on."

I noticed the boys all look at each other. It was as if they were having a silent conversation and I wasn't about to let it pass. "Come on, then, out with it. And don't tell me this Abington stuff that's all over the news has nothing to do with you. I'm not an idiot so don't treat me like one."

It was Adam who finally told me everything. The scale of the operation sounded insane.

"But we did it," he said. "Charlotte and her brother were arrested earlier, trying to leave the country. Abington senior's still out there but they'll get him. They have to. There are raids happening up and down the country."

"This has been the biggest operation on UK soil in years," added Daniel. "Multiple agencies are involved."

"And that's not all." Mike turned to me. "Since the news broke, Abington stock has taken a complete nose dive. People want to disassociate themselves from the scandal. But Heart Industries are in the market to purchase that stock –

which will ultimately save thousands of jobs across all their divisions."

Caleb smiled – a little smugly, I might add. "It also means we'll pretty much be able to buy their entire company, lock, stock and barrel, for peanuts."

I raised an eyebrow. "Well," I said, "I'd certainly like to be a fly on the wall when Rodger Abington hears that juicy little nugget ..."

Abington:

They'd caught Charlotte. Bastards. She'd been taken up north but I'd see to it they didn't hold her for long. I still had strings I could pull.

They had Trevor and my wife too. Well, I'd laid enough breadcrumbs at their door over the years so, as far as I was concerned, they could wing it. They'd be going down for a long time. No great loss after all. In fact, Trevor could make himself useful at last and take the fall for all of us.

As for what had been taken from me? Who the fuck cared? I'd always planned for every eventuality and I had more money stashed away than I could spend in two lifetimes. I had nothing to lose. But the Hearts? Oh, I'd make sure the Hearts paid for everything they'd done.

Daniel:

I was shocked when Mike called to say Mum had had a fall and quite seriously hurt herself. She was a force of nature and tough as old boots, but it brought it home to us that she was getting older.

We dropped everything and got to the house just as Mike was climbing into the ambulance to sit with her. I was glad Mike had been staying in Paul's cottage in the grounds. He'd been keeping an eye on Paul's dog and also acting as Mum's close security. I'd noticed how at ease he and Mum were with one another. But I wasn't quite prepared for the sight of him, sitting in the ambulance, stroking and kissing the back of her hand.

As we hung around in the hospital waiting room, Mike looked pale and uncomfortable. I put it down to the anxiety of waiting for an update from the doctor.

I got that so wrong.

He soon piped up. "You do know your mum has been putting off her knee operation."

"What do you mean, 'putting off'?" I exchanged a glance with Adam and Caleb.

"Well, you have to admit, there's been a lot going on," Mike replied. "And you know your mum – she's never one to put herself first. But, now she's going to have to. Her knee gave out. That's why she fell. It has to be fixed."

Adam blew out his cheeks. "We didn't know it had got that bad."

"Of course you didn't," Mike said. "You know your mum. She'd never say."

He hesitated. "Anyway, there's something else. And this is probably the worst time to tell you this but ... I love her."

Caleb leaned over and patted his shoulder. "We know you do, Mike. And we're so grateful you're there keeping an eye out for her."

"No, you're not listening to me." Mike shook his head. "I love her. I am in love with her. And ... I want to marry her. Time's short. Today has made me realise we're neither of us getting any younger. I want to marry your mum and I want to marry her soon."

He paused. Waited. The three of us were stunned into silence.

"Look," Mike began again, "I love you boys like my own, you know that. And I really would like your blessing. But, honestly? I do intend to propose to her, with or without it."

Before any of us had a chance to respond, a doctor appeared. He told us Mum was being prepped for surgery. As well as her smashed knee, she also had a broken wrist, which would need to be fixed with a metal pin.

"But your mother is in good shape," the doctor added. "I don't foresee any problems."

"Can we see her?" Mike asked.

"Of course," he said. "But – just one of you, if you don't mind."

Mike glanced at each of us.

After a moment, Adam smiled at him. "You go, Mike," he said. "Give her our love. And ... I'm guessing none of us saw this coming but" – he glanced at Caleb and me – "I reckon I'm right in saying we all wish you the very best. If it's what Mum wants too, then ... welcome to the family."

Caleb grinned.

"Yeah," I said, "welcome to the family, Mike."

The doctor looked a little confused as he led Mike away through some double doors.

When Mike returned a short while later, he had a huge smile on his face.

"The lady ..." he announced, "... the lady, she said yes."

Abington:

I still hadn't located Darcey, the tricky little bitch. Where the fuck was she hiding? It was as if she'd just vanished without a trace. I would find her, of that I was sure. Was she still in Ireland? I wanted her dead and I wanted it done slowly. This was all her fault. That nosey little fucker had caused all of this.

I rang my informant at the Office Angels job agency and was told she hadn't been back in the office. Caleb had apparently gone through numerous PAs/secretaries. Harry, meanwhile, had stayed over in Ireland as he was convinced she was still hiding out there.

I had to keep moving about, never staying in one place for too long. Over the years, I had planned for this. The authorities had raided my home, frozen my assets and everyone had been arrested. But those fuckers were going to pay for what they'd done. Every last one of them. That entire family had been nothing but a thorn in my side and I wanted them all dead.

Chapter Thirteen

Darcey:

Paul was sparing with his use of the burner phone – we really couldn't take any chances – but he did make a call to find out the latest on Sierra. The news was wonderful: she was out of hospital and now staying with her parents while she recuperated. We couldn't have had a better start to the day.

Later, I was due my next scan, and the maternity bras I'd ordered would have arrived. (Thank goodness. My boobs were now pretty impressive; I was almost busting out of the bras I currently had.) Paul, Tom and Travis took me to the village. Paul waited outside the shop while I picked up my order and the others went to get more food supplies.

It was an older lady who served me this time. She reminded me of Gloria. I was a little taken aback when she asked if she could touch my bump, but then I thought, Why not? As she placed her hands on my tummy, I felt a kick. A proper, actual kick.

We both laughed with the shock. Then I felt tears spring to my eyes because I'd turned into a watering pot, who cried at the drop of a hat; even at adverts on TV. Damned hormones!

Next, I went for my scan at the local women's clinic. I figured I'd be the talk of the village, turning up with three gorgeous men in tow, who all wanted to be in the room while I was scanned.

The ultrasound was performed by a rather austere-looking woman. I was so tempted to say that I'd invited all three men because I didn't know which one was the baby daddy. Imagining the look on the woman's face made me smile.

My jellybeans were certainly not jellybeans anymore. We all stared in awe at the screen, and these two perfect little people. Their heartbeats were strong and clear. Obviously, the tears came again but, when I looked up, the guys were crying too.

I thought of Caleb; of all he was missing. I couldn't help it.

"Would you like to know the sex?" the woman asked.

Before I had a chance to answer, three voices replied with an emphatic, "No!"

The woman gave the guys a cursory glance. "What about you?" she said, looking back towards me. "Would you like to know the sex?"

I didn't know how to keep a straight face. "Er ... no," I managed. "Let's make it a surprise."

Apparently, the babies measured slightly large, which was unusual for twins. I was also told they were monozygotic. This meant they would be identical bundles of joy. And I loved them already.

Travis took the roll of blue paper from the nurse as she offered it to me. Then he gently wiped my bump clean of the clear jelly. Tom helped me up off the bed and Paul carried my bags. Seriously, these three would have tongues wagging. The expression on the nurse's face said it all.

Paul:

That evening, I received a phone call from Simon telling me the good news about Mike and Gloria. Not so good that she'd had a fall, but good she was on the mend and they were finally getting married. I had always known the pair of them had feelings for each other. Darcey would be delighted because she adored them both.

I loved this time of day. We would all be out on the wraparound porch of my parents' old farmhouse, usually with the radio on low. Darcey and I sat on the porch swing. One of the geese, called Major, had taken to sitting between us and curling his long neck around Darcey's bump while she stroked his soft, downy feathers. Travis and Tom would either read or play cards and chat. We were all so relaxed, you could almost forget about the imminent danger Darcey faced. We'd fallen into such an easy routine.

I'd heard Travis and Tom fighting several times over who was the best shot, while they cleaned their guns. We decided to settle it once and for all and set up some old beer cans on the wood pile out the back. The boys were pretty well matched with their military backgrounds. They took turns and shot at all six targets, stepping a little further back each time until eventually it came down to one shot – and Travis won. He crowed over his victory, making us all laugh.

Unexpectedly, Darcey asked, "Can I have a try?"

"I don't see why not," said Tom.

The boys readied her gun and set the targets back up. Then Travis gave her a little demonstration and tuition on how the gun worked and how to line up the shot, as well as how to hold it correctly.

"Don't worry if you don't manage to hit any of the cans," he said.

"Yeah," added Tom. "We make it look easy because we're highly trained."

Darcey nodded. "Tell you what, let's have a little bet. Just to make things interesting."

Travis and Tom exchanged an amused glance. "If that's what you really want," Travis said. "So, if we win, you have to make the meals of our choosing for a full week."

"Fine," Darcey replied. "But if I win, I get to choose the next three DVDs, get daily shoulder rubs, and you two have to go into town to get me more bananas, pickles and crackers."

That's right: bananas, pickles and crackers. These were the latest food cravings. Darcey laughed and blamed her jellybeans for the sick concoction.

The boys couldn't resist a little smirk. They definitely thought they had this in the bag.

Darcey then stepped further back from the targets than the pair of them, and proceeded to give the lads a master class in target practice and reloading her gun.

I wished I'd taken a picture because they looked truly crestfallen. I couldn't stop laughing. Tears literally rolled down my face. Darcey asked if she could keep hold of the gun. The girl knew how to use it so I didn't see why not.

Travis:

Darcey looked beat this evening. The scan had gone well but all the excitement had taken its toll.

Tom went out to settle the animals for the night and close up the hen coop. If anything happened to those bloody chickens, Darcey would be devastated. She had named every single one of them. They seemed to know their names too; followed her around the yard and came running as soon as they heard her voice.

It was harder locking the geese away. They hated Tom and me. Major was one huge, particularly vicious bird and he regularly chased us both. Darcey was the only one of us he didn't attack. He seemed to adore her and guarded her constantly. He would rub up against her legs and she would coo at him, telling him what a good boy he was and stroking his long neck – the neck Tom and I wanted to wring!

When Tom came back in, he looked irritated.

"Problem?" I asked.

"Just the usual," he grunted. "Those sodding geese are a nightmare. I've had to leave them out – Major wouldn't stop charging at me. I hate that bloody creature. He can take his chances with the foxes."

Paul:

I took Darcey a hot chocolate before I turned in for the night. One glance at her told me something was preying on her mind.

"Wanna talk about it?" I said.

She gave me a long look. "Can I ask you something? Do you think Caleb would want to know about the twins?"

I hesitated. Darcey still couldn't know the whole truth. "If it was me ... I'd want to know," I answered. It was all I could think of, though I knew without a shadow of a doubt that Caleb was going to bust a nut when he found out. Preferably not mine.

As I left her to her thoughts and walked across the landing, I heard a noise. It sounded as though it might have come from the barn where we kept the Discovery. Instinctively, I drew my gun and headed downstairs.

The others had beaten me to it. Tom had laid cover in the doorway and Travis was already halfway across the yard.

Two seconds later, the noise-maker revealed himself: Major appeared from the barn and ran at Travis, hissing and flapping his wings like a demon from hell.

I was still chuckling when I got into bed.

Adam:

I was frustrated. After all this time, Abington was still on the run.

Caleb was being a pain in the arse in the office too. I completely got how he felt – I did. But it wasn't an excuse. He held everyone to impossible standards, including himself, and had had two temps in tears within a week. Mum was recovering well from her fall but we really felt her prolonged absence from the office. As for Darcey, no one even dared mention her name.

The positive news was that the case against the Abingtons was ironclad. There was no way they could wriggle out of the shitstorm we'd brought down on their heads, high-priced lawyers or not. Daniel had been able to recover a good chunk of the hard drive and had passed it over to the authorities, tightening the noose around their necks a little bit more. Their reach went further than we'd originally thought but, thanks to the information Daniel had gathered, the authorities were closing in overseas too.

My brother was a freaking genius. Thank God he was on our side.

Darcey:

I don't know why but I'd been feeling uneasy all day; some kind of weird sense of foreboding. Maybe it was because Major was acting strangely. He'd stayed by my side all afternoon and had even tried to come into the house – much to Tom and Travis's horror.

After we'd eaten in the evening, I decided to get an early night. I was just brushing my hair when the twins gave me such a hard kick that I dropped the brush. As I crouched to pick it up, I heard Major suddenly go insane in the yard.

Almost at the same time, there was a "pop" and something flew past my head.

I screamed and ducked lower. I was pretty sure someone had just taken a shot at me.

As I crawled to my bedroom door, I could hear more shots explode downstairs.

Then the lights went out.

I should have felt frozen with fear, but I didn't. I was raging – how dare someone try to kill me and my babies!

Paul had let me keep the gun after the shooting competition. I'd stuck it in a drawer. Keeping to floor level as best I could, I crawled to the chest and, stretching up, felt around until my fingers closed on it.

"Darcey! You okay?" I heard Paul shout up the stairs.

I yelled back, "I'm fine!"

The words were hardly out of my mouth when the sounds of Major's honking and the powerful beating of his wings suddenly stopped.

I heard a cry – Tom – then the smashing of glass.

With the gun gripped so tightly my knuckles had turned white, I inched my way to the top of the stairs.

That's when I smelt the smoke.

"Darcey!" The urgency in Paul's voice left no room for doubt.

Adrenaline surged through my veins.

The house was on fire. I had to get out.

I reached the kitchen to find it ablaze and the flames already spreading to the sitting room. The heat was intense.

As the smoke stung my eyes, a hand grabbed at me. Paul's hand. Seconds later, he'd steered me out to the porch, where we took cover.

Then I saw Major.

My beautiful, loyal goose was still in the yard. Dead, and laid out like an avenging angel. Angry, grief-stricken tears welled up in my eyes. Major had warned us; he'd sounded the alarm and gone on the attack. He may well have saved all our lives.

There was a spate of rapid gunfire; more shouting, though I couldn't make out the words.

Then silence.

With the searing heat of the fire at our backs, we were forced to move from the porch. Paul covered me as I ran to one of the barns. I found Tom there. He'd been winged but he was okay.

Just as Paul joined us, we saw Travis dragging a man in tactical gear across the yard by the scruff of his neck. I wasn't sure if he was dead or just unconscious.

I looked over towards the beautiful old farmhouse. It was well alight now, engulfed in a huge fireball. Plumes of smoke and embers spiralled upwards into the night sky.

Paul:

I had to get Darcey away. I handed Tom the keys to the Discovery and told him to keep her safe and get her out of there. I'd have to stay put. It wouldn't be long before every law enforcement officer within a ten-mile radius was beating a path to the farm.

I marched back to Travis, my eyes fixed on his prisoner. It was clear Travis had already introduced the man's face to his fists.

"Wake him up," I said.

Travis dragged the unconscious shooter over to the old stone animal trough. It was full of water and Travis dropped him into it unceremoniously.

He came to instantly.

I leant over him. "How many of you are there?"

"Fuck off!" was the reply.

Before I could even open my mouth again, Travis had grabbed a handful of the guy's hair and dunked his head back into the trough. He held it there, under the water.

When Travis released him, he came up, gasping for air. "I ain't telling you shit," he spluttered.

I shook my head. "Wrong answer."

This time, Travis held him till he started to thrash and twitch before he him let go.

The man's head shot up out of the water. He inhaled deep, rasping breaths.

"There were five of us," he managed at last. "We've been watching you. We were camped out near the river."

So we had them all; we knew four were dead.

I grabbed the shooter's collar and thrust my face close to his. "Who are you working for? Who sent you? Abington, right?"

He hesitated; until Travis looked set to dunk him again.

"Harry!" he cried out.

Who the hell was Harry? One of Abington's henchmen, no doubt.

"Keep hold of him," I told Travis. Then I took off with a flashlight and gun down to the river. I found a small camo tent. There wasn't much inside: a mobile phone, some local maps and a few pieces of clothing. As I slipped the mobile into my pocket, I heard the wail of sirens. The police would have a lot of questions. This was going to be a long night.

Darcey:

I stepped out of a hot bubble bath. I felt I'd finally managed to wash away the smell of smoke. Then I wrapped myself in the fluffy bathrobe provided by the hotel Tom had driven us to. It felt good – soft and warm – but it didn't cheer me up. I was so tired. And I was heartbroken that Major was dead. Tom had spoken to Paul, who'd told him he was going to bury my beautiful goose before they left. They just had to finish with the police first.

We weren't far from the farm and I had every intention of waiting for them to join us. I wanted updates. But when I rested my head on the pillow for five minutes, I must have fallen asleep instantly. I woke several hours later to light streaming in through the windows and Paul fast asleep in the armchair.

I wasn't looking forward to getting back into my smokey clothes. I'd need to buy some new ones and a few essentials. Everything I owned had presumably been destroyed in the fire.

As soon as the guys were awake, we went down to breakfast. I was starving and found myself wolfing down a full English breakfast, two slices of toast and a bowl of fruit salad, washed down with three glasses of orange juice. I had to smile to myself. Pregnant or not, I guessed I could eat what I wanted now since I didn't have anyone to impress anymore.

"We have to fly back to London," Paul said, when he'd cleared his own plate. "As soon as possible." He turned to look at me. "Abington knows you're here. Ireland isn't a safe place for you anymore. We'll be able to protect you better back home."

I nodded. I'd never quite been able to get my head round the fact that Abington had put out a hit on me. Even after last night, it still felt like some weird dream that was happening to someone else. But I wasn't about to argue. I had to trust Paul, Tom and Travis with mine and my babies' lives.

We checked out of the hotel and went straight to the boutique where I'd bought my other clothes. The lady who reminded me of Gloria was serving and seemed really pleased to see me again. As she rang the purchases up, I went to pay with some cash Paul had given me, but she began to apologise profusely.

"No, no, there's no charge for these," she began. "I'm so, so sorry, but it came to light that the young girl who took your deposit got confused and charged it to the credit card you left with us. We would obviously have refunded the card in due course but, since you're here again, we can use that payment for today's items."

I couldn't be angry – she looked so crestfallen. Anyway, what was done was done. At least we now knew how Abington had tracked me down.

As beautiful as Ireland was, I wasn't sorry to be leaving. The plan was to fly back as soon as possible from Dublin airport. Tom and I would then go to stay with Paul. That way, I'd be protected 24/7 – which was great except that Paul's cottage was in the grounds of Gloria's house. My babies wouldn't be a secret from the Hearts any longer.

Adam:

My head was banging; I had a raging migraine. I'd been helping my contacts trace the families of the people we'd rescued from the Abingtons' trafficking operation. We'd already managed to reunite eight of them. But it was a huge undertaking, needing help and cooperation from Interpol, the Missing People Charity, MI5 and various other organisations worldwide. We'd also loaned our support and resources for counselling and accommodation; as Heart Industries employed a huge number of ex-forces, and spouses of serving forces, we had a full support team at our disposal: doctors, counsellors, and experts in every field of health and wellbeing, all on hand to help the staff who needed it readjust to civilian life.

I couldn't get one of the captives out of my mind; the girl with the piercing blue eyes. In amongst the chaos, she'd seemed so calm and serene. She'd stepped out of that god-awful cage like a queen; head held high, spine ramrod straight. I read her file and discovered she'd been a translator before being snatched. How did someone like her get taken? Was it just being in the wrong place at the wrong time?

When I turned the page, I found those mesmerising eyes staring back at me from her profile photo. It had been taken after she was cleaned up and she was astonishingly beautiful. I had to speak with her. I had to know more. She might be able to give us more information about the trafficking network. We knew many of the women and children had been repeatedly raped. The captors liked sampling their goods by all accounts. Children had been left bloody and soiled in torn, filthy clothing, completely traumatised. They hadn't been fed regularly and were treated like animals. Judgement day for the traffickers couldn't come soon enough.

Something else wasn't helping my head: Paul was bringing Darcey back from Ireland and Caleb couldn't know. That would be a fun secret to have to keep. Paul was still wary about her being here again but it seemed to be the safest place for her right now. She'd be under constant surveillance by Paul and Tom. Not Travis this time, though. He was going north. I had to debrief him as soon as he was off the plane as we needed him on assignment with another specialist team immediately.

At least Caleb wasn't around. Daniel had arranged to take him and one of the crews to a supposedly unused site of Abington's. We'd only discovered he owned it through one of their shell corporations after Daniel had recovered the information on the hard drive from the warehouse.

Gloria:

The wedding plans were coming along marvellously. Things just seemed to fall into place. I was up and about again, and I felt great. Mike couldn't have been kinder or more attentive and I adored him. He barely left my side.

If I was honest, though, I had started to crave some alone time. I also knew how much my boys needed him, especially with everything that was going on.

My opportunity to shoo him off to the office came when Doris and Noreen popped in one day with bridal magazines. I told him he couldn't possibly be here while I was looking at wedding dresses. He eventually conceded and away he went, leaving me and the girls to pore over the magazines outside in the sunshine.

Mike and I had chosen a wonderful country house for the wedding. There would only be 150 guests. We wanted a celebration that was fun, relaxed and predominantly outdoors. As I looked at dresses that would suit the setting, and the ambiance Mike and I wanted to create, I was torn between an elegant 1950s style and an ankle-length, fitted gown, with a long, vintage-lace jacket that had a small train. Noreen, Doris and Julia, with baby Hope, were to be my bridesmaids and we needed to settle on those outfits too. If Darcey had been here, of course I would have asked her to be a bridesmaid. I would have loved it. But I hadn't heard from her in such a long time. Adam had told me she'd left the company so I didn't even know if she was in Ireland anymore.

Out of the corner of my eye, I caught movement. I turned to see someone approaching from the side entrance to the garden. In an instant, all thoughts of wedding dresses were forgotten.

"Paul!" I sprang to my feet – yes, I was pretty sprightly again by now – and began to laugh as I took in his beaming face. It had been months since I'd seen him. The boys wouldn't tell me why he'd had to go away; only that it was imperative and they didn't know when he'd be back.

He made a beeline for me, kissed me on the cheek and squeezed me in a tight hug.

"Oh, Paul, how I've missed you!" I cried.

"I've missed you too, Mrs H," Paul replied, finally releasing me.

I laughed again. Paul always referred to me as Mrs H.

I was about to ask how he was, where he'd been, why he couldn't be in touch – all the things I was dying to know – when I heard Noreen and Doris gasp in unison. I glanced at them and followed their gaze towards the side gate.

And I was struck utterly dumb.

Caleb:

We didn't expect to find anything. After our first raid, Abington would have made sure the place was cleaned out. And we were right. Whoever had been here had emptied the warehouse and left in a hurry. From the scrape marks on the floor, it looked as though something heavy had been stored here.

As much as I was desperate to find Darcey and bring her home, I knew it wasn't safe. Abington was unhinged. A psychopath. The more we uncovered, the sicker and more depraved we realised he was. The whole family was deranged. The fact I could have been married to one of them didn't bear thinking about. It was ironic that Abington's wife sat on the board of trustees for a children's charity, yet his own son raped and traumatised little boys. One in particular was no more than a baby. DNA evidence had been gathered from the kid's rectum and the rags he'd been wearing. I'd seen some disturbing sights during my time in the service and working special missions, but the look on that child's face – his tears as he shook with distress when we went near him – tore at my heart.

The recordings Daniel had recovered from the first raid were sickening. The bastards had raped quite a few of the captives and filmed it to add to their humiliation. We'd produced a most-wanted list of names and faces from that footage. They would be held accountable.

But that wasn't the extent of it. A police search of Abington's home had uncovered recordings of Rodger Abington himself with various women. The recordings had been kept in his private safe. The man was as sick as his son. He'd tied women up and beaten them to within an inch of their lives; you could hear his fists smashing repeatedly into their faces, heads and ribs. Once they were a bloody mess, bound and strung up from hooks in the ceiling, he raped them. None of the women on the recordings had been among the survivors we'd found. Fuck only knew what had become of them.

The authorities had seized all the personal assets they knew about belonging to the entire family. There were eyes on extended family too, and on close contacts who hadn't already been arrested. The Abington web seemed to have tendrils in every major city in the UK.

Simon:

With time racing by, the wedding plans were coming along at a fast pace. We had the day planned like a military operation; the security had to be tight. We couldn't take any risks so every available set of boots would be on the ground.

Darcey was back in the UK and staying with Paul. He'd left her under the watchful eye of Mike and a couple of the other guys while he went to pick Sierra up for the wedding. Sierra was finally out of hospital but still in a bad way. She was determined not to miss the big event, though. Paul was lit up from the inside at the thought of seeing her again.

Never thought I'd see the day Paul's head was turned by a woman.

I had to confirm final arrangements and security precautions with the hotel. We had exclusive access, and the teams were setting up comms both inside and out. The wedding was going to boast some pretty impressive guests. Nothing could be allowed to go wrong.

Darcey:

Gloria had asked me to be a bridesmaid, along with Julia, Noreen and Doris. Simon was dubious about my having such a public role at the wedding but I was adamant. If Gloria wanted me in her bridesmaid troop, nothing would stop me from being part of it.

"Besides," I reassured him, "you've covered pretty much every eventuality security-wise – I know you have. No one's going to be able to get within ten feet of me."

I had to admit though that, as bridesmaids go, I felt I looked like a busted couch. All four of us were to wear the same colour of blush, but the dress styles would be different to suit our figures and ages. Mike's daughters would wear blush too, in their roles as ushers.

At my dress fitting, it was decided not to alter my gown until the last minute. The girls had all chosen elegant heels, but I opted for ballet pumps for comfort. I also decided to wear my long hair down, with two beautiful vintage combs pinning it up on either side of my head. Naturally, it would be Franco doing hair and make-up.

Daniel would walk with us on the day and carry Hope down the aisle. I was excited but felt sick to my stomach at the same time. Caleb would be there. What if he brought a date with him? I didn't know if I could stand it. He'd never made any attempt to contact me since I'd landed back in the UK. His message could not have been louder or clearer.

Gloria:

Darcey being back with us for my wedding day was just the icing on my cake of dreams. I'd paired everyone up for the procession down the aisle: Julia would walk with Daniel and Hope; Noreen with her Jed; Doris with my Adam; and, though neither of them knew it, I'd put Darcey and Caleb together. I'd be walked down the aisle by Paul, and Simon was to be Mike's best man.

Mike and I had organised a trip to Italy for our honeymoon. I was so excited. It felt as though a weight had been lifted from the two of us – the fact everything was out in the open now and we didn't have to sneak about anymore was liberating, while having such wonderful companionship again was sublime. Some people go all their lives and never know what it is to be truly loved, but I was fortunate enough to have found love twice.

Chapter Fourteen

Darcey:

The big day finally arrived and we all piled into Gloria's suite at the hotel to get ready. There was an amazing breakfast spread on offer but I couldn't touch a bite. I was so happy for Gloria; at the same time, the sparkle was taken off my morning by the thought of having to see Caleb. I wondered if he might ignore me. Actually, maybe that would be best.

As Franco and his team worked their magic on us, Franco made the girls howl with laughter, Gloria looking positively radiant. I perched on the window seat waiting my turn, and looked out over the beautifully landscaped grounds. After a moment, Julia came and sat down next to me. I felt her place her hand on mine.

"How are you doing?" she asked.

I smiled. "I'm fine. Although the twins do seem to use me like a trampoline so I've not been sleeping too well – but you know what that's like. You're doing an amazing job, by the way. Hope is beautiful and happy and ... angelic."

"She is." Julia nodded. "But I don't know how I'd have coped with any of this without Daniel. He's been my total rock." She raised an eyebrow. "Cagey, though. Wouldn't tell me anything about you after you went to Ireland. Just said it was safer if I didn't know anything."

That made sense. I filled her in on some of the details, including what had happened to Sierra.

She looked shocked. "How could Daniel not tell me any of this?"

"No," I told her, "he was right not to. The fewer people who knew anything, the better."

When it was my turn in the stylist's chair, Franco and his angels had to work extra hard just to hide the bags under my eyes. However, once I was finished ... well, it almost looked like a different woman gazing back at me from the mirror. Then the girls helped me into my floaty gown. Thankfully, the fabric draped itself artfully over my huge bump and gargantuan breasts. The sparkle around the neckline caught the light and, miraculously, I felt quite pretty.

As I walked to the door, I was given a hand-tied bouquet of wildflowers that included vintage roses, freesia and some other heady-scented blooms. I inhaled deeply. This seemed to calm me and give me the fortitude I needed for what was to come.

Outside the door stood Paul. He looked so handsome in his suit. When he saw me, his entire face lit up and he twirled me round and planted a kiss on my cheek. Then he placed his hands on my belly.

"Okay, you two, listen up," he said in a stern voice. "This is your Uncle Paul and today is an important day. So you need to be good for Mammy. Got it?"

Paul spoke to my unborn babes a lot and it always made me laugh.

Then Daniel appeared. He smiled at me as he passed me in the doorway, gave Julia's cheek a swift peck, and scooped

Hope into his arms. The little girl's eyes grew big when she looked at him, and she clapped her hands in excitement.

Gloria and Paul left the suite first as Gloria had to meet with the registrar downstairs. Before she went, she gave me a hug.

"By the way," she said as she pulled back, "when you get downstairs, you'll find Caleb waiting to escort you down the aisle."

Someone needed to pick my jaw up from the floor.

Caleb:

This definitely wasn't your average wedding. The place was overrun with security teams – some in plain sight, others disguised as guests. We had every exit covered; all the staff had named ID badges; everyone had been vetted before they were allowed anywhere near. We'd swept the grounds, the sewers, all cars and delivery vans, lift shafts, rooftops; practically every inch of the place. There were teams positioned all over at strategic points. We still didn't know where Rodger Abington was. I wanted to keep the press out too – I wasn't taking any chances. Nothing was going to spoil Mike and my mum's day.

With the ceremony due to start soon, I decided to check in with the crews outside one last time. One of my guys told me he'd heard quadbikes in the woods. Three of them had gone to check it out but, by the time they got there, there was no sign of them, other than the ground they'd disturbed.

The hotel manager then came scurrying up to me to inform me they were having trouble with one of the lifts and they needed a part to fix it. There were two main lifts, though, so not too much cause for concern.

By the time I was finished, I knew I was cutting it fine – especially as I was supposed to play escort to one of my mum's friends. I dashed back to the foyer but, as I got close, I heard strains of music. The procession had already started to make its way to the gazebo. Shit ...

I rushed through the doors to see Mum being walked down the aisle by Paul, with the bridesmaids following behind. The women were all paired up; except for the one bringing up the rear. She had long, curly hair that hung prettily down her back. I couldn't think which one of Mum's friends she might be as I hurried to take my place beside her.

I offered her my arm, then turned my head to look at her.

And I froze.

Abington:

Finally, it felt as though I was at the top of the pile again. The fucking Hearts strode around as if they owned the city. Well, I wanted the lot of them dead. And with a Heart wedding in the offing, they'd soon all be gathered in one place. How convenient.

I'd been hiding out in my bunker for weeks now. It was comical watching all the security feeds I'd set up. The various properties I owned had been searched more than once, but they had no idea about the bunker.

It had come to my attention that a supposedly good friend had turned evidence on my baby girl. That's how she'd been found. That friend now sported a smile across his throat from ear to ear, and was generously feeding the fish in the Thames for his trouble. His family had been evicted from their home and his own little girl was getting a taste for nose candy – I'd made sure of it. No one fucked with me or mine.

My informants had told me my girl was due to be transported from Low Newton, County Durham, to Crown Court today to stand trial. As she was classed as low threat, getting her away shouldn't pose too many problems. I'd arranged for the transportation to be hit on the way to court. I had a colourful team of mercenaries on retainer for such tasks. Not very pleasant fellows but they got the job done. I didn't need to know specifics.

While it was inconvenient to have had so many of my assets frozen, surely the Hearts couldn't be so fucking stupid as to think I didn't have a backup. Once this business with them was done and scores had been settled, I was ready to get out. A fresh start. Lillian, my bitch of a wife, and Trevor could rot in prison for all I cared. Eventually, my baby girl would come join me.

As most of my men were needed to hit my baby's transport, I knew I'd have to get my own hands dirty with the Hearts. I took just a couple of men with me when I left the safety of the bunker. Three of us should be plenty for what I had in mind.

We passed through the woods near the wedding venue on our quadbikes and stationed ourselves at the waterfall just outside of the hotel grounds. We had multiple drones equipped with cameras and rigged with explosives; six in total. I only needed one to hit its target. The perfect time would be when all the family gathered for photographs. We'd strike then and wipe them out in one go.

Caleb:

I stared at her, not quite believing my eyes. So many emotions: excitement, lust, longing – and panic in case she disappeared on me again. The woman stole my breath.

It took a second for the obvious to hit me: Darcey was pregnant. Very pregnant.

I had so many questions. I wanted to kiss her and crush her in my arms. I never wanted to let her go. Unfortunately, she was glaring at me with contempt and utter disgust. And I had no opportunity to say a word because my mum was literally about to get married.

I guided us to our seats and sat down next to her. We needed to talk. I had to explain. I had to make her see that I never wanted to let her go – though the expression on her face told me I'd have my work cut out making her listen.

I tried to focus on the service. Mum looked elegant and happy, as she beamed up at Mike, and I was thrilled for her. But I couldn't concentrate. I had to keep glancing at the stunning woman who sat beside me.

Vows taken, Mum and Mike walked back up the aisle and I helped Darcey out of her seat. Begrudgingly, she took my arm, though without looking at me. On our way to the reception area, we were stopped multiple times by family and friends. I was a pretty sociable guy, but not today. Not right now. I just wished we were alone.

Flutes of champagne and of orange juice, and tumblers of whiskey were passed to guests. I snagged a whiskey first and downed it in one. I had a feeling I was going to need it. Then I grabbed a flute of champagne and one of fresh orange, passing the orange to Darcey. She still hadn't spoken a word. I could tell it was taking all her willpower to hold her tongue and I had the distinct feeling that when she blew her top, it would be spectacular.

"Everyone over here for photos, please," I heard Adam call.

I don't think I'd ever been less in the mood to have my photo taken, but we dutifully made our way over.

This was insane – I had to say something.

"You look beautiful," I managed. "Darcey, I'm so relieved to see you—"

She cut me off. "Yeah, well, don't worry. I'll be out of your hair as soon as the meal and speeches are done, so I won't embarrass you and your date."

"Wait – what are you talking about?" I took hold of her arm. Stopped her in her tracks. "I don't want you to leave ..."

Then it dawned on me what she had said. "Hang on ... What date?"

She shook her head and began to walk again.

I followed. "I had no idea you were pregnant. Look, Darcey, I know you don't want to talk to me but ... is it mine?"

I don't know what possessed me to ask. The words were out of my mouth before I could stop them. And I felt a stinging smack across my cheek. The force of it knocked my head sideways.

"Just go to hell, Caleb, do you hear me?" Darcey yelled. "You can just go to hell!"

She turned and walked off.

I made to go after her, but Adam was there in an instant and he stopped me.

I almost wanted to deck him on the spot. "This is all your fault. You and Daniel. Why did I listen to you? I could have protected Darcey here – I could've made sure she was safe."

Adam stepped in close. "Let's just cool it, shall we?" he hissed. "This is Mum's wedding day and you're not going to spoil it for her."

"Did you know she was pregnant before today?" I watched his face. "Yeah, of course you did."

He pinned me down with his eyes. "Everything we did, we did to keep Darcey alive."

I glared back at him. I still wanted to knock him flat but, as much as I hated it, I knew he was right.

"Now calm down," he said, "and let's go and join in with the photos."

I gave him a begrudging nod and followed him over to the photography area.

"By the way," Adam added, "what did you just say to Darcey?"

I told him and he stared at me in disbelief. "Seriously, man, do you honestly think that baby could be anyone's but yours? Darcey has never so much as looked at anyone else since she met you."

Adam:

Caleb had screwed up big time. Darcey looked pissed. Daniel had gone after her when she'd stormed off, to calm her down. I'm now of the opinion we should have told Caleb about the baby. He'd been totally blindsided and opened his mouth without thinking. I felt partly responsible.

We lined up for a photograph but that's as far as we got.

Out of nowhere, shots rang out. The sound of an explosion split the air; then another and another.

There was shouting and screaming; panic as guests scattered.

The comms I was wearing burst into life – one of the team on the roof.

"We just shot down a drone!" I heard. "Explosives attached – detonated on impact."

Mike was quick to spring into action. "Multiple drones coming in!" he yelled.

I didn't have to tell him to get Mum to safety. He was already shoving her and the photographer towards the hotel.

More shots were fired.

I went to run to where the ground teams were stationed. I figured Caleb would follow but, when I looked back, he was still standing there.

"Come on, Caleb – what are you waiting for?" I shouted.

His head whipped this way and that as he looked all around him.

"Where's Darcey?" he shouted back. The desperation in his voice was raw. "Adam, where the fuck is Darcey?"

I shook my head. "Daniel went after her!"

Darcey:

How dare Caleb ask me if he's the father! He knew he was the first man I'd ever slept with. Did he really think I was just going to leap into bed with the next guy who came along? What an arsehole. Not everyone moved on as quickly as he did.

My hand still tingled from where I'd slapped him. I hoped his face still stung too.

I needed to get out of there. I wanted to go home; back to Paul's. I was in no mood to party and was pretty sure Gloria and Mike would understand.

I headed back to Gloria's suite and grabbed my clutch bag and the keys to one of the company cars. They were all tagged with the registration numbers. Then I made my way back outside around the front of the building, found the right car and drove off down the long driveway. At the end, I turned left out of the gates. I saw the security teams talking into their headsets. There seemed to be a flurry of activity, but they let me go.

The road almost doubled back on itself and I found myself driving parallel to the hotel gardens. There was a dense canopy of trees overhead and the bushes along the garden boundary were thick. You couldn't see what was going on in the grounds. I guessed that was why Gloria and Mike had chosen this as their venue – because of the privacy.

I was lost in my thoughts, hurt feelings and humiliation, when I heard the boom and rumbles of a series of explosions. What the hell ...? In that moment, I remembered the security guys at the gate and the intense looks on their faces.

Something had happened.

I stopped the car, turned it around and headed back. I'd hardly gone more than a few metres when I caught sight of a quadbike moving quickly towards me along the verge on the hotel side of the road. It was being driven recklessly and the rider was without a helmet.

The rider sat high on the seat and kept looking back over his shoulder. Whoever it was didn't seem aware of me approaching in the car. He was more interested in what might be going on behind him.

It was only as he drew level, then passed me, that I got a proper look at him.

Abington ...

I don't even know exactly what went through my head. He was coming to the end of the woodland trail, almost at the entrance to the long hotel driveway, and just burst out.

I put my foot down.

That bastard had put a hit out on me. He'd turned my life upside down and he wasn't getting away.

Moments later, I smashed into the quadbike.

Abington was thrown into the air like a ragdoll and smacked into my windscreen head first. The glass spiderwebbed as his blood spattered.

I thought of Sierra; how she'd been hit in the same fashion at the command of this puppeteer of misery.

I wondered how he liked it.

I asked myself if I felt guilty. But if the truth be known, I wanted to drive over him again just to make sure I'd done a good job.

The seatbelt had tightened over my rather large belly, but I was okay as I'd braced myself for impact. I'd bumped my head too and there was a tiny cut, but I felt fine. I dived out of the car and grabbed my mobile to call Paul.

Slightly shaken, I stood and stared at Rodger. He looked pathetic. He was barely alive; his face and head a bloodied mess. One arm and leg lay at weird angles and the bone protruded through his shin and camo trousers. He wouldn't be going anywhere in a hurry.

Caleb:

A huge area of the gardens had been decimated; the gazebo was gone. Crews had descended from all over the hotel; helping get people inside the building; triaging the wounded. Two shooters had been caught so one team were in the process of loosening their lips. I told them I didn't care how they did it.

Mum and Mike were fine. Julia and Hope too, thank God. But, according to Daniel, Noreen, Jed and Doris had all been hit. He didn't know how badly.

I heard Paul yell. "Darcey's at the bottom of the drive!"

And I ran.

Oh, God, no ... Let her and my baby be okay ...

I pumped my arms and legs till my chest was on fire.

I reached her in record time ahead of my brothers, and took a moment to scan her over. Darcey leant against one of the company cars. She didn't seem aware of me until I was there in front of her. When her eyes flicked up at me, I thought she might run but she didn't.

The car windscreen was smashed and bloodied. Her head was cut but there were no other signs of injury.

And I couldn't help myself. Relief and yearning fully overcame me. My arms wrapped around her and I kissed her hard, pressing her up against the car. I felt frenzied; I couldn't get enough and my hands were all over her. I was only vaguely aware of the sound of sirens approaching. I could hear Daniel and Adam talking. They must have run after me. But all I wanted was to hold on to this woman in front of me.

She didn't let me.

"What are you doing?" Darcey demanded as she pulled away. Contempt for me still burned in her eyes.

I cupped my hands either side of her face. "I have so much to explain to you. But just know, I never stopped loving you for a moment. You're it for me – you're mine."

She almost laughed as she shook her head. "Really, Caleb? I don't think so."

Pushing past me she asked, "Is he dead?"

I turned to see Adam and Daniel crouched over someone on the ground. I hadn't noticed him before. There was a lot of blood, and limbs were snapped and twisted. Only then did I notice the wrecked quadbike upside down in the hedge.

Only then did I realise this someone was Rodger Abington.

Darcey:

I was absolutely wiped out. A paramedic came to check me over. Caleb had insisted on it before he was dragged off to help with some of the more seriously injured guests. A couple of people had arrived at the hotel in their own helicopters, so those were commandeered to take the worst affected to hospital. Unsurprisingly, my blood pressure was raised, but other than the cut on my head, I'd escaped miraculously unscathed.

My brain, however, was in a whirl. What was with Caleb? He'd ignored me for months on end and now he was all over me again? If I hadn't felt so confused, I'd have been furious.

I had to talk to the police to explain how I'd come to hit Rodger Abington. I was convincing when I told them we'd simply collided: he wasn't looking where he was going and had swerved into my path. There would obviously be further enquiries but I wasn't worried.

Afterwards, Paul walked me up to my room and said he'd bring my bag through from Gloria's suite.

"Now you need to get some sleep," he said, giving me a peck on the forehead.

I wanted a bath first. I turned on the taps and watched the water fill the huge tub, swirling in some expensive-smelling, golden-amber bubble bath and watching it froth up. Then I piled up my hair and undid the zipper of my bridesmaid dress. It fell to the floor in a pool of blush-coloured tulle. As I lay back in the scented water, the bubbles caressed my skin and I closed my eyes. I wanted to be able to process all that had happened in the last few hours but there was too much of it.

When I heard the door of my room open, I called, "I am going to sleep, Paul, I promise. Needed a bath first. You can just leave my case on the bed – thanks."

I'd hardly finished speaking when I felt a pair of strong hands on either side of my face. I tensed and my eyes flew open.

Caleb was on his knees at the side of the bath, his face inches from mine. Before I knew what was happening, he was kissing me hard once again, like a starving man. I tried to hold on to my anger towards him, but who was I kidding? I was emotionally and physically worn out and my traitorous body betrayed me as my nipples instantly pebbled.

With a huge effort of will, I pushed him away before I simply gave in.

"How dare you …" I managed. "Just get out, Caleb. I'm exhausted."

He didn't budge. "No. You have to hear me out."

"Have to?" My hand clenched into a fist. I was ready to swipe him again. "You knocked me up, then you abandoned me and sent me away. I don't have to do anything for you."

Caleb rolled from his knees and sat on the floor beside the tub. "Darcey, truly I didn't know about the baby. There had been a threat to your life. Abington had a professional hit out on you and he wasn't messing around. The guys felt it was better to get you out of the way till all the shit had gone down with Abington and he was behind bars. I couldn't risk any contact with you. The boys made me see that. If Abington had tracked you down …"

He paused. "You have to believe me, Darcey. It's been literally torture without you. My heart's been in bits. But you had to be safe."

I studied him. Every inch of his face. The depths of his eyes. He meant what he said. Only it made no sense.

"But I saw you, Caleb, at that gala. I saw you with that beautiful woman on your arm."

"That was all just part of a ruse." He gazed at me in desperation. "That woman was Charlotte Abington – my ex. Adam and Daniel thought that, if Abington believed I was getting back with her, it might take the heat off you. I swear to God it was all just for show. I didn't even want to go to that sodding gala."

He was on his knees again, one hand stroking my cheek. "I adore you," he said. "You and my baby – you're my future."

All my defence mechanisms melted away – my anger, my self-preservation barriers, my indignation; even my hurt seemed to dissipate.

I leaned forwards and kissed him for all I was worth.

It was as if we'd never been apart. He played my body like a finely tuned instrument, kissing, nibbling and licking his way down my earlobe, neck and across my breasts. The taste of the soapy bubbles on his tongue didn't seem to bother him and his hands were everywhere.

Then suddenly he was naked and had climbed into the tub behind me. He played with my huge, sensitive nipples, stroking my breasts and caressing my round belly. God, I needed his touch; the man set me on fire.

He reached round and gently strummed my clit in small circles with just the right amount of pressure. I started to ride his hand – I couldn't get enough. He had it so right and as he rolled my nipple with his other hand, I came apart in the tub as my body shuddered through the climax. It had been so long but my senses hadn't forgotten.

Caleb had to help me out of the tub. He dried me off then tugged me to the bedroom. There, he bent me over and placed my hands on the high bed. And he entered me from behind. Sex was a little trickier with the size of my belly. But I was so wet; so sensitive and highly aroused.

The stretch felt wonderful as he slowly nudged my pussy with his length. When I cried out for more, he pushed all the way in, curling over my back and massaging my breasts, as he held me in place. The burn felt delicious; he was so deep and thick. I could feel him pulsing. Then he began to move – gently at first but I needed hard and fast. We set a punishing rhythm until, once again, everything tightened, and a second orgasm crashed through my body. Caleb came at the same time, spilling inside the depths of me.

Afterwards, we both collapsed onto the bed. My legs had turned to jelly and sleep pulled me under almost instantly.

Caleb:

Darcey curled up in my arms and I heard her breathing change. She was asleep in moments. As I stroked her belly, I felt my baby kick against my hand. It was an entirely incredible feeling. It made me realise how much I'd missed out on already. I was determined I wouldn't miss another moment.

As I clung to Darcey for dear life, I fell asleep too, breathing in the scent of her hair. God, had I missed that.

I don't know what time it was when I felt her leave the bed. But even in my sleep-hazed state, I knew I truly loved this woman and I couldn't imagine a life without her. I saw the shape of her move towards the bathroom.

Before I could so much as focus my eyes, I called out "Marry me!"

Darcey whirled around.

"I love you and I love our baby." I stretched my arm towards her across the bed. "I mean it – marry me."

She gazed at me; placed her hands on her belly. "So, about the baby thing ..."

I raised my head from the pillow.

"It's babies, Caleb – not baby."

I stared at her. My brain felt sluggish.

"Two babies, to be precise."

One more moment passed. Then I got it.

Darcey:

It was early morning and I had to get up and pee. I washed my hands and began to brush my teeth but, as I stood, resting against the basin, I had the overriding urge to pee again. I figured the twins must be jointly pressing down on my bladder – hard, because I began to pee before I even made it to the toilet. You never read about the real stuff in romance books: the sensitive nipples, swollen ankles and almost permanently bursting bladder. At the thought of giving birth twice in one go, I wondered if my poor lady garden would ever be the same again.

I'd just stepped into the shower when I felt Caleb before I saw him. He washed my hair and soaped me up, paying particular attention to my swollen breasts. (Clearly, they were very dirty as he spent a lot of time on them.) I became instantly aroused. I soaped his shaft, which was again thick and fully erect, and had begun to nudge my butt cheeks. Reaching around lower, I played with his balls and I heard him groan.

There was a tiled seat in the shower. Caleb lifted my nearest leg onto it. I was wet in more ways than one and I was so ready for him. He entered me from behind as his hand sneaked around the front of me and rubbed my clit. The hot water beating down, the feeling of my pending orgasm and being deliciously stretched were more than I could take. We both shattered together.

It was only 7:00 a.m. when we got down to the dining room for breakfast. From what we'd seen as we made our way downstairs and along the hallway, the interior of the hotel hadn't been too badly affected by yesterday's violence. There were a few broken windows and doors, and a little fire damage, but nothing as severe as what had happened to the gardens.

We were soon joined by Paul, Sierra, Gloria, Mike, Daniel and Julia. Daniel had Hope in his arms and I noticed he was holding Julia's hand. I needed to find out the story there.

Caleb had gone to get our breakfasts and I stood up to fetch some orange juice for us. But as soon as I got up, I felt a tiny trickle of pee. I sat back down quickly and clenched my pelvic floor to stop the flow. Fortunately, I was wearing loose-fitting black maternity trousers and a long floaty shirt, so it wouldn't have been noticeable. But that didn't stop me flushing beetroot-red with embarrassment.

The flow seemed to stop when I sat down. I gave it a moment to be sure, then headed to the ladies' toilets, where I purchased a sanitary towel from the vending machine.

When I got back to the dining room, I was delighted to see Jed, Noreen and Doris. They looked a little banged up but had refused to go to hospital. It really could have been so much worse for everyone.

Adam:

It was early morning when I got the news about Charlotte Abington. She'd escaped custody yesterday on the way to court. It was a professional job, I was told – very clean – and she'd vanished without a trace. Her father would have been behind it, of course, but it wouldn't be long before she was caught. I was sure of that.

As soon as I appeared at breakfast, Caleb tugged Darcey to her feet. It looked as though he'd been waiting for me because he was out of his seat as soon as he spotted me.

We all knew what was coming. I heard Mum's excited intake of breath and saw Mike grin at her. Caleb had always been one of the good guys, like our dad before him. But Darcey completed him.

I tried to catch the girl's eye. She'd been through so much and I wanted her to know how happy I was for her. What I saw was the colour drain from her face as her legs buckled and she blacked out.

Paul:

Darcey had been checked over yesterday and pronounced fit and well but now things didn't look so good. I paced the hospital waiting room with such anxiety, you'd have thought I was the babies' father. Surely Darcey and those cherished little ones couldn't have come through all they had in the last few months to not make it now. Caleb had looked terrified as he'd disappeared through the double doors of the maternity suite, following the trolley that carried his precious girl.

I was terrified too. This had to be one of the longest few hours of my life. The girl had come to mean so much to me. She was family now.

When Caleb finally reappeared, he was flushed and wide-eyed. I froze. He stared at me for one second – then his face cracked into probably the widest grin I'd ever seen. In that moment, I knew everything was going to be fine.

Darcey:

So much for my leaking bladder. Turns out that was actually my waters breaking. The babies weren't due for another two months, so, in hospital, I was given an injection to help harden their lungs. But as they were showing signs of distress, eventually they had to be born by Caesarian section.

And there they were. Our identical twins. So tiny – just short of three pounds each – but so perfect.

We called them Paul and James; James after Caleb's dad and Paul as a way to thank the man who had helped me survive so much.

Our amazing boys went from strength to strength. After two weeks, we were able to take them home – back to Caleb's apartment for now, but we'd soon start house-hunting for somewhere more suited to our growing family.

When I finally went back to work part-time, it was only for one day in the office. The other two days, I worked from home. I had no shortage of childcare. Between Noreen, Doris,

Gloria and Mike (who retired officially when they got back from honeymoon), they had it covered.

At a special meal that Caleb had organised, with all the family and extended family present, he proceeded to get down on one knee to propose to me properly. We married exactly six months later.

And love must be catching because, although Daniel and Julia were adamant they were just friends, they held hands everywhere they went; Adam had begun seeing a lovely lady called Aria, one of the women he'd rescued from the raid on Abington's warehouse; and Paul and Sierra were officially a couple at last, and I adored them both.

As for me, I finally had somewhere to belong. I had a whole new family.

Epilogue

Lillian Abington:

Oh, Rodger, darling ... You truly are an arrogant, conceited arsehole. It wasn't your finest moment when you decided to set me and our son up to take the fall for all your and Charlotte's sick business dealings. You have no idea exactly how much I know about your rotten business and the misery you perpetrated, do you? You thought I didn't know about all those pert little secretaries you've had in your office, the affairs; about all your sick sex tapes. You condescending prick – you thought it all went over my head. Well, Trevor might still be behind bars for the time being but I'm out on bail. And once I've made sure there's nothing to implicate him, I am so ready to talk.

They tell me you have multiple life-threatening injuries – you're basically a paraplegic now, dear. So silly to go racing about on a quadbike at your age. Without a helmet too. It's only the machines keeping you alive. And, baby, I know you wouldn't want to exist in a vegetative state. We've had that very conversation many times. You'd want the machines turned off to save the last remnants of your dignity. You always said you couldn't think of anything worse if your mind was intact but your body wouldn't co-operate.

So, for that reason, my darling, I've told them to keep you on life support. I'm going to look for a nice, cosy hospice for you. Somewhere where you can suck jelly through a fucking straw for the rest of your days for all I care, and where the only hands you'll have touching your broken body will be those of the male nurses when they wipe your arse, give you a bedbath or change your nappy.

Never mind, sweetheart. You might learn to enjoy it. And anyway, it's like they say – Karma truly is a bitch.

Acknowledgements

Writing this book has only been possible because I have an amazingly supportive network of friends and family.

I need to give a special mention and thank my fabulous long-suffering husband Neil and my family for their unwavering support and belief and for giving me the space, encouragement and freedom to write.

Also, my crazy fantastic friends Mel, Chris and Dawn whose advice, dedication and passion for my characters have kept me on the right path. There is also the fabulous Carrie McGovern (author) and her husband whose friendship, help and advice have been invaluable.

About the Author

Donna Caldwell was born and raised in Washington in the North East of England where she still lives with her husband and three children. She works full-time but writes purely for pleasure.

Writing has always been something Donna aspired to do and she finds it an outlet for her creativity and a way of switching off and relaxing. Her laptop goes with her pretty much everywhere she goes and she finds inspiration for characters and situations in the strangest of places.

A weird little-known fact about Donna is that she is a very artistic and creative person and can pick things up very quickly but for the life of her, she can't knit or crochet.

You can find Donna on:
Website: www.donnacaldwellauthor.com
TikTok: @donnacalwellauthoruk
Facebook: @donnacaldwellauthor
Instagram: @donna_caldwell_author

Coming Soon...

STICKS & STONES

COMING SPRING 2025

"Will Adam's past prevent him from having a future?"

Book two of The Hearts Saga takes Adam and Aria's story into darker, more harrowing, and twisted territory that will leave you breathless. *Sticks & Stones* reveals the dire circumstances that led Aria to be trafficked like chattel, found in a cage, and sold into the sex trade as retribution for her husband's actions.

"Her life has never been her own... Can she survive the deceit and treachery from those supposed to love her?"

Aria has never known a true loving touch. The heat between her and Adam is undeniable, and the sparks between them refuse to be extinguished. Both are haunted by the ghosts of their pasts. Just when Aria begins to feel safe, her world is shattered once again. She is kidnapped, and Adam will tear the universe apart to find her.

"Will their love withstand the ultimate test? Can Adam and Aria overcome the darkness threatening to consume them?"

Sticks & Stones is an intense, emotional rollercoaster that you won't be able to put down. Prepare yourself for a story of love, survival, and redemption that will captivate you until the very last page.

Karma is a bitch!!